TIME KILLER

TODD M. THIEDE

iUniverse LLC
Bloomington

TIME KILLER

iUniverse books may be ordered through booksellers or by contacting:

iUniverse
1663 Liberty Drive
Bloomington, IN 47403
www.iuniverse.com
1-800-Authors (1-800-288-4677)

ISBN: 978-1-4759-7235-1 (sc)
ISBN: 978-1-4759-7236-8 (hc)
ISBN: 978-1-4759-7237-5 (e)

Library of Congress Control Number: 2013901011

Printed in the United States of America.

iUniverse rev. date: 03/19/2014

This book is dedicated to my beautiful wife, Courtney.
I would have never been able to finish this book
without her help and encouragement.

Stephen Bjornson wakes up and tries to roll over toward his wife, only to find he cannot move at all. His thinking feels slow and hazy, as if he has been drugged. He opens his eyes slowly to see that the room is dark, with only a small beam of light from the full moon breaking through the drapes. He had opened them earlier to make sure the front gate was shut. His son rarely remembers to shut the gate when he comes home for dinner from the neighbor's house. He surveys his room and continues to fight the fog in his brain, as he can feel something is very wrong.

He tries to stay calm, but his mind and heart are racing. He slowly tries to raise each arm and finds that he is tied down to the bed with duct tape across his chest, torso, and legs. With his arms pinned to his sides, all he can do is turn his head far enough to the left to see that his wife, Gwen, is still there, but she is also taped to the bed. Stephen notices Gwen has tape over her mouth. Her brown eyes are wide and look very dark in the moonlit room. Her hair is splayed out and crowns her head like a halo. At first Stephen thinks he must be dreaming. He can't imagine why he would be tied to his bed and his angel, Gwen, tied next to him. Then he shakes his head, as nothing is making sense. He closes his eyes and reopens them. He focuses on Gwen and realizes that the halo was created by her messy blonde hair as she struggled to break free from the bonds. She keeps sweeping her gaze away from him to stare toward the foot of the bed, and Stephen slowly focuses his gaze on the shape of a person behind the footboard. He is terrified at the thought of some stranger in their house. However, he is having a hard time maintaining focus on any one thought.

Stephen starts to remember the early days of their marriage, when they fought over silly things like furniture. He and Gwen had spent three months shopping for bedroom sets, picking at each other's tastes for traditional or modern furniture. The young couple had taken almost every Saturday to go shopping to fill their home. Giddy and in love, their fights never lasted long and often ended in the bed. In hindsight, maybe that was why they had been so careful in their choices. Stephen wishes their lives could be that easy now—just make love to end an argument. He is not able to remember the last time he and Gwen had made time for intimacy. He keeps thinking that now isn't the time for memories—like having a daydream at work—but he can't think about what is more important than remembering the good times with Gwen.

He feels a bouncing sensation next to him on the bed and rouses from his drug-induced reverie. Gwen is bouncing her head and moaning beneath the tape. She keeps staring at him and then jerking her head toward the foot of the bed. He remembers that there is a person standing over him and his wife, just staring across the bed at them, waiting for him to wake up. Stephen vaguely wonders how Gwen can be so awake when he is so tired.

He tries to swallow, but his tongue feels like lead. His mouth feels like it is full of cotton. After a few tries, he squeaks out, "Who are you? What do you want?" He is disappointed at the quiver in his voice so he tries again, hoping to sound more intimidating. "Who do you think you are, coming into my house? What do you want from us? We don't keep large sums of cash in the house."

The man just stands there, staring down at Stephen and Gwen, not saying a word. Stephen thinks that it must be a man based on the wide shoulders and body shape. Besides, there is no way a woman would do this, he thinks. This man is wearing a dark ski mask. He is also wearing black leather gloves, which particularly frightens Stephen. He has watched enough forensic shows to know that gloves can make identification of criminals much harder. As he begins to become more aware and able to focus, he sees that the man seems to be very well-dressed, wearing an expensive suit, button-down shirt, and tie. The ski mask and leather gloves clash against the business attire and Stephen wonders who would dress so nicely to commit a crime. He feels like he is going to drift off again, so he shakes his head and tries to maintain focus on the intruder.

Just when it seems like an eternity has passed since he first tried to roll over in his own bed, he jumps as the man yells, "You wasted my time!"

The voice is so loud and deep that Stephen believes he feels the rumble through the floor into the bed. He jumps and his eyes open wide. He instantly tries to put on a brave face again and stares the man down. After all, this man is threatening his family. Then he starts to worry if his kids will be woken up by this man. He doesn't want them to wake and see any of this. He writhes wildly against his bindings, but they don't give. Fear raises his neck hair. *This isn't a normal burglary.*

He decides that he is getting nowhere and tries conversation, which is what he is best at, anyway. "What are you talking about? Why are you doing this?" Stephen says, his voice quivering. All he can do is lie there, thinking about his children just across the hall from him. He has no idea what this madman knows about his family and whether he knows the kids are sleeping right across the hall. While he is very concerned for his and Gwen's safety, he closes his eyes and quickly asks God to protect his children from harm.

It seems like hours that the suited man continues to stand over them, but only minutes pass. Stephen is scared to speak more, worried that any noise will arouse the kids. Just when the angst is going to force Stephen to say something again, the stranger finally speaks again. "You wasted my time. Time is money!" Gwen had been fighting her restraints up until that second yell. She lies completely still aside from ratcheting her head towards Stephen. He looks back at her and can see the tears spilling from her eyes. The moonlight catches the tears so that they remind him of his playtime with his daughter the other day, when they blew bubbles in the backyard and the sunlight glistened off the bubbles in the air.

The man grabs a pen from the top of Stephen's dresser. He starts pacing back and forth in front of the bed, clicking the pen over and over again. CLICK! CLICK! CLICK! The clicks echo through Stephen's head and return him to the moment. The man continues to mumble, "You wasted my time…you wasted my time…you wasted my time." Gwen, still staring at Stephen, nods toward the man. He understands that she expects him to do something, but he is at a loss. He cannot free himself so he focuses on what he can do—continue to try to talk his way out of this.

As he is trying to come up with a plan, the man finally kneels down next to the bed, pen still in hand. He leans over and says, "Stephen—is it okay if I call you Stephen?"

Stephen nods his head in reluctant approval. Stephen starts thinking, *How does this man know my name? Have I met him before? What does he want from me?*

"Stephen, I know you and your type. You don't have a care in the world outside your family's own little bubble. You don't think that your actions have any effect on other people's lives. You see, Stephen," he continues, "I once had a nice wife and a daughter, just like you. We were happy, just like you. We had the perfect life, just like you. But you see, things are not always as they appear. Are they, Stephen?"

Stephen decides not to answer, fearing that the answer to the question is nothing that he wants to hear, particularly from an aggressive stranger. "Answer me!" the suited man shouts directly into Stephen's ear. Stephen shakes his head no. "You see, Stephen, my wife packed up all her things one day and decided she was taking my daughter away from me. It seemed that she was leaving me for another man. She said I was wasting **her** time. I couldn't provide her with what she needed. She needed financial stability and even though I had a good job that kept us afloat, it wasn't enough. Stephen, it wasn't enough because every so often, people like you waste my time and I don't make any money. People like you cost me money, and **you** cost me my family." That comment was chilling. The man walks over to Gwen.

"Please don't hurt us!" says Stephen, whimpering now, his bravado completely gone. "I love you, Gwen," he murmurs as he starts to sob. He turns his face away so that Gwen does not see him. He feels compelled to turn back as the man approaches his wife, whom he loves dearly, despite their distance.

"Oh poor Stephen; poor, poor Stephen. You didn't tell him, did you, Gwen? I can call you Gwen, can't I?" Gwen nods her head reluctantly. She is between sobs because the bed is only shaking on Stephen's side. She starts fighting at her restraints again, trying to push away from the approaching masked man with her feet, trying to dig her heels in. The tape keeps her from being able to arch her body high enough to move toward the head of the bed. Stephen is sickened watching her suffer this way, and he starts to fight his restraints, too.

"You see, Stephen, ever since you and I met a month ago, I have been following you and your family, watching you and Gwen, little Billy and Sandy in your daily lives. Now, I haven't been able to watch you every day because I have a job and time is money, you know. Nonetheless, I have been watching all of you. And what I have learned from watching you is that you enjoy wasting people's time. Gwen here is not only wasting other people's time, she is also wasting your time, Stephen. You see, Stephen, your precious little Gwen is having an affair," he states matter-of-factly.

At those words, everyone in the room freezes. Stephen lies completely still, weighing whether there could be truth to the words of this madman. Gwen has stopped moving, either because of his words or because the mask is now only inches from her face. She is staring into his eyes and cannot drop her gaze.

Stephen decides that whether it is true or not, this man is not their marriage counselor and has no right to intrude in or reveal their issues like this. He musters up more courage and exclaims, "No, that's not true. I know my Gwennie loves me and would never do that!"

The suited man now leans over and whispers into Gwen's ear, "Tell him, tell Stephen the truth! He deserves that, at the very least. Tell him the truth now." What had started as a whisper has turned into a menacing hiss in her ear. She flinches as he says truth so loud that her eardrum hurts. Stephen watches, helpless, as his wife pulls her head as far away from the man's face as possible.

The masked man suddenly rips the duct tape from her mouth in one quick jerk. Gwen screams in pain and then throws her head toward Stephen. "It's not true, Stephen! I love you with all my heart and would never do that to you or our family!" She is crying again, and Stephen is not sure who to believe. Why would a man break into his house and lie to him?

"Lies, lies, lies...you are wasting my time again, Gwen. Now tell him the truth. Stop wasting my time. Stop it, stop it, stop it...time is money!" he shouts and hits the bed next to her. "Tell him now!" Stephen is feeling impatient about what this man wants and worries about why his children haven't come in to see what is going on. He starts to fear the worst about their fate, but asking will only remind the man that they are close by.

Between sobs, Gwen begins to choke out her confession in a small pitiful wail. "Okay, it's true, Stephen. I met someone else. But I love you and I love our kids! You have to believe me, Stephen, I do love you." The silence hangs in the air, thick and palpable. Stephen feels a gulf widening between them—the woman he so desperately wanted to protect a minute ago has indeed betrayed him.

Stephen's eyes widen and he struggles against the tape. A slow look of realization comes across his face. His tears stop and his eyes start to narrow to slits. "So that's why you missed my work luncheon? Is that why you weren't there that day to pick up Billy from soccer practice? Have you been busy sleeping around?" Stephen's voice begins to roar, forgetting about anyone but the two of them. "Who is it, Gwen? Who is he?" he yells, struggling violently to face her. He succeeds in partially turning his body toward her. The suited man steps back, folds his arms, and watches the argument as it progresses. A smile of accomplishment is visible in the mask's mouth opening. He seems proud that he has caused the two of them to fight.

Gwen continues to cry and shake the bed. "I have been seeing David, one of the dads from Sandy's daycare. I never loved him, Stephen. I just needed more than you have been giving me." With the last statement, her words sound hollow, as if she is wrung out and tired. Guilt creates an ugly mask on her face as she looks into Stephen's eyes.

The masked man takes advantage of her pause. "See, Stephen? Do you see how she is wasting your time? It's just like you did to me last month when you wasted my time. Now, here's the difference between you and me: I am here to help you, Stephen; I am going to rid you of your problem, so you are no longer wasting time with Gwen."

As soon as he finishes this statement, he begins clicking the pen again, as if he is nervous. Stephen starts to fight his bonds again to stand between the masked man and his wife, who he knows he still loves. The masked man places his hand between Stephen and Gwen. Then he crawls on top of her, positioning himself so he is straddling Gwen. After the humiliation he has faced—being told by a total stranger that his wife is cheating—seeing him on top of her is too much for Stephen. He manages to get a leg free from the tape and starts kicking toward the man. However, the bed is wide and he just grazes his arm. He is waiting for the man to pull up her nightgown and rape her, but that doesn't happen.

The man looks back and forth between the two, savoring her fear and his anger. He then thrusts the pen directly into Gwen's right eye. He jams it in so hard and so fast that she dies almost instantly from the pen penetrating the brain. Blood spatters everywhere and the suited man takes a few seconds to survey the results. Stephen can see the man's teeth in the mouth hole of the mask. His smile is demonic and growing. Viselike grips of trauma lock his body. He feels numb. It is a blessing.

"As I said, Stephen, I am here to help you. I'm here to stop you from wasting everyone's time." The man stands up from the bed and walks around to Stephen's side to sit next to him. He stops talking directly to Stephen, but he can hear him mumbling, "You wasted my time, you wasted my time, time is money," over and over again.

Stephen, still lying there in shock, wakes up as if from a dream and starts to scream, "No. No. No. Why are you doing this to me? What did I do to deserve this?"

"Okay, Stephen, here is the situation: I'm going to need you to pay me for the time you took from me. After all, time is money. So for the three hours of my time you wasted last month, I figure you owe me $633. That would make us even for the three hours. Heck, I won't even charge you for the time I just saved you by taking Gwen out of your life; consider that a gift from me to you," he says in a very calm, business-like voice.

Stephen thinks he must have fallen back into a dream; this cannot be real. *Money for the time I took from the suited man? Three hours? This was all about three measly hours of time? Where did I meet this guy? How did I waste three hours of his time?* he keeps thinking.

"Where is my money, Stephen? I am going to have to start adding to the bill if you don't tell me where my $633 is. Time is money! You wouldn't want to waste any more of my time, would you, Stephen?" the suited man asks angrily. Stephen shakes his head slowly, still not understanding.

As the man starts rifling through their things, Stephen finally comprehends he is looking for *his* money. He proceeds to tell him that his wallet is on his dresser in the corner of the room and that there should be enough to cover it. The suited man walks over to the dresser and grabs his wallet, takes out the money and counts it. "You only have $450 here, Stephen. Where is the rest of it? Quit wasting my time!" he screams.

"My...my...wife may...have some money in her purse. It's in the closet...probably on the floor," Stephen says, his voice choked.

"You know, Stephen, I kind of like you," the man says calmly as he goes to the closet. "I liked you last month, too—well, that is, before you decided to waste my time. I like the fact that you want me to take the money from your wife's purse. I mean, it isn't like she needs it anymore anyhow and, after all, it is your money, anyway. Am I right?" The man's laugh is high-pitched and evil. He reaches into the closet, pulls out the purse and takes out some money. "All she has in here, Stephen, is two 100 dollar bills." With that, the masked man takes out his own personal wallet and puts exactly $17 on Stephen's dresser. He puts the $650 into his wallet and proceeds to sit back down by Stephen. Stephen tries to take note of the wallet to tell the police later, but then he realizes that he may not be alive much longer, either.

"Stephen," he says, "like I told you earlier, I've been following you and your family for about a month, and I've noticed that you like wasting people's time. I mean, you went to the appliance store and talked to a salesman about a new television for almost an hour two weeks ago and didn't buy it. Then you went into an open house just last week and walked around talking to the realtor about how you were considering buying a new home. You took about two hours of his time with no intention of buying the house, or even calling him back. You were just there wasting his time! Like his trying to make a living was a joke to you and Gwen."

"That isn't true! I was going to call him back. I was very interested in that house!" Stephen spits out.

"Sorry, Stephen, I know better. Remember, I was watching you closely and the moment you walked out of the house, you threw the realtor's card away, while you and your wife laughed. You both thought the house was disgusting and way overpriced. You discussed how you love your house right now and would never leave it. Now quit wasting my time with lies and accept the fact that I know you better than you think I do," he says with some finality. "I am going to do the rest of the world a favor here, Stephen. You are right-handed, is that correct?" he asks. When Stephen nods his head, the man grabs the duct tape from the floor and duct tapes Stephen's mouth shut. He then walks out of the bedroom, only to return a few moments later with bolt cutters. He leans over Stephen and whispers into his ear, "I am going to cut off your thumb and index finger on your right hand." Stephen blanches. The man continues, "That way you can no longer fill out any paperwork or sign anything and waste anyone else's time like you wasted mine, the realtor's, and the appliance salesman's."

He then stands up and cuts off Stephen's thumb and finger. As Stephen lies there in unbearable pain, unable to scream with his mouth taped shut, his face blood red, his temple veins bulging, the suited man leans back in and whispers, "Don't worry. You won't die from this. I want you to live and learn not to waste other people's time anymore. I also want you tell everyone else to stop wasting people's time. Tell them all how time is important to you now that you have a second chance. Tell them that they need to be considerate of other people's time and not just their own. You can do that for me, right, Stephen?" Stephen nods frantically as tears flow from his tortured eyes. He feels himself slipping in and out of consciousness as the blood pumps out of his hand. The masked man tears more duct tape from the roll and wraps it around Stephen's hand, almost like a bandage. "We wouldn't want you bleeding to death before you can get that message out, would we, Stephen?" Stephen shakes his head no.

The man now rips back the tape from Stephen's mouth, taking part of his moustache off with it. He tastes blood. The tape has ripped off some skin. The man then picks up the phone next to the bed, lays the mouthpiece on the pillow next to Stephen's mouth, and proceeds to dial 911. He picks up Stephen's bloody finger off the floor and uses it to write, "*DON'T WASTE PEOPLE'S TIME*" on the wall as the phone rings. He then calmly walks out of the room, whistling as if he has no care in the world. The song he is whistling is very familiar, but Stephen cannot place it. Stephen recognizes the sound of his back door opening and closing. The man is finally gone. As he starts to feel light-headed, he wonders if he is in a nightmare he cannot escape.

The tickle of the blood dripping down the side of his jaw brings him back to awareness. He hears the operator repeatedly asking if anyone is there. Stephen yells hoarsely into the phone as best as he can, "Please help me; there was a man here in my house! He killed my wife. He…he hurt me. I'm bleeding and I'm tied up. Please hurry—I've lost a lot of…" As he drifts in and out of terrible dreams and thoughts, his mind keeps returning to his children. *Did the man hurt them? Are they even alive?* He prays that they will not find him like this. With tears now flowing along with the blood, he finally closes his eyes to the darkness of what has happened, his body numbing with the shock. Stephen passes out.

It takes almost ten minutes for the ambulance to arrive, followed shortly by the police. The police knock on the door at first; hearing nothing, they break down the door and rush into the house. They yell as they rush around the house looking for the family, but no one responds.

The smell of copper from the bloody mess the murderer has left behind gags them as they move up the stairs. With the medics behind them, the police clear rooms one by one, potentially destroying evidence. The master bedroom is the first room the paramedics enter upstairs, as the door stands slightly ajar. There they find Stephen unconscious, with blood dripping from the duct tape bandage on his right hand. His right cheek lies in a small pool of blood from his torn moustache. He is still duct taped to the bed, and next to him lies his dead wife. The first officer in the room takes one look around and runs to the master bath and vomits up his lunch. Today is his first day, and the pen in her eye and the blood surrounding Stephen is just too much for him to handle.

The police officers go back into the hall to allow the medics to work on Stephen. James is fairly new to the force and has never seen such a violent crime. While he is upset that this happened to the family, he is also excited to be involved in what will likely be a big case for his station. His partner, Bob, is tired and waiting to retire soon. He is trying to pass on his knowledge to James but feels sometimes that James lacks compassion for others.

James enters six–year-old Billy's room. Above the red race car bed, Billy's name is carved into a piece of driftwood. There are little green army men scattered around the floor, resembling the beaches of Normandy. James sees numerous trophies for various sports on his dresser top. James wonders how Billy could have slept through all the mayhem in his parents' room. He doesn't want to startle the boy, as this is going to be a terrible night for him. The officer wants to take him out of the house before he can see what has happened to his parents just down the hall. He tries to lift the small boy up very carefully, as not to wake him.

However, Billy isn't ever going to wake up. Billy lies in James' arms like a limp doll. The murderer smothered him with his pillow and after he was sure he was dead, he cut off his right-hand finger and thumb. The lack of bruising around the cuts indicates Billy's heart was not beating at the time. James says a silent prayer that his future children will never go through this and gently places the boy back down.

Written on the wall in blood, only visible after James turns on the car-shaped lamp, is, "***LIKE FATHER, LIKE SON***". James can only imagine what this monster has done to the little girl.

He gets a huge lump in his throat as he sees Bob walk out of her room, shaking his head.

For some reason, James has to see this other room. Maybe by seeing the chaos, he can understand and control it. Sandy's room is very upbeat. There are pink walls, a princess bedspread, and dozens of stuffed animals on her bed and dresser. He can feel her presence and happiness just by walking into her world. She was only three, yet she has been smothered with her own pillow. Her finger and thumb are missing, and just like her brother's, they were removed after she was murdered. Written in blood on the wall is, "*WHORE, JUST LIKE MOM*".

Bob drops to his knees and starts sobbing right as he thinks of his grandchildren, who are about Sandy and Billy's ages. What would he do if this ever happened to them? *How could a human being do this to children?* he thinks. James doesn't know what to do except pat Bob on the shoulder. He is having the same thoughts, but isn't as affected since his kids do not exist yet.

As James and Bob re-enter the master bedroom, they see Stephen being transferred to a gurney. He has an IV in his arm. He looks up at them and says in a hoarse voice, "Please check on my kids. They're down the hall." The officers exchange a quick, knowing look. They assure Stephen that they will take care of everything while he gets treated.

Stephen starts to feel woozy from the painkillers administered by the paramedics and finally closes his eyes into a deep sleep. As they push Stephen out into the hallway, the paramedics ask the police officers if they need to help the children. Bob shakes his head no, putting one finger to his lips to indicate silence; he then puts his head down again to pray.

T he Rockton Police Department is quiet at the moment. The station was built fifty years ago and the wear on the building during that time is evident. The bricks in the façade are old and chipped, worn down from years of Illinois winters. One window is boarded up where a brick had been thrown through it in retaliation by a convicted man's friends. The fixtures, carpet and furniture are at least two decades old.

Detective Max Larkin enters the squad room. He feels light-hearted and happy because he has just finished solving a case. It wasn't a high profile case but there hasn't been much crime in Rockton lately. Max is one of the best detectives Rockton has ever seen. He advanced quickly from patrolman to detective because of his natural instincts and great people skills. He has been able to get a confession from the hardest of criminals. Having graduated top of his class from the police academy, he broke many records there.

This morning he has tried very hard to get to work early, as he wants to get in a quick workout before the Captain comes in to hand out assignments. The case he just closed requires him to type up some reports and he really hates doing paperwork. He often wishes he could just solve cases and have someone else do the menial work. He has a post-case hangover, where he is too tired to really want to start a new case but also feels the desire for a new puzzle to solve. If he is lucky, today will be a light day of check-up on some smaller, less urgent ongoing investigations. Then he can finally go out for a beer at a bar after work rather than getting home at ten with beer and pizza for one. Maybe he can even meet a girl. He doesn't miss his last girlfriend or the drama, but he does miss having someone to look forward to after work.

He sits down heavily at his desk, wishing he had gotten up a little earlier, as he can see the Captain is already in his office. *There goes my workout,* he thinks. While Max is only twenty-nine, he has been trying to maintain the physique he has been losing since he made detective. It's hard to balance the heavy workload with good eating habits and regular exercise. His average height and regular features already make it hard enough to get women's attention, so he feels that having a good physique can only help. His co-workers often tease him that his military-style haircut, high and tight, isn't doing him any favors—they comment that he looks like a jarhead gone to pasture. He always takes their joking as a bit of jealousy since he knows he is regarded by many police officers as the best detective on the force and he has earned their respect.

His mom had called while he was in the shower so he now picks up the phone to call her before he forgets. "Hey, Mom. What's up? Yes, I know Dad's birthday is coming up. I haven't forgotten. I don't know what to get him this year. He seems to have everything." Max chats with his mom as he warily watches the Captain get up from his desk and walk toward the door, eyeing him.

"Hey, Max, come in here, would you?" Captain Perry calls out.

Max holds up his finger. He wraps up his call with his mom and heads to Perry's office.

He walks into the Captain's office to the sounds of 'oooohs' and 'aaaahs' of the other detectives. He even hears one of them say, "Nice working with ya, Max. Good luck!" He waves his hand in dismissal at the guys.

As he heads toward the back offices, he calls, "Hey, Captain. I was just planning on going to the gym for a quick workout. Can this wait for thirty minutes?" The captain denies his request.

Max is always impressed by the numerous awards and commendations on the Captain's office wall, including a Purple Heart from Vietnam. He thinks, *If I had a dollar for every time the Captain told me the story of how he got that Purple Heart, I could have retired already.*

Although Max has been a detective for six years now, he still gets butterflies every time he goes into the Captain's office, like a kid getting called into the principal's office. "What did I do this time, Cap?" Max says with a chuckle.

"It isn't what you did. It is more of what I am going to do to you," Captain Perry says with a grin. "You are getting a new partner today."

Max drops his head and shoulders and slowly shakes his head from side to side. "You know I work better alone. Can't you give McCarren the rookie? He needs a partner bad. If not just for the help on his cases, how about just to babysit him—you know, hold his hand, give him a pacifier, that type of stuff?" He winks at Perry.

The Captain assumes a serious face and leans forward. "Look Max, you haven't had a partner for two years now, ever since Curtis suddenly decided to move to L.A. I mean, come on. He was a detective here for over ten years and then after only six months of working with you, he feels the need to move to a warmer climate. You are getting this partner, no matter what. Besides, she has a lot in common with you."

Captain Perry barely finishes his sentence before Max cuts him off. "She? Are you kidding me? I graduated top of my class at the academy. I was a patrol officer for only one year and then I became the youngest detective in town at the age of 23. I have been your best detective ever since then. For the past six years, I have solved your toughest cases and with the exception of Curtis, I have been pretty fair with my fellow detectives."

"Someday, Max, you are going to have to explain to me what happened with Curtis. He said it had nothing to do with you and you deny it as well, but I still think something fishy went on," Perry says.

"Six years, Captain! Six great years and this is how you repay me?" Max's resentment is clear in his voice.

"Like I said, Max, you are getting this partner, no matter what. Here, take a look at her file and you'll see why I think you'll make great partners." He hands Max a manila folder.

Max starts flipping through the file. "Graduated top of her class at the academy. Family lives here in Rockton. Her father was a cop here. He was killed by a disgruntled man on a routine traffic stop when she was young. The guy shot her dad when he approached his car to issue a speeding ticket. It says here she had offers from all over the country but stayed here to be with her mom. She has great connections around town and is very good at research. I could certainly use that ability in a partner—if I wanted one, that is." Max puts the file back on the Captain's desk.

"Ok, Captain, I see that there are some similarities between us. But she has been on the force for four years already and is just getting promoted? Why did it take her so long? I figure with her dad being highly respected and dying in the line of duty, not to mention her exemplary history, that she would have been fast tracked." Max decides he better get this information up front if he can. He doesn't want the Captain to think he is going to take this lying down. He isn't at all comfortable with having a partner, let alone a female one.

Captain Perry sits down in his big leather chair and leans in to Max in a confidential manner. "Well…she has a chip on her shoulder and doesn't take male authority figures very seriously…but I still think she is going to be a great detective. It just took some time for me to convince the Chief to give her a shot. I knew her old man and he was due to be a detective before he was murdered. If she is half as good as him, it will be a great promotion for her and we'll get a great detective added to the team."

The phone on Captain Perry's desk rings. He picks it up, listening, "…Ok, I'll put my best team on it, Chief." Captain Perry hangs up the phone and looks directly at Max. "Well, Larkin, I have more good news for you. You and your new partner just got your first case together. And it's a doozy. There was a family murdered. The entire family was murdered, with the exception of the father. The perp left him alive, but cut off his finger and thumb. That's all we know so far. I'll send you some more info via email or text as I get it."

From the door of his office the Captain calls, "Fairlane, get in here on the double!"

A young woman stands up from a desk in the far corner of the squad room. She is twenty-six years old and strikingly beautiful. Max had seen her around but never really had a conversation with her. She stands 5'8", about 4 inches shorter than him. Her long black hair is swept back into a ponytail at the nape of her neck. She is wearing glasses that accentuate the bones in her face and is dressed very casually for a detective, in jeans and a button-down blue shirt. *At least I wear a sports coat with my jeans,* he thinks. Her white tennis shoes shine like they are brand new and have not been worn before she took them from the closet to wear today.

"Yes, sir, what can I do for you?" Jesse says as she steps into the Captain's office.

"Here is your new partner. Max Larkin, meet Jesse Fairlane," the Captain says while smiling at Max.

The two detectives shake hands and smile at each other uneasily. Max feels lucky that despite her beauty, she isn't his type and he's never been one to get tongue-tied around gorgeous women. He is having a hard time getting past her looks to take her choice to be an officer seriously. However, he also sees that he has no choice.

"Wait a second here, Captain?!" Jesse says with glee. "I get to work with *THE* Max Larkin on my first day as a detective? This is too good to be true!" Jesse turns and beams at Max as he puts his head down, blushing a little bit.

"It is an honor to work with you, Detective Larkin. When I was going through the academy, I heard so many stories about you and how you advanced so quickly to detective. I wanted to be just like you. Heck, I even broke some of your records at the academy, including your time on the combat firing range."

"Nice to meet you too, Josey," Max says, smiling and winking at his boss. He intentionally miscues her name, retaliating for her own sarcasm.

"It's Jesse, Sir. Jesse Fairlane."

Max chuckles under his breath. "Whatever."

Jesse is astonished that he can't remember that they have actually met many times before. She feels the need to speak up. "Actually sir, we have met before today—quite a few times, at that. I am often the first officer on the scene of the cases you investigate."

Max looks her up and down. "I guess I didn't recognize you out of your uniform. I usually don't pay attention to patrol officers because most of them use Rockton as a résumé builder to get a job in a big city like Chicago. I don't really get to know them personally. I figure if they're not going to care about my city, why should I care enough to get to know them?"

"Okay you two, enough. You have a case to work on and according to the Chief, the Mayor is looking for a quick solve on this one because he doesn't want to be known as the mayor of a town where this type of thing happens. Get over to the hospital ASAP. Based on what the Chief said, the father was taken there after he was found, but then heavily sedated. The officers didn't get any information from him, as he was grief-stricken by the death of his family. Try and get some info from him and then head over to the house and take a look around." A moment of silence passes before he blurts out, "What are you two still standing around for? Get going already!" The two detectives quickly leave his office like scolded kids.

Jesse and Max head toward their desks and then meet by the front door. There are only four other detectives on the force besides them: McCarren, Phillips, Johnson, and Salvo. All four of the men are huddled around McCarren's desk, having a good laugh. When Max and Jesse walk by, the remarks include, "Good luck, Max! Be careful and don't break a nail on this one." With that, they all burst out laughing. Jesse bristles at the comments and walks away faster, swinging her arms. Max, however, just mockingly laughs with them and salutes as he follows Jesse more slowly to the parking lot.

As they exit the side door, Jesse heads for her own car. "Hey, rookie, we'll take my car and I'll drive," Max yells.

Jesse curses to herself. She has been waiting for a case like this and never thought she would be paired with Max Larkin. She spent so much time as an officer that she started to doubt her dream of becoming detective. Now, she finally is here and she can't even follow her new partner to the car correctly. *I need to calm down and breathe, or I'm going to constantly worry about what he thinks rather than doing my job,* she rationalizes.

Jesse jogs over toward Max as he gets into his 1982 Black Firebird. *It's a cliché that he drives this kind of car, but I can't say I blame him,* she jokes with herself.

"Nice ride, Detective," Jesse says as she lowers herself into the car and examines the mint condition interior.

"It belonged to my dad. He bought it brand new in 1981, right off the showroom floor. He took good care of it and when I turned 18, he gave it to me for a birthday present," Max says as he fires up the car. "It still roars like a lion after all these years. I really love this car. I mean, my dad wouldn't even let me in this car until I was three. He used to say, 'I didn't want your diaper leaking all over the leather seats,' whenever I asked him why there were no pictures of me in the car when I was a baby. All the pictures show only my parents in the car, or just the car by itself. I wasn't in a single shot with this car. Who knows - maybe that is why he gave it to me. Maybe he felt bad for not including me when I was younger."

Max looks down at his phone and checks his email. He reads a little bit of the case information the Captain sent over and starts filling Jesse in. "The killer mutilated the father, but left him alive. However, he killed the rest of the family. It is truly a brutal murder for our little town."

Max can tell that Jesse is still distant and upset. He guesses that it must be from the other detectives' comments. He isn't sure what to say, but he also thinks she might not focus if she doesn't get her head in the game. "Don't let them get to you. Despite women being officers for many years, very few make detective. The guys are just like that—always cracking jokes and taking shots at each other. It's not personal."

"Well, it certainly feels personal! It seems like no one takes me seriously; everyone thinks, *Why would you want to do that job and see those horrible things?* I want to achieve what my dad didn't, but I don't need all this macho B.S. and 'women don't belong here' crap. I've done everything right and they still don't want to let me in!" At this, Jesse's shoulders slump and she stares out the window dejectedly.

"You did do everything right, kid, so just ignore them. When you are better than them, someone will always try to bring you down. I mean, you broke my records at the Academy—you must have something to hold over them. Hell, McCarren can barely perform this job right now due to his divorce—so preoccupied! Don't let them drag you down and distract you. We have a murderer to find."

Jesse faces Max and grins. Max can see why the guys give her such a hard time. They are trying to treat her like the other guys, but they don't know how to talk to her with her striking good looks. They are being overzealous when they pick on her, to hide their attraction. He hopes this is the end of this personal stuff and tries to turn her attention to the task at hand.

"When we get to the hospital, I think it would be best for me to take point and talk to this guy. I think this is too big a case for you to jump into right away. We can work your way up to it after this one."

Jesse is abashed. *Great, this guy thinks I can't do this job either, despite what he just said. I am going to have to prove him wrong, just like I have proved everyone wrong before.*

As they pull up outside the hospital, Max reiterates, "Remember, rookie, let me do all the talking. Just sit there and take notes. This guy is our only witness."

"I hate hospitals," Jesse whispers as they ride the elevator up to Stephen's room. "They remind me of the perils of our job. I remember visiting my dad once after he was attacked with a knife. We spent a lot of time visiting my grandma, too, before she passed away. Not good memories here."

Stephen Bjornson slowly opens his eyes. The room is very bright, not just from the lights, but because everything is so white. His head is spinning and he can't seem to focus well on any particular object. He remembers sirens and flashing lights and being carried from his house. Then the terror returns. He stifles a mental scream. Still, it creeps up on him as he recalls. He closes his eyes and starts to cry as he realizes that he may be in heaven. Everything is so bright, clean looking, and quiet.

Then the sound of beeps from machines and voices from the next room permeate his consciousness and confirm that he is still earthbound. As he tries to raise his arms to wipe away tears, he feels the I.V. tape pull on his arm. He can vaguely make out thick bandages and senses the wetness of blood seeping through on his right hand. He feels bandages on his lips. He closes his eyes as the room starts to spin, but then he pictures the masked man kneeling over his beautiful wife with the pen in his hand. He bolts straight up, screaming her name. The medical staff burst into the room to stabilize him. It takes two big orderlies to hold him and strap him down.

The detectives walk into Stephen's room just as he is calming down. In a very direct manner, Detective Larkin says, "Mr. Bjornson, I'm Detective Larkin and this is Detective Fairlane. I know this is going to be very difficult, but we need to ask you some questions so we can find this guy. He needs to be stopped before he can do this to another family."

Stephen interrupts the detective before he can go any further. "Where are my kids? Are they okay?" he asks in a slightly slurred voice. He appears panicked and he can't form the words well. Max realizes there is only a small window of opportunity to question him.

As gently as he can he explains the fate of the Bjornson children and, as expected, Stephen is distraught, shuffling in his bed. His head is tossing back and forth as he fights his restraints. The detective asks him another question, hoping he will answer. "Mr. Bjornson, I know you're in pain. We want to help you and are truly sorry for your loss. We also need to catch this guy before he kills again. Please help us!" Max says as he reaches down and touches Stephen's arm.

Stephen bitterly wails, "What do I care? He took everything from me. I have nothing to live for!"

"If you truly feel that way, Mr. Bjornson, then you're wasting my time," retorts Detective Larkin. Slowly Stephen lifts his head up, his whole body goes rigid, and he blanches visibly. He gasps for air, as if he is having a hard time breathing.

"I've heard that before," Stephen says, his eyes wild. "The man in the suit said it to me many times, and he kept mumbling those exact words over and over to himself. 'Quit wasting my time; you're wasting my time; time is money'—over and over again. I'll hear those words in my head the rest of my life!" He then drops his head, looking down at his bandaged hand. "He kept telling me that I wasted his time a month ago and it cost him $633. He actually had me pay him $633, but that is not the weirdest thing. He collected $650 between my wallet and my wife's purse, but he left $17 as change on my dresser. If he was robbing me, why wouldn't he take all of our money? Why didn't he take any of our stuff? He even left my wife's jewelry."

Larkin zeroed in on the comments. "What did you do last month? Where did you go? I need to know exactly everything you did and everywhere you went. Do you think you can remember all of that, Mr. Bjornson?"

"We did nothing out of the ordinary. I went to work; Gwen took care of the kids." Abruptly he blurts, "Can I please just be alone right now?"

Detective Larkin tells Stephen to call him if he can remember anything else and hands him a card. Upon exiting, he turns to Stephen and says, "Remember this, Mr. Bjornson: there may be other families on this man's list. What if he could have been stopped before he took your family and you learned that another man chose not to help, as you are doing right now? How would that affect your life and how you feel about this situation? You can help us stop this man and prevent another family from suffering like you are. Please call me if you can remember anything at all, no matter how small a detail; it could be important."

As the detectives walk out of the room, Jesse grabs Max by the arm in the hallway. "He knows a lot more than he's saying. Why did you let him off so easily?"

"Think about it this way…only a few hours ago, his whole family was brutally murdered. His wife was killed right next to him. His kids were killed in their sleep. He has lost his entire family at the hands of a man that he can't identify and evidently all over a few hundred dollars. He is still in a state of shock. I just refreshed a memory from that time when I said, 'You are wasting my time.' He went pale and talked about it even though it upset him. If I push him now, all that will do is make his brain put a mental block over it all and he will get angry at us. He needs to open up on his own time. Who knows, maybe he truly cannot remember anything at this time, but if we leave him be, his mind can relax and let details come back to him naturally. This is why I wanted to be the one to talk to him. You might have cost us a valuable witness had you pressured him." His explanation is not haughty but it is not far from it.

"I completely understand what you mean, sir. I guess I might have been a little too anxious and pushed him away. Maybe that's why the Captain put me with you." Actually, despite her conciliatory tone, Jesse is seething but decides humility will work best with this chauvinist.

"Let's get over to the house and see what we can find out there, providing that the original officers and paramedics didn't destroy all of our evidence already," Max says as he continues to walk away from Jesse.

As they get back into Max's car, he can't help noticing that Jesse doesn't seem right. She is dragging along like she has the weight of the world on her shoulders. Max closes his door, puts on his seatbelt, and watches as Jesse does the same. Once she is situated, he fires up the engine. The loud roar always puts a smile on his face. It reminds him of his father and the good times with him and this car.

Just as they are about to drive away, he pushes the gearshift back into park. Despite his better judgment, he asks, "What's eating you?"

Jesse seems stunned by his reaction. *We just left a man that lost his whole life in one night, and the great Max Larkin doesn't understand why I'm upset? He just ripped me for wanting to push him harder for information. Nothing seems great about this day so far!*

"I just feel like this day couldn't get much worse. That poor man lost his family. I get stuck with you. I looked up to you for the last four years, trying to be like you, and I feel like you don't want me anywhere near you. I'm a great cop and will be a great detective, but you haven't even given me a chance. You've already made up your mind that I'm not going to be good just because I'm a woman!" she snaps back at Max with such an attitude that he snaps his head back as if she just struck him in the face.

Max stares straight ahead and steps on the gas a bit too hard. The tires screech as he accelerates away from the hospital. He pretends he's concentrating on his driving as he absorbs her words. He is actually impressed that Jesse stuck up for herself and realizes maybe she's right. Maybe he is being too hard on her and being unfair.

As they get closer to the Bjornson's neighborhood, he glances sideways at her. "Hey, Jesse, I apologize. Maybe you're right. I *am* being too hard on you. I truly didn't want a partner, but if I have to have one, I am glad that I have a person that can admit mistakes and still stand up for themselves."

This lightens the mood and she offers a small grin and even snickers.

They ride in silence through quiet streets. "The truth is, Jesse, my last partner was thought to be a good detective for Rockton. He was a detective for ten years and had a great closing ratio on his cases. The only thing was, he was doing some things that were not proper. There was one time we were investigating some home robberies and we determined it was most likely women because of some long blonde hair found at two of the scenes. The hair didn't have a skin tag on it, so no D.N.A., but we were able to determine it was a woman's hair. We brought in a woman for questioning, based on an anonymous tip. Her alibi checked out, but she was still a good suspect based on the information the tipster gave us. About two weeks went by and there was another robbery. I decided one night I would follow her and see what she was up to. I got to her place and lo and behold, my partner was going into her house carrying a bottle of wine. He wound up staying the whole night."

Max sighs and continues, "When I confronted him about it the next day, he tried to defend it, saying, 'Her alibi checked out so I figured why not?' It was at that point that I lost trust in him and told him either he could leave on his own, or I'd tell the Captain about it. It turns out the woman he was sleeping with didn't have anything to do with the crime. The anonymous tipster turned out to be an ex-boyfriend and he just wanted her to suffer. The ex did get charged with submitting a false report. Thank God for telephone tracking software. That's how we were able to find out who the tipster was.

"The point is that my partner shouldn't have crossed that line. You do not socialize with suspects. No way, no how! I promised him I wouldn't sully his reputation at the station so he could still get a job elsewhere. I kind of regret that, but at the time, I thought it would be best to not ruin his life over one mishap. Please don't say a word about this to anyone. You're the only person I've told about this. We need to have trust as partners. I need to know I can trust you with this and everything else that being a partner entails." She nods.

As Jesse sits there listening she realizes two things, Max is very serious about his job and that he is genuinely sorry for the way he has been treating her. "I understand. I'm not your old partner, though. I care a lot about this community. I'm here to help keep this town safe. Please don't lump me in with him. You can trust me with anything and everything," Jesse says emphatically. "Of course, I know those are only words; time will tell what I'm really made of."

By the time the two detectives pull into the Bjornson's driveway, there is a sense of growing mutual trust. The two detectives are smiling and cheerful—as cheerful as two people could be as they were about to enter a murder scene.

"Ok, Jesse, what do you see?" Max asks his new partner as they walk into the Bjornson house. The smell of cordite and iron has mostly dissipated, but Max still catches a faint whiff of it—a hint of the horrors that had taken place fourteen hours ago.

Jesse looks around the Bjornson home for a second and responds confidently, "I see the door kicked in, but according to the first officers on the scene, they had to break down that door to get into the house. I see smudged bloody footprints. I think those are the paramedics and police officers because the imprints look like the type of shoes I was issued as a patrol officer. Other than that, I see nothing out of place, which likely means it was not a robbery. This was very personal and all about killing them—not stealing anything but their lives."

Max stands there in awe. He's not sure he was this quick on his feet during his first case as detective. "That's good, Jesse. You do have an eye for details. Now, let's go into the master bedroom. According to Mr. Bjornson and the evidence, that's where the killer spent most of his time. Once we're done in there, I want to check out the kids' rooms, as well. But let's start there and work our way back."

The first thing both detectives see is the bloody writing on the wall. They both stare at it, trying to fathom the mind that would do this. They scan the room looking for anything that would stick out to them. Their eyes meet in the middle of the visual search, and they each can tell that the other is just as astonished at the carnage and the malice.

Jesse can't hold back her feelings anymore. "This guy is a monster. We need to catch him, and fast." Max nods his head.

"Jesse, come look at this," Max says as he stares at the bed. "What's missing right here?" He points to the area where the wife had been sleeping.

"There are two very large dents on this side of the bed. These large spots are on either side of where Mrs. Bjornson was lying in the bed." Jesse points at the right side of the bed and draws a line where Gwen would have been lying. "Do you think the sick bastard was kneeling over her when he killed her?"

Max nods his head in agreement and continues to look around. Jesse takes some pictures of the bed and surrounding area, thinking that maybe she will see something in the pictures later, after they put some of this together. Of course, she hasn't seen the Crime Scenes guy's photos yet, but she still wants her own. She figures it would also give her a fresh look, without the emotional trauma.

"Well, besides the big dents on the bed, there isn't a single thing that sticks out here. This guy was very careful to not leave anything that could help us. What do you think?" Jesse asks, shaking her head.

"I am going to head to the son's room and take a look around." Max takes one last look around the room as he heads down the hallway to the Bjornson boy's room. As the two enter the room, they once again see the bloody writing on the wall. Max looks over to his new partner and sees her lips moving like she is saying something under her breath.

"What? Did you say something?"

She looks over at her partner with very sad eyes. "I was just saying a prayer for this little boy. It just isn't fair!" Jesse bows her head and continues her prayer. She then raises her head and continues into the room.

They both take a look around the room. Again, nothing seems out of place. The killer came into the room, did what he set out to do, and left. There is no evidence the killer was even there except for the writing on the wall and the empty bed.

Both detectives continue to look over the room and when their eyes meet after a few minutes, Max gestures toward the exit. They both head toward the door, Jesse trailing her fingers over a picture of the boy with his parents, smiling at the camera. Max follows behind and they both head down the hall to Bjornson's daughter's room.

There it was, the bloody writing on the wall, staring at them. They stare at it like deer caught in the headlights. There is no way to avoid the writing, as hard as they try. It seems so out of place with the brightness of the room. Jesse once again bows her head and starts praying for the little girl who once slept peacefully in this room, and for the terrible waste of innocence.

She glances over at the bed and scans the initial notes from the arriving officers. She looks at the bed and back at the notes, over and over. One paragraph stands out and makes her gasp. When the officers had found the little girl, there were deep indentations in the bedspread on each side of her body.

"This guy has a thing for showing his power over females, even little girls. Do you see this?" Jesse points to the notes in her hand. "He probably straddled her and knelt over her as he killed her, just like he did with her mom. They didn't find anything like this around the areas where the father and son were, but he did it to both of the females," Jesse says as she takes pictures of the bed and surrounding area. The evidence of his kneeling is gone since the covers had been moved, but Jesse feels a need to document this room, if nothing else than to remind her of the heinous crime.

"Good catch. I think you're right. He definitely has issues with women, that's for sure," Max tells Jesse as he continues searching. "I think we have seen all we need to see here. Let's get out of here and take a look at the forensic pictures back at the station. What do you say?"

"I think you're right. Maybe there is something in the notes from Bjornson's interview, as short as it was," Jesse says.

The short drive back to the station is silent. The detectives are still wallowing in the backwash of the crime, their senses still reeling. Neither remembers anything this evil happening in their town. It seems like something that happens in other cities—bigger cities—to other people, and gets shown on the national news. They have had their share of homicides in Rockton, Max more than Jesse, but this level of carnage is new to them.

Once they arrive back at the station, Jesse sits at his old partner's desk, right across from him. It is quiet once again as they look over all the evidence and statements. It seems like there is a lack of something— statements, witnesses, and motive.

Who kills someone for wasting their time? Max stares at his desk and starts thinking about what Bjornson had said at the hospital. *Why did the* *killer wear a suit? Why did the man want only $633—no more, no less? What job makes $211 an hour?*

"Jesse, Captain Perry says you're good at research, so I need you to dump all the phone records from the Bjornson cell phones—who they talked to, for how long, their texts, and their emails. I need to know who they were talking to and about what! Maybe they know this guy." Jesse walks away to see where the tech team is on gathering the data she needs.

Max continues staring at the pictures and the evidence, hoping that he will see something. The man must have been covered in blood if the bed was that messy. Besides, he had used the blood to write on the walls so it's likely that some of that got on him as well. "So there was a well-dressed man covered in blood, leaving the Bjornson house early this morning," Max says out loud to no one in particular. He scans over each picture and each page trying to find something—anything—that can help. *How does one clean a nice but bloody suit? The victim said he was well dressed. I know blood is hard to get off things, especially clothes. Would he dump the suit? Would he have it dry cleaned?* He's used to tossing questions like this around during a case. Sometimes it's useless; sometimes it stirs up something in the dark, musty corners of his mind.

It only takes Jesse about an hour to get the information Max requested. The first thing that she points out is the emails and text messages to David Pierce from Gwen Bjornson. There are some hot and steamy messages between the two. The last text message to Gwen from David was last night, just around the time Mr. Bjornson had told the officers he and his wife went to bed, trying to set up a meeting for today at lunch. Her response had been less than enthusiastic. She had sent him a message saying she was starting to feel bad and thought that they should stop seeing each other. She had even mentioned changing daycare providers for Sandy. "Jesse, I need you to get me info on David Pierce: his address, his job, the whole works, ASAP!" Larkin's eyes brighten. "Mr. Pierce just moved to the top of our list."

"Already on it. I came to the same conclusions. We should be getting that information any minute now," she says, excitement in her own eyes.

It turns out that David Pierce lives just a few blocks away from the Bjornson's house. He is a mostly stay-at-home dad with a part time job as a barista at the local coffee shop in the mornings. Max wants to make it to the coffee shop before David's shift is over. He figures he can pair that with getting something light to eat and some coffee. Since his day had turned from paperwork to homicide early this morning, he hadn't had more than a cup of coffee to keep him going. David was scheduled to work this morning so this would be a good time to get him to talk without his wife and kids around.

"David Pierce, please?" Larkin asks a young woman cleaning tables at the coffee shop. She points to the counter, where a relatively young man is working. David Pierce is making coffee for a client. He is a good looking man, younger in appearance than Mr. Bjornson, but lacking the confidence that Mr. Bjornson exuded, despite his trauma. "David Pierce?" he asks the man.

"Yes. What can I get you, sir?"

"I need to ask you some questions, Mr. Pierce," says Detective Larkin.

"Sorry, sir, but, if you don't order anything, I can't help you."

"But I insist!" Detective Larkin intones as he flashes his badge.

With fear in his eyes, David tells his co-workers that he is going to take a break. He tells Detective Larkin to have a seat in the far corner of the coffee shop, where he will meet him in two minutes. As David starts walking toward the table, the detective senses he's nervous. David has a muscular build. Larkin briefly wonders if that was what attracted Mrs. Bjornson.

"What can I do for you, Officer?" David says, a bit sheepishly. He keeps glancing over at his co-workers to see if they are watching the conversation.

"How do you know Gwen Bjornson? What is your relationship?" are Detective Larkin's first questions.

"She's a good friend. Her daughter goes to the same daycare as my son and she comes into the coffee shop a lot. We've had lunch a few times, talking about our kids and stuff. With a quick glance he asks, "Did something happen to Gwen or Sandy that I should know about? Is something going on with the school?"

"Mr. Pierce, I know that you know Gwen better than that!" Larkin says as he pulls out a few printed emails. "I think you know her very well, based on what I'm reading here. You may know her better than her husband. So you need to come clean and quit wasting my time with your lies," snaps Larkin.

"Okay, okay, we did know each other outside of what I said earlier," David says his eyes darting about. "We have been having an affair for over a year now. Did her husband, Stephen, tell you about us or something? Oh my God, does he know? I don't understand why the police would care about me having an affair! It's not against the law." David starts to look scared.

"Last night you sent her a text message trying to set up a meeting today, but she declined. Were you upset by this?" asks Detective Larkin.

"Yeah, I was upset!" David exclaims. "I wanted to meet to tell her that I'm falling in love with her and that I am hoping we can leave our spouses and run away together. We're both so unhappy, but we love our children. But then she sent me a message back saying that she wanted to break it off—stop seeing me. So yes, to say that I was upset is an understatement. What did she say happened? Did she file some charges on me for harassment or something?" David says. "Is Stephen harassing her? Is she okay?"

His voice even, Larkin says, "David, Gwen was murdered last night in her home, along with her son and daughter. Her husband is still alive, but barely survived. The murderer cut off his thumb and finger to send him a message."

The man blanches; his voice turns shaky. "What message?"

"The message was to not waste anyone's time anymore. The murderer said Stephen wasted his time and that the whole family wasted others' time."

Max waits a beat to gauge David's reaction. But he just sits there, silent and wide-eyed, with tears running down his cheeks. Detective Larkin asks the next obvious question. "Where were you last night?"

"You don't seriously think I did this? I love Gwen! I would never hurt her. You should check into her husband Stephen more. He is always biting off more than he can chew. He would take her out shopping all the time and buy stuff they didn't need. And sometimes he would take her out shopping for things that he couldn't afford, like cars, boats, and houses, just to look like a big shot in her eyes. Truth be told, she said it annoyed her. She said that all those shopping trips did is to remind her of stuff she would never own with him. It made her feel inferior to the people that worked there and the people that did have those nice things. She told me that Stephen also borrows money from a lot of people and some of them are not on the up and up, if you know what I mean. This really scared her, but she was telling me that he was getting better at paying them off on time as of late."

Detective Larkin listens quietly and says nothing. He decides that David can go. For now, everything he says appears to be the truth, but he tells him to not go far. He hands his card over and says to call if anything else occurs to him, such as any names of Mr. Bjornson's associates. He stays at the table to watch Pierce return to work. He notices that he avoids eye contact with his co-workers and says it was nothing. He curses under his breath, as he forgot to order anything before his discussion with David and, now he wants to get away from the coffee shop. He decides he'll pick up some food on his way back to the station.

Back at his desk, fast food in hand, he decides he needs to start planning better for the unexpected rather than eat junk because it's convenient. Instead of sitting at his desk, he picks up the food, moving to an interview room to be alone with his thoughts. He just can't believe that David Pierce is involved. David is just a lonely man who was in love with another man's wife. If David were to kill anyone, he believed he would have killed Bjornson, not his wife. Besides, being a father meant he was less likely to kill the children. At least, that's what Max thought. Not being a father himself, maybe he was wrong.

"Jesse!" Detective Larkin yells out the door after finishing his lunch. Jesse comes running into the room. "I need you to pull the financial files on the Bjornson family. I want to know all I can about what was going on with them." She returns to the other room, slightly winded, nodding her head in assent.

Jesse is fast—the request takes only thirty minutes. The Bjornsons have nothing out of the ordinary. Two mortgages, two car loans—one of which was just opened about three weeks ago — student loans from Mr. Bjornson's college, and about $25,000 in credit card debt, which is nothing out of the ordinary for a family of four these days. They have two bank accounts, a joint checking account and a joint savings account, each one with about $10,000 in them. Mr. Bjornson has a great job, making about $125,000 a year as a Vice President for a local restaurant chain. Everything seems normal. It turns out that Mr. Pierce was being lied to by Mrs. Bjornson about their money problems. Granted, they are not able to afford all the things they shop for, but they are not hurting by any means. It wouldn't make sense that Mr. Bjornson owed all kinds of money with $20,000 sitting in the bank. People who borrow money from criminals don't save their money. Detective Larkin wonders briefly if Mr. Pierce found out about her exaggerations, but then remembers the pain on David's face when he learned about Gwen's death. He still can't see any involvement from him. He knows he can't rule him out, but he's positive that they need to focus on someone else.

Something gnaws at Larkin. He feels that he has to be missing something. There is more to this than meets the eye. He goes back to the evidence. First up is the $17 the killer left behind. He was smart enough not to leave any fingerprints, so that's out. Next up are the bolt cutters that were used to cut the fingers and thumbs off. Again, no fingerprints. *Damn!* Detective Larkin thinks. *Ever since television has started airing forensic-style shows, everyone wears gloves!*

Detective Larkin heads back to the hospital. It seems like the only place to go for more information at this time. *He has to know more than he told me last time. Maybe the shock and medications have worn off, and he is thinking more clearly than before.* Besides, they have to catch this guy before he does this again. Something about the murder scene says that this isn't the last they will hear from this monster.

The first thing Max notices is that Mr. Bjornson looks less likely to speak than before. His confidence is gone and his shell is all that is left lying in the hospital bed. The loss of his family is settling in deeply.

Max starts out by apologizing again for his loss. "Mr. Bjornson, is there anything you can tell me that you may have remembered since last time I was here? Anything, no matter how big or small, could be a great help."

Bjornson sits up in the bed, finally looking more awake than he had since his admittance. "No! I can't remember anything else. I didn't see his face; he was wearing a mask. All I can remember is the suit he was wearing. It was a nice suit—nothing too cheap or too expensive. I know it was a dark color—either blue or black. He wore a white buttoned shirt with what might have been a silk tie. It was very dark at the time he was in there. All I can see when I close my eyes is Gwennie's blood splattered across that white shirt and his cuff links glistening with her blood," Bjornson says, looking as if he is going to break down again. He becomes less animated with every word, and his eyes glaze over as he remembers the look on Gwen's face as the pen descended toward her face.

Detective Larkin interrupts him as he starts mumbling "Poor Gwen" over and over.

Max says, "I have one more question for you, sir, and this one may be the toughest of them all. When he was using your bolt cutters, did you notice if he was right-handed or…?"

Bjornson shakes his head and cuts him off. "They weren't *my* bolt cutters. I have never seen them before in my life. I have no use for such a tool in my house. I can only assume that he must have brought them with him."

Larkin's face brightens. "This could be the break I am looking for, Mr. Bjornson. Like I told you before, no matter how big or how small, anything you tell me can make a difference. Now, do you remember if he was right- or left-handed?"

Unfortunately, Mr. Bjornson can't remember that detail. He says that he was too scared and in too much in shock to pay attention to something that small, but he has given the detective a very important piece of information. The bolt cutters belong to the killer and not the Bjornsons.

Detective Larkin rushes back to the police station and looks over the bolt cutters that are still in the forensics lab. He has Jesse find out all she can about their make and model and where they are sold locally. Jesse comes back into the room with a huge list of retailers.

It turns out that there is nothing special about the bolt cutters. They are sold at every home improvement and hardware store throughout the country. The darn things don't even have serial numbers—another dead end. This guy is either really smart or he is really lucky.

Jesse and Max sit there for awhile looking over the bolt cutters, still in their plastic evidence bag. The techs hadn't gotten to them yet so they were hoping to see a fingerprint in an odd area, a piece of skin caught on the handle—anything at all.

Max picks up a legal pad and starts jotting. When he is done he stares at his writing and says, "The killer is unlike other killers. What is the most different thing about this killer?"

"I d say motive. He doesn't kill for the average motives people kill for. Seems like he isn't in serious financial problems, so it isn't a mob kind of thing. And so far, from what we know it isn't a love triangle type of thing considering our former prime suspect there, the young man in the coffee shop."

She hesitated, then said, "We do know the Bjornsons like to shop but don't always buy."

Max nodded, wanting more.

Jesse didn't speak as she lapsed into deep thought. "Well, the most telling thing to me is this business of wasting time and collecting money. He's definitely whacked. But on the other hand, he has a responsible job and probably deals with the public."

He said, "Are you thinking some kind of pissed off, whacko salesman?

"It's as good as any other suspect. The wasting time. The collecting of money. Maybe some high ticket salesman that's off his rocker."

"And that leads me to another avenue."

"And that is?"

"That's the damn uniqueness of the crime. Nobody does stuff like this. Nobody sane, that is. The collecting and all. The message on the wall. It's so unique one has to ask if this or something like it has been done before around here!"

Larkin tilts back his chair, thinking about one more cup of coffee to get him home for the night, when Jesse exclaims, "I'm going to run a nationwide search on this type of murder. I think this guy may have done this already. Maybe not here, but he has definitely killed before!"

"Good thinking, Jesse," he tells her with a smile. She smiles back and heads back to her desk to search the database.

It is getting close to 1 a.m.—way past quitting time for Detectives Jesse Fairlane and Max Larkin, but they don't care now that they have a new direction to go toward. All they care about is finding this guy before he strikes again. The street lights' luminescent glow is poking through the high row of windows near the ceiling. The inside fluorescent lights flicker slightly. They used to give Max a headache, but now he finds their hum familiar and comforting. They sift through boxes of unsolved murders while the computer searches for similar cases. Sitting at adjacent desks, they are looking for any similarities to the Bjornson family case. Nothing from their precinct looks quite the same as what they saw at that house. They can't recall ever seeing a whole family murdered like this—not in their lifetime. There is a stack of boxes that clerks brought up earlier that they haven't even begun to sort through.

Detective Larkin jumps up suddenly, upsetting his chair and spilling the coffee that was in his left hand all over the floor. "Wait just a minute!" he exclaims as he puts a story in front of Jesse. "Here he is! This is our guy. Ten years ago, he killed a whole family just twenty minutes from here in Clinton, Wisconsin. He cut off the thumb and finger of the husband and wrote on their wall to stop wasting people's time. The search was widened to this area, so we have a file here in Rockton. You were right, Jesse, he has killed before. We need to find this guy."

"I remember that story now," Jesse says, thinking back. "I was in junior high when that happened. We were all reminded not to talk to strangers and to be home before dark the week that it happened. It was assumed that it was a man who broke into their home in the middle of the night and then tied them up and tortured them. The sick bastard even killed their cat. Do you remember that one, Max?"

"Actually, Jesse, I don't," he says with some confusion in his voice. "I was in my freshman year of college in northern Wisconsin. That's weird that my parents never even told me about it. Rarely does something that big happen around here in Rockton. Maybe they just didn't want me to worry about them."

As Detective Larkin ponders why he was completely unaware of such a terrible murder so close to home, Jesse moves from the stack of papers over to Max's desk. She starts a second computer search for murders with the key words 'stop wasting time.' As she pores through the various hits, thinking that the Clinton murder must have been the first, she sees a reference to a town east of Rockton, outside of Illinois in Indiana.

"Oh my God!" Jesse says as she sits straight up in her chair, the color draining from her face. "Here is one from twenty-five years ago in the northern part of Indiana—Merrillville, Indiana to be exact. He killed a man and a woman, but left their three-year-old son alive. He actually woke the kid up and dragged him into his parents' room, making him dial 911. Then he had him tell the police he was sorry for wasting their time with his parents' murder. Can you believe that he actually did that to that poor little boy? He wrote the same thing on the wall in blood… STOP WASTING PEOPLE'S TIME"

Larkin is excited. "Let's start with that case from ten years ago. It should be the fresher of the two and is closer. We can put the two files together and compare them when we get back tomorrow. I am going to head over to Clinton first thing in the morning, after I go home and get some rest. You should go home and get some shut-eye also, Jesse. Two fresh pairs of eyes could make a huge difference on this case. Get out of here, and I'll catch up with you after I get back from Clinton," Detective Larkin says as he grabs his coat and heads out the door. He is not sure if he'll get any sleep, but he has to try to rest if he is going to complete the marathon that every murder investigation becomes.

anush Patel lies in his bed with the sounds of the ocean coming from a white noise machine. He feels a slight pain in his neck like a bee sting. His eyes open wide; he's shocked at the sight of a man wearing a black ski mask and a dark colored suit staring down at him. He reaches out toward him, only to discover his arms are restricted by something. Hanush is in his fourth month of residency at St. Joseph's Hospital. Given his medical background and experience, he knows he has been drugged and will likely either die or fall asleep very soon.

Hanush's eyes come open ever so slowly. *Is he gone? What just happened?* are the only things that come to his mind. He must have blacked out, as he feels like he has lost some time from his life—like minutes have gone by that he felt pass subconsciously. He is able to look around but still cannot move his body. Feeling the muscles trying to work, he notices that no limbs will move from their current position, either. He is able to tilt his chin toward his chest a little to see that his entire body from the neck down has been duct taped to his bed. There are rows and rows of tape strapping him against the sheets. Oddly, he becomes concerned about the glue from the tape ruining his sheets. These sheets are satin and one of the few luxuries he allowed himself during med school.

He hears a small noise toward the foot of the bed and raises his eyes to see a suited man watching him. The man is sitting in a kitchen chair. The chair is turned backwards and the man is straddling the seat. He seems to be just staring at Hanush, waiting for him to wake up.

"Who are you? What are you doing here?" Hanush tries to yell at the man. "What do you want? How did you get in here?"

The words come out mushy and slurred but the man understands enough to get the gist.

The masked man stands up and walks slowly over to Hanush. "I've been waiting for you to wake up for a while now, Hanush. Can I call you Hanush?"

"My friends call me Hanush, my patients call me Doctor Patel, and you are neither, so I would rather you just leave here right now before…" Hanush slurs through his words quickly, but the man interrupts.

"Before what? Before you get up and attack me? Good luck with that; you are taped up nice and tight. And if you somehow miraculously free yourself, I'll kill you before you can get one foot on the floor. I suggest you be nice to me, Hanush, or this is going to be a short night for you, if you know what I mean." The man walks around the left side of the bed and slaps Hanush's face. "You see, Hanush, you wasted my time earlier today and time is money. So I have come to get my money from you. You wasted two and a half hours of my time today. That means you owe me $527.50. Does that sound okay to you, *Doctor* Patel?"

"I am not going to give you one cent. I owe you nothing!" Hanush replies angrily.

"Here are your choices, Hanush: You can pay me my money right now and I leave, or you can stick to your principles and not pay me. Then I will torture you until you do pay. Either way is fine by me. What's it going to be? I leave that decision entirely up to you. I suggest you make up your mind quickly, because time is money and I want my money. You wouldn't want me to add more to your bill, would you?" He reaches into his pocket and pulls out a Swiss Army knife. He exposes the corkscrew attachment and waves it in front of Hanush's face.

"Okay, okay," Hanush says, his voice quavering. He has quashed his anger because he sees it is getting him nowhere. "You can have your money. My wallet is in my pants pocket on the floor on the other side of the bed." The suited man goes over to the other side of the bed and grabs the pants. He pulls the wallet out and finds a solitary $20 bill.

"That's it? Twenty bucks? I said you owe me $527.50. Heck, I am even willing to round down to $527, but I am not settling for anything less than that," the man says as he throws the wallet onto the bed next to Hanush's head.

"That is all I have here. Look around here; I have nothing. I am just a resident med student. Take all that I have and leave, please. I am a doctor and I help people. I do not deserve this," Hanush says with just a touch of courage and conviction in his voice. "Just leave."

The man is now pacing alongside of the bed mumbling, "Twenty measly dollars. Time is money. You wasted my time and time is money. Twenty dollars will not do. It will not do at all. Time is money and you wasted my time, and now I want my money."

Hanush lies in his bed, struggling to break free quietly, to no avail. The drugs have started to wear off so he is hoping he has a chance to take this guy or get past him to get away. "Please, Mister, I am begging you to let me go. Take the money, take anything you want, but leave me be, please," he says as the fear in him grows with each passing moment. "I just want you to leave me alone, please."

Hanush closes his eyes and thinks of his family in India—of his mother and sisters who begged him to stay in school there rather than go to America. His betrothed is there also, but he is starting to wonder if he'll get to have his wedding after all. He just wanted to get the best medical education he could, with the best technology. Now he wonders if he will pay for that decision with his life.

The man keeps pacing and mumbling. He puts his right index finger, indicating he will be back in a moment. He leaves the bedroom and Hanush lets out a sigh of relief. He starts thinking about his day. *How did I meet this guy? Who is he?* keeps running through his mind. He continues to push at the tape as his muscles burn off the drug effects.

The suited man walks out of the bedroom and looks around for something that is worth $507. The apartment would be considered a studio if not for the door to the bedroom. The kitchen is attached to the main living area. There is a small wooden table with one wooden chair along the wall under the only window in the whole dark, dreary apartment. The only thing that he can see of any value is a coffee pot that is sitting on the counter top between the sink and stove. He mentally evaluates it and shakes his head in disgust. He walks toward the bedroom door.

The suited man walks into the bedroom and sees Hanush pushing calmly against his tape restraints with his knees and elbows. Hanush's head jerks up to meet the man's glare as the color leaves his face.

"Did you really think I left without my money? Come on, really? You have no TV, no radio, no nothing! Hell, even your coffee pot is a piece of junk. There is nothing of value at all in this apartment. How do you live? And most of all, how do you plan on giving me my money?"

Hanush is now gasping for air as fear consumes him. He had thought the man had left and he had worked out a plan to slowly push the restraints until they broke or gave. "I am a poor immigrant from India. I told you, I am just an intern with massive student debt. The only money I have is in the bank, and I use all of that to pay for food and gas to get to the hospital and back."

"You have money in the bank, you say? How much, exactly?" the masked man asks as he turns his head inquisitively. "Maybe I can get my money after all."

Hanush eyes his wallet. "I just got paid from the hospital, but I did buy some things today. Maybe there is enough to give you. Take my debit card out of my wallet, and go to the bank and get it. My pin is 7812. Please take it from my wallet and leave me be now. You will have your money. Go."

The masked man starts laughing. "Sorry Hanush, it isn't going to be that easy. You are going to have to come with me to the bank and get it out of the ATM yourself. I'm not going to take the risk of me leaving here and you getting loose and calling the cops or even worse, cancelling your debit card. Now, how should we do this?"

"I will not call the cops or cancel the debit card. I promise," Hanush says with some hope in his voice. "I just want this to be over and if you get your money, you said you would leave."

Hanush awakes inside his own car with his right hand duct taped to the gearshift knob. He remembers seeing the man remove a needle from his pocket—most likely the drugs coursing through his system for a second time. The man is still wearing his mask and is holding the pocket knife in his right hand.

"Hanush, I know you feel a little groggy, but I'm sure you can handle driving to the bank just a few blocks away. I'm glad you have a basement apartment. I'm not sure I could have gotten you here from the third floor so quietly." The man chuckles and pushes a needle next to Hanush's right shoulder with his left hand. "This syringe is full of air. If you try anything, I will inject it directly into you. Since you are a doctor, you know what this will do to you. Right?"

Hanush nods his head. "Yes, it will go to my heart and kill me. It is a very painful way to die. Don't worry; I will do as you say." The masked man reaches over and starts the car. He places the knife on his thigh and puts his right hand over Hanush's hand on the gearshift to slide the car into drive while his left hand still holds the needle to Hanush's shoulder.

The roads are clear, without a car in sight. The only light that can be seen comes from Hanush's car and a few streetlights that barely put a dent in the darkness. Hanush thinks that Rockton must be facing a budget crisis since the lamps seem so far apart, or they need to put up more street lights because it is so dark. He is struggling to see beyond his headlight beams. He is having a hard time keeping focused, so he wonders if his perception of the lights is just due to the haze from the drugs he has been given twice tonight.

The bank is only five blocks away from his apartment. Hanush pulls his car into the ATM drive-thru lane and uses his left hand to hit the switch that lowers the window. The man hands him his own ATM card and watches him enter the pin. He notices that he types different numbers than 7812. "Hey, you lied to me earlier. I can't believe this! You tried to waste my time even more. Get me my money now!"

Hanush requests $520 and hands the crisp bills to the man. "I am sorry I lied earlier. You're right. I just wanted you to leave. I'm truly sorry. Please, will you leave me alone now?"

The man shakes his head no and tells Hanush, "Let's get back to your place and we can go from there. You have some explaining to do."

Although the ride back to the apartment is short, Hanush can hear the man mumbling, "You wasted my time. Time is money. You wasted my time and then you lied to me." The distance might have been short, but it seemed as long as his first plane ride between home and New York. He cannot shake the feeling that he is going to be punished for lying to the man. He can feel his weak muscles shaking, but he isn't sure if the drug or his fear is causing it. Either way, he just hopes that the man will let him go. Foreboding grips him as they approach his building.

Hanush pulls into the parking lot and puts the car in park. His left hand is shaking as he reaches around the wheel to turn off the car. He can barely squeak out, "What now?" as he turns to the man holding a needle at his arm. Hanush briefly entertains using his left hand to push the needle away so he can escape and only then remembers the tape on his right hand. He could probably not pull that away quickly enough to escape. An air embolism frightens him.

The man looks at him and chuckles under his breath. "Well, Hanush,

I am fresh out of my drug of choice to knock you out. I'm not going to kill you here in your car. So that leaves me one choice…" The man reaches his left hand behind Hanush's head and forces it forward onto the outer edge of the steering wheel, knocking Hanush out.

The man uses the knife from his right hand to cut Hanush loose from the tape. He quickly climbs out of the passenger side of the vehicle and pulls Hanush out of the driver's seat to the hard concrete. He stretches himself before dragging Hanush to his apartment window. All of this work isn't sitting well with him—not at all in line with how he had planned his evening. Pushing the body in feet first, he is surprised at the dead weight for such a small person. Leaving Hanush hanging half in and half out, he pulls him the rest of the way once he reenters the apartment.

Hanush is again bound with duct tape. He may have run out of his drug of choice, but he had plenty of duct tape with him tonight. This time, he decides to bind Hanush in the chair near the window. No one else is around to hear, but the man is whispering about wasted time and time costing money under his breath.

At the sink he gets a glass of water and throws it in the young doctor's face. Hanush splutters, "Hey!" and shakes himself awake. He seems limp until he begins quaking with fear. The stranger has what he came for but hasn't left yet. Hanush is starting to think he isn't going to make it to work in the morning.

"Good morning, sunshine," the man says cheerfully. "Like I said earlier, you now have some explaining to do. I get why you lied to me. I truly do. I think I would have done the same thing if I were in your shoes. What I do need to know is where you got that car and how much you paid for it."

Hanush just sits in the chair, again wrestling with his dilemma. He thinks, *He wants to know about my car? He doesn't care about me lying to him or how much money I have in the bank. He didn't even ask how much more money I could get him or even check my balance on my receipt. The car? That's it?*

"Come on, Hanush. How much? It seems new. Is it new? Everyone likes to talk about their shiny new car." Hanush nods his head. "Were you able to pay cash? I mean, I did see your balance on the receipt after I knocked you out, so I know you've got that kind of money. How much was it?"

Hanush just sits there for a moment, without saying a word, before the madness finally gets to him. "Take my car if you want it. Take it, but please, just stop torturing me like this! My head feels like it is splitting open and you've drugged me so much that I feel sick."

The man moves behind Hanush now and pulls the doctor's head back by his hair to whisper in his ear. "I have no need for your car. I just want to hear what you paid and where you got it. They are pretty simple questions, I think. You should be able to answer them easily if you would just stop stalling." He is bellowing now.

Hanush jumps as the man goes from whispering to shouting in his ear. The man hasn't let go of him but has moved to see his face. Hanush winces as he says, "Okay, I bought it today. It is new and I paid $22,000 total, with tax and everything. I bought it just before closing time. My dad said that is the best time to go because they will give you the lowest price right away because they want to go home after being there all day. There, is that what you wanted to hear? Can you leave now?"

The man releases Hanush. "Thank you, Hanush. That wasn't too difficult, was it?" He again leans in to whisper into Hanush's ear. "I thank you for being honest with me and it is time for me to go, but first I need to do something. Be right back."

The man walks out the front door, only to return a minute later with bolt cutters in his hand. "I need to end this time-wasting ability you have. I need to rid the world of your being a nuisance. The man walks behind Hanush and slaps duct tape over his mouth. He then puts the bolt cutters to his right hand. There is a crack as the bolt cutters cut through the bone of Hanush's index finger. Hanush's scream is silent; the only person able to hear him is the man inflicting the pain. Another loud crack echoes in the mostly-empty room as the bolt cutters cut through the thumb this time. "Now you cannot sign anything anymore. This should stop you from wasting people's time again." The suited man drops the bolt cutters and then picks up the amputated digits and walks over to the wall. He proceeds to write in Hanush's blood, using the severed finger, HE WASTED MY TIME.

He drops the finger and thumb at his victim's feet, and then the masked man carefully jumps on the table, staring down at the doctor. Hanush, still crying from the pain, looks up at him. He can see the smile building on his face. The man's head is tilting back and forth. He is very pleased with his latest work.

How do I know this guy? Why is he doing this to me? How did I waste his time? Hanush wonders.

Now going into shock from the blood loss, he looks up at the man with guilty puppy eyes full of tears. The pain is unbearable. Based on his medical training, he recognizes the symptoms of shock, but he cannot stop the bleeding to stabilize himself.

Suddenly, the man rips off his mask in a grand flourish. Hanush snaps back into full consciousness. The man notices that Hanush does indeed recognize him and grabs his knife from his inside pocket. He opens it to the biggest blade and walks behind Hanush. He leans again to whisper to him, "That's right, it is me. Now you know why I did this to you. I don't think you have learned your lesson at all. I think you will leave here and still waste people's time, just like you did mine earlier today. And now that you know who I am, I am going to have to make sure you don't tell anyone about me. I have so much more work to do. This world is full of time wasters just like you. I am afraid I am going to have to remove you and your time wasting from this world."

The man takes the knife and jams it with great force into the back of Hanush's neck, right under the base of the skull. He pulls the knife out and stares at the blood dripping from the blade. He walks toward the sink, whistling the whole time, while he cleans the blood from his gloves and knife.

"Why did you have to waste even more of my time tonight? Why did you have to lie to me? I am so angry right now that getting rid of you and your time-wasting ways is not good enough. I'm going to have to take care of another time waster tonight. So thanks, Hanush, thank you very much for making it impossible to sleep tonight. I was going to give my next victim more time, but thanks to you, I can't tolerate any more time wasters from today. If I don't do something about her right now, I will not be able to live with myself. I wonder how long it will take Rockton's finest to find you. Even in death you will waste someone's time. Goodbye Hanush, and good riddance to you and your time-wasting ways." The man walks away from the bloody mess and leaves, still whistling as if he hasn't a care in the world.

5

"AHHHHHHH!" Detective Max Larkin bolts upright in bed, bathed in sweat. He's breathing very rapidly and his heart is thumping in his chest. He looks around his room to make sure he is actually at home. There is his high school football trophy sitting on his dresser, next to the picture of him getting his detective shield. "Thank God! It was just a dream!" he exhales as he gathers his bearings. Slowly he relaxes, and his heartbeat and breathing slow down to normal. He cannot believe how real that dream seemed. *It's 7 a.m. I only got about five hours of sleep. Man, oh man, this is going to be one of those days.*

As Detective Larkin stands in his shower, slouched over, he can't help rethinking his dream. He is standing near a couple lying in a pool of blood. They are tied to their bed just like the Bjornson couple. He can barely see the couple from where he is on the side of the bed—like he is kneeling next to the bed.

Only it wasn't the Bjornsons lying there; it was a totally different couple. He didn't know who they were, but they seemed very familiar to him, like he had seen them before. He just can't place where or when. The déjà vu feeling is strong, yet he can't quite recall what it is.

In his dream, he watched as the man lay there, gasping for breath and then, all at once, stopped breathing as blood flowed from his mouth and his eyes glazed over. He could clearly see the blood flowing from the man and woman's chests and stomachs, as if they had been stabbed there several times. Max was crying in his dream. He felt like the room was very familiar to him—that he had slept on that very comforter his dream hands were gripping so tightly. He knew it was common to piece together dream rooms from daily scenes, but it wasn't his comforter that he had squeezed so tightly in the dream.

He then heard a deep voice say, "Do it, kid! Do it now, or you're next!" It was then in his dream that he looked up and saw a man standing over him with a knife in his hand. There was still blood dripping from the knife, right next to his foot. He could feel the fear as he was seeing through the child's eyes. He could actually feel it deep in his bones—a shiver of fear—a portent that he would never be safe again.

As he kept looking upward in his dream, he started to focus through his tears on a black suit with a light blue shirt. His gaze followed the beautiful silk tie upward toward the man's face. He could see that the man was wearing a ski mask and a big smile. He began to back away from the smiling stranger and then slipped on something wet that must have been the couple's blood. That was when he woke up screaming.

Apparently, that story of the three–year-old boy from twenty-five years ago that Jesse had found really had upset the normally iron-nerved detective. *I need to focus on the case and not on a dream. I need to stop this guy and stop him now, or these nightmares are going to be reality for some other kid and his parents. I hope that feeling of familiarity with the dream's surroundings and that bone-chilling fear doesn't plague me for the rest of the day!*

Detective Larkin decides he is going to swing by and pick up Jesse on his way to Clinton. "Hey, Jesse, I'm thinking I should swing by your place and grab you to come with to Clinton. This way, we will be on the same page. And you might pick up something I might miss otherwise. What do you say?"

"Great idea! See you soon," she says with youthful exuberance. He can tell she is excited to be included. He wonders if he was motivated to invite her to avoid thinking about his dream while driving alone.

He pulls up to Jesse's apartment building and notices she is already waiting for him in the front doorway. Her hair is still wet from her quick shower. *Wow, she is really excited to do this. I hope she can stay focused; I can use that analytical mind of hers.*

As Jesse hops in the car she pulls her auburn hair back into a ponytail. If he were a little younger, he muses he might find her attractive, but he feels too old for her and he himself frowns on office romances.

"Good morning, Detective Larkin!" she says cheerfully.

"Jesse, if we are going to be working this closely together, you can drop the Detective Larkin and just call me Max. You are just as important to this case as I am. Now with that said, let's get this guy!" She nods her head vigorously in agreement.

It is quiet during the ride. Max is still brooding about the aftereffects of the nightmare.

They are only a few minutes outside of Rockton, headed to Clinton, when Jesse breaks the silence. "Detective Larkin, er-uh, Max, you seem distracted. Are you okay?" she asks tentatively. Max can't make up his mind whether to tell Jesse about the dream he had last night. After all, this was the first time in his career that he dreamed about a case. And it wasn't just a dream. It was a full-blown, heart-thumping nightmare that seemed all too real to be a coincidence.

"Last night, Jesse, I had a dream about this case. I dreamed I was that little boy 25 years ago. There were two people lying there in pools of their own blood. I am telling you, it felt very real to me. Their bodies weren't just images—they were real and I could swear I knew them." He shook his head. "This case is really getting to me. I have never dreamed about a case before. We really need to get this guy. He's been doing this for at least 25 years and nobody has caught him yet. Let's be the ones to bring this son of a bitch down!" he says with authority. It is as much for his benefit as hers that he forces conviction into his voice.

Jesse nods in agreement and looks directly at him. She can see how seriously upset he is. "We're going to get him, Max. I know it in my heart. This guy has been maiming and murdering for over 25 years, that's true, but he has never gone up against a detective as good as you. Not to mention, you have a great sidekick in me," she says with a little chuckle. Max is able to smile along with her. She can see that her attitude seems to lift some of the weight off his shoulders and his tension eases.

They speak very little as the traffic thins out and the roadside trees thicken. Jesse loves quiet country drives, as she doesn't often leave the city. She turns up the radio that Max has on low volume and begins to hum along with the country song. Max watches her carefree look and feels some of his unease creep back into his thoughts. But watching Jesse fiddle with her ponytail and lighten up as she gets more into the music is making it difficult to stay gloomy. He starts singing along with the next song, and soon the rural countryside thins out and houses spring up alongside the road.

They drive through the Clinton city limits and spot the police station up ahead. It's a small police station compared to Rockton.

In the small station they flash their badges and IDs, and ask to speak to the Chief of Detectives. An older man standing not too far from the front desk overhears them and says, "I'm Captain Williams. How can I help you?"

Larkin says, "We're detectives from Rockton, and we recently had a murder that was almost identical to one you had here about ten years ago. We would like to see the file on it, if you don't mind. Our Captain can give a formal call if needed. There were some skeleton files in our office, as it looks like we helped out with some initial manpower, but not a full set of information on what occurred. If possible, we would also like to talk to the detective that was in charge of that investigation and maybe even see the crime scene."

"Come with me to my office and let's see what we can do," Captain Williams says as he approaches one of the few offices in the small station.

In the office, Larkin notices a lot of awards on Captain Williams' walls. Included in them is the key to the city of Clinton.

"Very impressive awards wall, Captain Williams!" exclaims Jesse.

"Thank you very much!" he says with a smile. "Most of those are quite old, back from when I was young and energetic. Now, what case are you looking for? I'd be happy to help however I can."

Detective Larkin starts outlining the case that brought them to Clinton. He describes how a guy had killed a couple and how he wrote on their wall, just like he did in the case in Clinton ten years ago. He details how the murderer left the Bjornson husband alive this time so he could tell people to stop wasting other people's time.

Captain Williams's eyes glaze over as Larkin explains what happened to the Bjornson family. He starts fidgeting in his chair, waiting for the story to end.

"That was my case," he says, exhaling a sigh, as if he had been holding his breath through Max's entire synopsis. "I admit I couldn't get a damn thing on the guy. I had no clues. He killed both husband and wife, leaving nothing behind. This was the only case I was never able to solve," Captain Williams says, lowering his eyes. "I looked over photos; I checked for fingerprints and hair samples. I checked on the bolt cutters and still nothing. Hell, I even checked for footprints outside the house, and all I found were prints made by the inhabitants. There wasn't a darn thing out of place anywhere! It drove me nuts for almost a year before we finally moved on. I finally gave up and listed it as unsolved. It still haunts me to this day, since it's the last one left on my record."

Captain Williams opens the bottom drawer of a file cabinet containing only one file. The file seems relatively thin for a murder investigation, but Larkin figures it is because of the lack of evidence and manpower in Clinton. The captain stoops to grab the file, places it on his desk, opens it and turns it toward the two visiting detectives.

The first thing they notice is a photo with the writing on the wall, 'STOP WASTING PEOPLE'S TIME,' written in blood. The two visiting detectives thumb through the pictures, looking for anything that might lead them in a new direction.

"Wait just a minute. What is this?" exclaims Jesse, standing up in her excitement and pointing at the picture on top. "Look at this picture of the wife! I can see dents on both sides of her legs, like the killer was kneeling over her as he stabbed her. The blood spattered onto the killer when he was stabbing her. I know it isn't much, especially ten years after the fact. However, it shows that he wants dominance over women. He did the exact same thing to Mrs. Bjornson and her daughter. He can't control himself when it comes to these women. He has to hold them down and make sure he shows that he is more powerful than they are."

Max asks, "Captain Williams, can we see the crime scene? Is the house still vacant? I know it has been a long time, but maybe if we see the same thing the killer saw, we can put some more pieces together in this truly messed up puzzle."

"You're not going to believe this, but the house is still abandoned. It seems that no one in this small community wants any part of that house. We actually wanted to tear it down, but no one wanted the land so it never happened," states the Captain. The Rockton detectives can see how different things must be in Clinton. No house remains vacant in Rockton for very long, no matter what happened there.

Captain Williams walks Max and Jesse out to his car and they set out. The two detectives take a good look around the town. They can see the local gas station with only two pumps. The station even still has a gas pump attendant on duty for full service fill-ups. Across the street from there are various small storefronts ranging from hardware to fabric stores with a small local bar stuck in the middle. This is truly the epitome of

American small town living. There is even an old tow truck that looks about 50 years old but is still operational.

Right next to the gas station is a new car dealership. It's the only thing that doesn't seem to fit in. The place is shiny, new and large, compared to everything else in town. It doesn't look like much business comes through its doors, though. The building is huge with a very large lot, but the number of cars doesn't come close to filling it up.

"What's the deal with the car dealership? Why so big for this little town?" inquires Jesse.

"Well, that dealership opened up with a lot of fanfare behind it about eleven years ago. They had a really full lot, with tons of new cars. The big town news teams came out and shot stories about the grand opening. It was going to help put this town on the map. There were plans to build a highway that had an exit right near the dealership, and that was going to bring even more businesses here. Our whole town was based around that one auto dealer. That place used to have fifteen salespeople in there at any given time, with a total of 20 salespeople on staff. They brought in top-flight salespeople, service people, and management from other dealerships both in and out of state. Business was booming for the dealership and for the whole town in general. People were making a ton of money and things were looking great!" the Captain recounts with a smile. "That's when the murders that you're here for happened. Suddenly nobody outside of town wanted to come here for anything anymore. Who wants to say they bought anything from Clinton after that couple was brutally murdered? The owner went bankrupt and the manufacturer took over the dealership. Now, you are lucky to find more than five salespeople there at a time. All the big-shots that they hired left town and took the money they earned with them. The murderer did more than kill a local couple; he killed this whole town," Captain Williams sighs.

"Wow, that's terrible!" exclaims Max. "Have there been any other major crimes since the murders ten years ago? Any attempted murders, armed robberies or anything like that?"

The Captain looks perplexed by the question. After thinking about it for a few minutes, he says, "Not a one. Things went back to normal around here. We have barely given out a parking ticket in this town since those people were killed. I received some of those awards for having such a low crime rate, but there hasn't been much crime to fight."

They soon arrive at the crime scene. As they walk up the steps to the porch, there is a placard next to the front door that reads, "Welcome to the Ostrowski House", with a small set of painted pictures of a house and family. The door is unlocked, but it doesn't matter, as nobody has opened it for years. There is dirt on the knob and dust that lifts off the floor as the door opens. Dust bunnies and dirt greet them, with no signs of recent activity. Thick layers of dust have settled on the furniture, floor, and mantles. They now twirl in the morning light like cigarette smoke. Everyone is careful to not touch anything. Max mentally compares the Ostrowski residence to those old movie houses where monsters live and horror stories take place.

Jesse holds back a sneeze with a wrinkle and pinches her nose. They proceed upstairs to where the murders occurred. She can't help but wonder if there are vermin living in this house, but she sees no signs of their footprints among her own on the floor. She wishes she had brought some allergy pills with her, as she is quite allergic to dust.

When they approach the master bedroom, they see the door is already open and they catch a glimmer of light in the room from the windows. The three detectives walk into the bedroom. Light is streaming in through the shadeless window; the only thing that catches the detectives' eyes in this otherwise normal dilapidated bedroom is the writing on the wall from the killer: QUIT WASTING PEOPLE'S TIME. It looks so eerily familiar. It is faded compared to the red of the original photos and the Bjornson scene, but it only makes the statement seem more prophetic to Detective Larkin.

As they stand there, looking around the room, Detective Larkin notices something very interesting. "What is that at the end of the bed?"

The two detectives look at the bed. They all move in unison to have a closer look, leaning toward the bed without touching. There is a pattern in the dust on the bed, as if someone had sat at the edge recently. The void is in the shape of a person's butt and upper thighs resting on the edge of the bed.

"It looks like a person sat at the edge of the bed staring at the wall with the writing on it," says Jesse, dumbfounded. "Someone came here very recently to look at this, but how did they get in here? There are no footprints leading up here to the bedroom from downstairs. One of us would have noticed the disturbance in all that dust."

The three detectives take a look around and see some faint footprints in the dust next to the window and leading toward the bed. They also notice that the window has been opened because there is a dust void on the windowsill. "Could it have been the killer, come to admire his old work?" Jesse muses. As she ponders the situation further, it is the only answer that makes any sense without more background on the family.

Captain Williams puts in a call from his shoulder radio. "This is Captain Williams. I need someone down here at the old Ostrowski place with some evidence gathering equipment. It seems as though we had an intruder on the premises."

All three of them carefully back out of the room. They don't want to disturb anything as they retrace their steps back down. Outside they see some impressions in the dirt directly under the upstairs window in question.

"It looks like the person used a ladder to get to the window, for sure," Jesse says, turning to face Max as he also peers around the flower bed.

"Why come back here after all these years? Why now?" Max asks.

"Maybe he was reliving the moment. Maybe he wanted to refresh his memory before he killed his next victims, the Bjornson family. It has been ten years that we know of," Jesse replies. "Maybe we just don't know about the murders in between, or maybe something set him off again."

"I think you may be hitting the nail on the head with that one, Jesse," Max states. "Our killer wanted to bask in his glory a little and remember how he got away with it. He might have needed to relive this to get started again. His visit here might have triggered his renewed interest in murder."

It is at that moment that a police car and black SUV pull up. There are two police officers in each car, and all four officers excitedly walk up toward the house. Two officers go to the house, carrying forensic kits. The other two come running over to Max and Jesse. Captain Williams is perplexed by the officer's excitement. "Why on earth is everyone here?"

"Come on, Captain, we haven't had a crime scene in Clinton for a long time. I guess we were just a bit overzealous," replies one of the officers. "Sorry, sir."

Max and Jesse point out what they believe to be the impressions from a ladder and suggest they get photos and plaster casts. They wait for forensics to take pictures and then go back to the house to look around some more.

Back upstairs, they talk more with Captain Williams, paying attention to everything in the house to make sure they don't miss anything. Jesse snaps some shots with her cell phone to fill in memory gaps until the Clinton police can share their official photos.

As they reenter the master bedroom, they are told that the shoe impressions in the dust by the window are from a men's size 14 shoe. They are not sneakers or sports shoes, but look to be a popular style of men's dress shoe. The toe of the shoe was not in style ten years ago but matches the style that most businessmen wear these days.

"The person that was in this room was here within the last three days or so," one of the officers states. "We had recently done a routine sweep of the house after a tipster called in to make sure no kids were partying in here. None of these footprints or the ladder impression was here. It looks like he tried to cover up his shoe prints by dusting behind him with some cloth as he left, but he was unsuccessful. The dust is thick and would have required a broom or something with more weight.

"However, he didn't try to conceal the impression on the bed at all. He wanted us to know he was sitting there, quite likely for some time. You can tell by the dust displacement that he sat in just this one place and didn't fidget or move around a lot. He just sat and likely stared at the wall. This guy is sick and creepy!" The forensic technician shakes his head in disbelief.

Max closes his eyes and envisions the murderer sitting there to relive his handiwork, with his eyes closed as well. The smell of the blood from the Bjornsons' and the uneasiness of his nightmare come back behind his eyelids and he shudders. He quickly looks around to make sure no one notices his body quiver and focuses on the writing in faded blood on the wall between family portraits of the couple's wedding.

The forensic team proceeds to check for fingerprints on the window and the window sill, but the person who was in the room must have worn gloves. There are large marks in the dust, but they are just impressions of large hands, probably a man's hands in gloves.

After the evidence gathering, they come to the conclusion that a man with a size 14 shoe, wearing gloves, entered the master bedroom from the lone window in the room from outside via a ladder he brought with him. He then proceeded to sit down on the bed and stare at the wall. There is no evidence of him leaving this room for any other part of the home. All other rooms of the house were left untouched.

Jesse and Max return to the station with Captain Williams to gather copies of the pictures from today and from the decade-old crime scene. Small talk between Williams and the detectives is sparse as they work. The Captains will work out details of how the towns can further cooperate. Larkin can tell Williams doesn't want to let go of the case for personal reasons.

The two head back to Rockton. It is another quiet ride, as each reflects on their own ideas of what the murderer is after and his motives. This guy almost seems sentimental about his own gory murder scene, or why else would he return? This time, Jesse turns the radio off, also forgetting her rumbling stomach, while she flips through the file again.

Max tentatively queries Jesse about her father, unsure if it is a difficult topic for her. He wants to escape this case for a few minutes, until they get back to Rockton. She gladly obliges. "I decided to stay close to home, as Mom never fully recovered from the loss. My siblings have moved away and don't stay in touch much. Someone has to make sure she eats and takes care of Dad's old dog." Jesse abruptly turns away, staring out the window and playing with her hair. Max determines that is enough for now without making her uncomfortable.

"This case is getting stranger by the minute," Max says as they arrive back at their own station. "I can't believe he went back to the scene of the crime a decade later. What is this guy doing?"

6

5 A.M. WEDNESDAY MORNING, APPROXIMATELY 8 HOURS EARLIER...

here is a light emanating from the television set that has been left on to help her sleep. It is a small cramped room in a one-bedroom apartment. The king size bed is too big, leaving just enough room for a small dresser at its foot to hold the glowing television. The shabby furniture has clearly been pieced together. The room has a lived-in feel, though, that reminds the man of a teenager's first apartment. But the woman lying in the bed is no young adult, recently moved out from her parents. She is a whore who looks angelic in her slumber and the glow of the television. This somehow angers him even more than the reason he came.

"Wake up! Hey, wake up!" the suited man says as he smacks her face. She jerks awake and tries to put her arms defensively in front of her face, but she can't move them. Her limbs are not able to move at all, and her mouth is taped shut. She starts struggling against the tape and trying to lift her body up, looking like a fish out of water as she wiggles helplessly.

She sees the shadowy figure of a man standing before her, between her bed and the television. He is dressed in a dark suit and a ski mask. He has a knife in his hand and is pacing, mumbling something to himself. She can't quite make out what he is saying.

"Do you remember me?" he yells at her, once she lies still. "Do you remember me, you stupid bitch?" he screeches, leaning in closer to her face. She smells the faint aroma of coffee on his breath.

The woman shakes her head. She has no idea who this crazy man is. He takes off his mask. Her eyes become the size of silver dollars as she realizes how she knows this man. He smiles at the terror on her face.

"Now do you remember me?" he yells at her. She nods her head slightly. "Good! Now do you know why I am here?" This time, she shakes her head no slowly, unsure whether to lie or tell the truth.

He rips the tape from her mouth and asks, "Where do you remember me from?"

"I—I remember you because you were behind me in line at the coffee shop in Clinton. You were yelling at me to hurry up with my order," she stammers. She licks her numb lips.

"Ding, ding, ding, ladies and gentleman—we have a winner!" he says with a laugh. "You took forever to place your order for a cup of coffee! You wasted my time. You see, my time is valuable. And you took time from my life so you could get your coffee order just right. You wasted my time. You wasted my time, and time is money. I am so sick of you people wasting my time. I am going to put a stop to this," he shouts as he continues pacing.

"I am really sorry! I didn't know what I wanted and they have so many choices. I just wanted to get exactly what I wanted. I'm very sorry, please don't hurt me!" she whispers between sobs.

She is hoping the sobbing will drown out the rustle of the bed sheets as she wiggles around, trying to get loose, since he seems preoccupied. He looks strong and big, but that may mean he would move slowly enough that she could get past him and out the front door, down to the street where someone could help her.

"I wish I could believe that, but I don't," he says. She lies perfectly still whenever he looks directly at her. "You see, Amber—and yes, I know your name from the barista at the coffee shop—you see, Amber, here is the thing: after you wasted my time at the coffee shop yesterday, I was pissed but went to work anyway. After work, I grabbed a drink with a friend and, lo and behold, I saw you again at the bar. I found out I was not the only person whose time you wasted. I watched you scarf down drinks from a guy that seemed very interested in you. He came over to talk to you after the first drink and you talked with him for about an hour. He bought you three more drinks during that time, and when he asked you for your number, you said you weren't interested. You not only wasted his time; you wasted his money. That makes you a terrible person in my book. You need to be taught a lesson," he says, grinning at her coyly.

The man tears off a big piece of duct tape to put over her mouth again. "We can't have anyone hearing you scream, now can we, Amber?" he whispers into her ear.

He can hear her trying to say, "Please don't hurt me. I'm sorry," over and over again from under the tape.

"The way I see it, Amber, you owe me for my time that you wasted. The question is: how much do you owe me? The way I figure it, you wasted 15 minutes of my time, so you owe me $52.75. I won't charge you for the time I spent watching you at the bar. I did consider taking 30 extra dollars for the guy that bought you drinks, so he could at least get his money back, but I think he learned a valuable lesson about women, so he got his money's worth from that. So let's just round it up to $53 and we can call it even. Does that sound okay to you?" he asks Amber.

Amber just stares at him, unable to move or even think of what she would say if her mouth was not taped shut. She is completely dumbfounded by this. All of this over $52.75? He sees her eyes move toward the closet and walks over to see if he can find her purse.

Amber gestures her head in the direction of the closet in the corner of the room again, realizing he is following her thinking. He rifles around in the closet for her purse. When he finds it, he walks over to her and pours everything out on the bed. He then grabs her wallet hastily and takes out three $20 bills. He reaches into his pocket for a $5 and two singles. He throws them on the bed next to the other items from her purse while whispering into her ear, "This is your change." His breath gives her chills as it moves across her neck. She is drenched in sweat from the encounter and can feel the tape chafing her skin.

The man sits on the bed next to Amber. He holds her hand with his own and squeezes it softly. "You know, Amber, I was going to let you go for a day or two. I just didn't want to deal with you right now. We are only talking about fifteen minutes, after all, but earlier today, I had a man waste my time at my job. He wasted over two hours of my time and was more blatant than you, too. He just didn't care at all about me and my time. I had to rid the world of his time-wasting. So I did. Now pay attention here, Amber, so you can tell the cops the story later." He proceeds to tell her the ghastly details of his encounter with Hanush.

The man squeezes her hand a little tighter. "He upset me so badly that ridding the world of one time waster wasn't going to be enough. I had to get rid of one more. Since you also wasted my time earlier today, you're the one that had to be stopped. So here I am!"

He picks up his mask, pulls it back on, and starts walking toward the door. He stops suddenly, as if he has forgotten something. He stands there for what seems like an eternity to Amber as she stares at his back.

He slowly turns around and Amber starts struggling as a big smirk crosses the man's face. He has a gleam in his eyes that reminds her of a dog ready to attack. Like a hunter, he approaches her and climbs over her, straddling her body.

As he looks down on her tear-soaked face, his blood courses quickly through his veins and his heart beats faster. He feels so alive right now, and so much better that he is saving this town from another time waster. "I'm sorry. I planned on leaving you alive so you could tell everyone about not wasting people's time anymore. But then I realized you saw my face. Now I can't leave you alive. I'm sorry, Amber."

He pulls his Swiss Army knife out again from an internal jacket pocket and slowly opens it to the largest blade—the very same blade he used earlier on Hanush. Amber tries pleading with him again and struggles against the tape, trying to knock him off her. She is bound too tightly to knock him off, or maybe he is too strong. She stops struggling as she realizes the knife is poised above her chest. She whimpers and turns her head away, cringing, as he thrusts the knife deep into her chest. He can hear the bones in her chest crack as the knife passes through them, puncturing her heart. He quickly pulls the knife out. Using the knife, still drenched in her blood, he carves *TIME WASTER* into her stomach. Putting his gloved hands into the blood, he walks over toward her wall with the window. He proceeds to write *STOP WASTING PEOPLE'S TIME* on the wall in Amber's blood.

He picks up the knife from the bed and thrusts it into her neck to be sure that she is dead and decides to leave the knife with her, buried in her neck. Looking over the scene one last time, he turns toward the door, whistling as he walks through her living room to the front door.

He walks out Amber's front door and is surprised by another person entering the hallway as well. Amber's neighbor from across the hall is leaving for work. She has her briefcase in one hand and a cup of coffee in the other, juggling her keys to lock her door. The suited man is still wearing his ski mask, so she stares at him. He says to her, "Your neighbor wasted my time. I'm pretty sure she's dead so she won't be able to waste anyone's time ever again. Have a nice day!" He starts whistling again as he calmly walks down the stairs.

Almost unable to breathe the neighbor thinks, *This guy has to be kidding. Probably one of Amber's one-night stands trying to be funny. Wait, he did have blood all over him.* She drops her briefcase and coffee and runs into Amber's apartment through the open door unable to believe the sight that greets her. Amber is lying in bed with her eyes open, taped to her bed, with a knife stuck in her neck. There is blood everywhere.

The neighbor runs out looking for him. She stops when she gets to the second floor landing of the stairwell. He is still whistling as he goes out the first floor exit.

She asks herself what she could possibly do if she did catch up to him. What would he do to her? What could she possibly do to him if she was able to catch up to him?

She runs back into Amber's apartment and looks for a phone. Once inside she starts hyperventilating. Her heart is racing as if she has been running a marathon and she passes out.

As her eyes gradually flutter and try to open, she can hear her cell phone ringing from her briefcase in the hall. Still feeling groggy and with her mind in a haze, she walks out to the hall and opens her briefcase and digs out the phone. It's her boss calling.

"Hello?" she says in a low monotone voice.

"Where the hell are you, Melissa?" the voice on the phone screams at her. "You were supposed to be here over two hours ago."

Still stunned and confused, she answers, "I don't know." Melissa stops and looks around. She sees a ratty brown couch and some beer bottles on the floor. *Where am I?* Looking at the door she is standing next to, she realizes she isn't at home. Then she recognizes Amber's hand-me-down furniture and starts to remember everything. "Oh my God! My neighbor—she's dead. I saw the killer. I must have passed out after that," she says, her voice halting. "I have to call the police right now." Melissa then hits the end button on her phone and immediately dials 911.

The phone rings only once before the 911 operator picks up. "911, what is your..."

The operator doesn't even finish her standard greeting before Melissa starts screaming, "My neighbor's dead. She was murdered. I saw the killer. Please help!"

Melissa's ragged breathing is making her choke on her sobs. "Calm down, Miss. I need to know where you are," the operator calmly asks her. "Did you say you killed your neighbor?"

"No! I didn't kill her! I found her in her room, and the killer talked to me as he left her apartment. He told me he killed her. Please send someone right away. I am afraid he's going to come back. Please send someone now!" Melissa's voice quivers with fear; she is starting to feel light-headed.

"I need your address, please, so I can get police there," the operator reiterates to Melissa.

"I'm at 865 Van Street, third floor, apartment 8. My neighbor lives in apartment 9. Please hurry!" Melissa says as she picks up her keys and unlocks her apartment door. "I'm in my apartment now." Hurriedly she locks her door behind her—first the knob, then the deadbolt, and finally the chain. She double-checks them all before she sits down behind her door.

"I'll stay on the line as long as you wish, ma'am. You need to slow your breathing so you don't pass out," the operator says, trying to help reassure Melissa.

"Thank you very much," Melissa says between choked sobs. "Why would someone do this? Why kill her, and then walk right past me and not kill me?"

"I wish I could answer those questions for you. I truly do. You just need to understand that you are alive right now and that there is nothing you can do for your neighbor. You cannot let yourself feel guilty for being alive. You need to know that," the 911 operator says. "Miss, I just got notification that the police are at the building's front door, heading up the stairs. I told them to knock on your door as soon as they come up."

"Thank you for staying on the line with me. I needed someone. Goodbye," Melissa says as she hits the end button on her cell phone.

The moment she puts her phone down, Melissa hears a knock on her door. "Who's there?" she asks as she squints through the peephole.

"Detective Larkin, ma'am."

"Could you please show me some ID?"

"Of course." Max puts his badge and ID up so she can see it. "I am going to go across the hall for a few minutes, and then my partner and I will be back to talk to you. There'll be an officer posted right in the hallway to keep an eye on you. Is that okay?"

"Yes. Thank you," she says through the door.

In the apartment across the hall, Detective Larkin can immediately feel the negative energy in the room. Morale is bad for everyone working on this investigation, as the killer just keeps going and there is so little evidence to go on.

Jesse pokes her head in the door and greets him with, "You're going to want to see this."

In the bedroom Max spots the sign. *STOP WASTING PEOPLE'S TIME* is written in blood, just like the others. "What's going on, Jesse?"

Jesse points at the victim's stomach. *TIME WASTER* is carved into her body. "Well, that's new!" he exclaims. "This guy is getting worse. First, he removed fingers and now he is actually carving into the body."

"Look at this," Jesse says as she points to the sides of the lower body. "He was kneeling over her, just like the other women before. I am telling you, Max, he has a thing for being in power over the women he is murdering. It is not enough for him to just kill them; he needs to feel them squirm while he is doing it."

"Well, look what we have here. There is $7 scattered on top of her purse, and it looks like her wallet was left open as well. The money and all this stuff is covered in blood, which means that it was there before he killed her," Max points out to Jesse. "Take a look in her wallet and see if there is any other money in there, would you, Jesse?"

Jesse shifts her weight forward to look at the contents on the bed. "Here is a receipt for an ATM withdrawal of $60. It was at 2:05 this morning," she says as she continues to rifle through the objects. "No cash, though, besides that $7. Hey, wait a minute. I know this location. It's right next to that new nightclub downtown. What is the name?"

"You mean *Heat of the Moment* night club?" interjects Max.

"Yeah, that is the one," Jesse says. "I'm willing to bet she stopped at this ATM after she left the club. They close at 2 a.m. and, with this ATM being so close, it makes perfect sense. Look at her left hand and tell me if there is a stamp on it that resembles a flame."

Max lifts her left hand and there it is—a bright red flame stamp on her hand.

"Here is a receipt from that club for $120, including tip, that she paid with her credit card. It's time stamped at 1:55 a.m," Jesse says as she put down the victim's purse.

"Okay, here we go. She was probably at the club last night until it closed, spending a good amount of money on drinks. Paying with the credit card was her only option. As she left the club, she decided she needed some cash just in case, and started looking for the nearest ATM. She saw the one across the street, withdrew 60 bucks and came straight home. But the only money she has now is $7, and that money is sitting next to her head," Max says out loud so everyone in the room can hear. "Now the big questions are...was she alone at the club? After all, 120 bucks is a lot to spend on drinks just for yourself. If she was with someone, who was it? Was it our killer getting to know his victim? Was it friends? I guess we have to take a trip to *Heat of the Moment* night club to find out. Now, what about the $7? Based on what Mr. Bjornson said about the man that killed his family, he took his money, but gave him change back. He said that $633 was what he was owed from the Bjornsons wasting three hours of his time. Let's see, that comes to $211 per hour. Is this $7 change from the $60 she took out of the bank? If it is, that means she wasted..." Max runs the figures in his head.

"Approximately 15 minutes, Detective," blurts out one of the officers in the room.

"Thanks. I would have gotten it," Max says with a chuckle.

"Okay, this guy killed her over fifteen minutes of his time wasted?" Jesse says with a look of shock and disgust. "Fifteen lousy minutes. I think you're right Max, this guy is escalating. Escalating, big time!"

Turning to one of the forensic team members, Max tells them to check for any identifying fibers on the money in case it came from the murderer's wallet. Then he motions for Jesse's attention and points to the front room. "Let's go talk to the neighbor, Jesse. She told 911 that she saw this guy. Maybe she can give us something to go on," Max says as he guides her toward the door.

Max and Jesse knock on the door. "It's me, ma'am, Detective Larkin, and I brought my partner, Detective Fairlane. May we come in and ask you a few questions?"

The two detectives hear the deadbolt being unlocked, and the door starts to open slowly. The detectives catch their first glimpse of Melissa—a young, attractive red-haired woman. Melissa's eyes are puffy from crying; her hands shaking with fear and anxiety. When she stumbles away from the door, she barely keeps her knees from buckling. Her suit jacket is ripped, possibly from when she passed out or scrambled home during the 911 call.

"Come in, detectives. Please have a seat. Can I get you anything to drink?" Melissa asks.

"Please, miss, have a seat and relax. You have had a very traumatic morning and we don't want to take much of your time. We need to know if there is anything you can tell us about the man you saw leave your neighbor's apartment, Miss…?"

Before Detective Larkin can finish Melissa speaks up. "Davenport, Melissa Davenport."

Looking around the room, Max can tell this is a single, career-oriented woman. She has a lot of paintings on the wall that would be considered modern art by many people. She has a relatively modest entertainment system with an old tube television and VCR. *Who has a VCR anymore?* Max wonders. On top of the entertainment system are diplomas and degrees. Melissa was a member of the national honor society in high school and got her Master's degree in Business Management from Florida State. Outside of those personal items, there isn't much to her place. She has no family photos up and, as a matter of fact, she has absolutely no photos of herself or anyone else in her whole apartment. She is apparently more concerned about her career than about personal possessions and relationships.

"Ms. Davenport, I know today has been very rough for you, but if you could please walk me through this morning… Please don't leave out any details, no matter how small or insignificant they might seem. Even the smallest thing could help us catch this guy," Jesse says. She takes a seat on the chair adjacent to the couch where Melissa has slumped over. The woman is playing with a piece of frayed cloth from her jacket while the detectives speak to her.

Melissa takes a deep breath and closes her eyes. Jesse reaches over and takes her hand.

"It's okay, Ms. Davenport…take your time," Max says with deep care in his voice.

Melissa opens her eyes and looks straight at Jesse. "I woke up late this morning because I was working late last night on some loans that came in for approval. I showered, dressed, and grabbed my briefcase and my coffee. After locking my door, I turned around to see a well-dressed man in a blue pinstripe suit. The suit was a four button, and he was wearing a white shirt that looked professionally pressed and a bright blue silk tie. He was also wearing a black ski mask. I could see his eyes: they were brown but very bloodshot. He had a lot of blood on his suit from the knees up. His shirt had a little bit of blood on it, but it's hard to say how much because he had all four coat buttons fastened. It was just much more noticeable on the shirt because it stood out against the white. The spots on the suit and tie looked more like grease stains because the backdrop was so dark." She pauses, continuing after a small gasp. "I froze right there in mid-step. I couldn't move at all. I was terrified. I kept staring directly into his eyes." She starts crying again.

Jesse squeezes her hand again and Melissa takes another deep breath to continue. "He looked right at me and said, 'Your neighbor wasted my time. I killed her so she won't be able to waste anyone's time ever again.' And then he wished me a nice day, turning toward the stairs. He was whistling some little tune as he walked away—nothing I could name offhand, but vaguely familiar. I was in shock. I kept thinking it was a joke played by one of Amber's 'boyfriends'." Melissa does the air quote thing with both hands and a sarcastic look on her face. "Amber was… what's a nice way of putting it? She was a very promiscuous person, bringing home a lot of guys, some of whom were pretty sleazy, in my opinion. But I couldn't get past the fact that this well-dressed man was covered in blood. I ran into her apartment and saw her lying there with the knife stuck in her neck. I didn't think anymore—I just reacted. I ran to the stairwell and could see him leaving the building on the first floor. Just as he got to the door, I saw him reach up to take his mask off. I could see that he had brown hair, with some gray mixed in. He was starting to go bald on the back of his head. It looked like a skin beanie, if you know what I mean?"

Both detectives nod. Max diligently writes down all he can of what Melissa is saying since she has Jesse's hand locked between her own. "Is there anything else you can remember, Ms. Davenport?" Jesse asks her.

"No. After that, I just went back to her apartment to look for a phone, but wound up fainting. I realized that anything I did to try and stop him would likely lead me to the same fate as Amber. I'm sorry—I can't remember anything else," Melissa says, with a very sad expression.

Max jumps right in. "You did great, Ms. Davenport. We are going to keep a policeman outside your building for today to make sure this guy doesn't come back. Okay?"

Melissa nods her head and when she thanks Jesse for all she did, Jesse hugs her. As she pulls away from Melissa's fearful embrace, she hands Melissa her card. "Here's my card, Melissa. Call me if you can think of anything else or even if you just need someone to talk to. I'll be here for you."

As the detectives are leaving Max turns around and says, "Thank you very much, Ms. Davenport. You have been a tremendous help."

They leave her apartment and, while walking down the hallway, they decide to go down the stairs and see if anything at all was left behind by the killer. As Max and Jesse descend the stairs, they check every stair, the railings, and the wall. Nothing seems out of the ordinary. They finally get down to the bottom of the stairwell.

As Jesse is about to grab the door knob on the exit door, Max yells, "Stop! There is blood on that!" He reaches into his pocket and grabs a small cloth handkerchief. He dabs the blood stain enough to remove most of it from the knob. "For Forensics," he says.

Jesse nods. "Thanks, Max! That could have been costly. I am curious as to why you wiped up some but not all of the blood. What are you going to with that?" she asks.

Max stares at the red dot of blood on his handkerchief. "I have a friend in the lab. I want him to process it before anyone else does. If it is our guy, I want this evidence on the top of his pile. This guy will do it for me. I left the rest of the blood for the Forensics people. I didn't want to contaminate the crime scene and remove evidence from it. This way we all win. But most importantly, I win," he says with a huge smile on his face as he raises his eyebrows.

Jesse can't help herself from smiling. "I knew there was a reason why you got things done so well and so quickly. You have that station loaded with your friends. Okay, let's get back to the station and look at all we have to piece this together."

Jesse runs upstairs to Forensics to tell them about the blood. Max walks back to his car at a slow pace, lost in thought. As Jesse approaches the car, Max stops short of opening the door. "Jesse, let's go back to the hospital and visit Mr. Bjornson. Maybe he can remember something more. If not, we will have to see if we can jog his memory by telling him that this guy has struck again and is getting worse."

"I agree. I think that guy knows more than what he told us," Jesse says. "Melissa remembers a lot more about our killer than Bjornson did, and he saw him and talked to him a lot longer than she did. I don't know if he is just afraid or if he just doesn't care. Either way, we need him to spill his guts—and now."

Max can tell Jesse is very upset after talking with Melissa. "Wait a minute. Did you just refer to her as Melissa and not Ms. Davenport? And what was that 'I will be there for you' remark?"

Jesse's face goes pale for a second before her answer. "I was just trying to help her feel better. I figured that another woman to talk to would be good for her, since we already met and she seemed okay around me. I just figured I would be a good candidate. I mean, did you see that hug? It's obvious that she feels comfortable with me."

All Max can do is shake his head and smile as he sits down in the car. He knows something just made Jesse very uncomfortable, but there isn't time for that now. He's more concerned about catching this killer than any personal feelings he has about his partner or any witness. Personal feelings just slow cops down.

Max and Jesse are sitting at their desks staring at pictures of all the crime scenes they have seen in the last three days. First, they look at the Bjornson house and the carnage the killer left there. He did all of that for just three hours of his time being wasted.

Then there is Amber Swanson's apartment. She had nothing at all—no money, no real possessions to speak of—yet he took her life for a measly fifteen minutes of his time that she wasted.

Max rubs his eyes for a moment and looks down at the case file that was faxed over from the Indiana murder twenty-five years ago. "Maybe we should take a look at the case where it appears he began. The one in Merrillville," he says to Jesse. She reaches over to grab the file from him. He will not let her have it. He pulls it closer to his chest. "I don't want to see the pictures, Jesse. When you told me about this case the other day, I had that nightmare. I don't want any more nightmares like that. I'll look at the case, but not the pictures," Max reaches into the file and grabs the paperwork, but leaves the pictures for Jesse.

Jesse is concerned about what Max has shared. It seems the case is really getting to him. She wonders if she should bring it up to the Captain, but decides to give it some time and see if it gets worse.

Max flips through the file, just glancing at first. He is looking for something to jump off the page—something so obvious that a child would see it. He gets distressed at the primitive report writing from twenty-five years ago. "How did these guys work twenty-five years ago? I can barely read their handwriting. I hope we can get something out of this. I don't like the fact that we may be wasting our time on this." As Max finishes his last statement, he puts his head in his right hand and starts to shake his head. "Sorry about that. I wasn't thinking. I may never be able to say, type, or read those words again without thinking of this guy."

Jesse looks up from the photos when Max stops talking, "I hear ya, partner. I'm the same way. You know what else? I'm going to be nicer to others. I never realized how I took so many people for granted. I sit in a drive-thru and can't make up mind, and people actually honk at me for taking too long. There was a lady at the coffee shop just the other day that couldn't make up her mind what she wanted and finally a man just yelled at her about taking too long. I heard this happen and didn't even look up to see what was going on. I just sat there reading my newspaper. Thinking about it now, I guess I never really thought about other people's feelings or the time constraints in their lives.

"Today, it seems like everyone is running to this place or that. Nobody seems to stop and enjoy the time they have. Everyone is in such a hurry. I, for one, am going to slow myself down and enjoy the little things in life. If I find myself in a line, I will just accept that I need to wait. If someone seems in a hurry behind me in a line, I will let them cut in front of me."

While Jesse is learning patience for her fellow man, Max is getting frustrated with their lack of leads. "Ugh! I can't look at this file anymore. Do you have any plans for the night, Jesse? I am going to call Merrillville P.D. and see if we can go there tonight. I am more of a visual person. Yes, I know what you are going to say, Jesse: if I am visual, I should look at the pictures. Well, like I said earlier, I don't want to see the people in the pictures. I do want to see the house if I can. I also would like to talk to the guy who did the investigation and hopefully get some of his insight, as well. What do you say? Want to take another road trip with me?"

Jesse leans back in her chair and contemplates the thought of going to Merrillville. "Sure, why not? We are getting nowhere here. It's only about a two and a half hour drive from here. Give them a call and see if we can get some extra information that these files are not giving us."

Max picks up his desk phone and dials the Merrillville Police. Jesse can hear him explaining what he expects to get out of this trip. He tells them how he wants to sit down with the lead detective on the case and wants to see the area where the murders took place. He hangs up the phone. "We're all set, Jesse. They even offered to put us up for the night at the motel in town. The chief detective is the guy that was the lead detective twenty-five years ago on this case, and he said he will do whatever it takes to help us get this guy. I'm going to talk to the Captain to clear it with him and we'll get on the road."

Max drops Jesse at home to pack an overnight bag and then runs home himself. They then drive out of Rockton due east to Merrillville, Indiana. The windows are up and the radio is on low. Tension is high between them as they silently go over the little information they have. They both know that it would be best to try and build a bigger profile of the killer but worry if he'll strike again while they chase a very old case. Maybe by going back to the killer's beginning, they'll be able to identify him. This is the first place that he took a life. It is also the only place that he left a witness. Granted, that witness was only three years old at the time. They are truly hoping that going over their current case files with the lead detective will help shake loose some important facts.

After fifteen minutes on the road, Max says, "I hope this detective can remember some things that aren't in the file. This guy has killed in three states and all we have so far is that he wears a suit, has brown and gray hair, is balding and hates people wasting his time. Outside of those things, we've got nothing." At the end of that statement, he makes a fist and punches his steering wheel in frustration.

Jesse flinches. She has never seen him this upset. "Max, calm down; we are going to get this guy. Deep down in my heart, I just know we will," she says as she puts out her hand for a fist bump from her partner. He happily obliges.

Max concentrates on driving as fast as he can while Jesse looks through all of the cases. Eventually she says, "Max, something is weird here. Twenty-five years ago he killed, and then it took him fifteen years to do it again. Now here we are, ten years after that, and he has killed three times already. Why did he wait so long the last two times, but this time he is acting so quickly? Do we have copycats? Or did something set him off each time?"

Max adjusts himself in his seat. He is a bit uneasy about this guy. "I've been thinking about that exact thing. Fifteen years, then ten years, and now one day between kills. My educated guess is that something changed in his life each time and he felt the need to kill people rather than deal with the situations. I think this time is different than the last two times. This time, the thing that set him off is huge. It's so big that he feels like he may never be right in his sick, twisted mind unless he gets rid of all the

69

people who wrong him. That includes the people from twenty-five years ago and ten years ago. Whoever set him off then had better watch out now, because I think he's coming after them this time. He wants to finish everyone and everything this time, and I don't think he will stop until he is done with his work."

Jesse listens to Max discuss his theory. She has not had enough experience to dispute any of it. "I truly hope you're wrong about continuing on this pace. This is my first case and already I have seen more murders than McCarren, Salvo, and Phillips combined. I must say, I'm having a heck of a week."

Camaraderie grows between them as they volley theories back and forth. Max sees a lot of potential in his partner and he can't help but feel proud of her. *She really has a great mind for this job.*

They arrive at the Merrillville police station around 8 p.m. Wednesday evening. The station is well lit, with big glass doors going to the entrance foyer. It is more modern than what they have in Rockton and way more modern than the one in Clinton, Wisconsin. Max is the first to notice the big differences in the appearances of the three police stations. "Wow, Jesse, we are definitely not in Rockton anymore! Clinton is like the Stone Age, Rockton is like medieval times, and Merrillville appears to be from the not too distant future. I think we are going to be in for a big awakening on the technology differences between our station and this one. So what do you say, Jesse, ready to go see the wizard?" Max jokes at his partner as he holds out his arm and places his hand on his hip so she can wrap her arm in his, like the Scarecrow did for Dorothy. Jesse just pushes it away and laughs.

As both detectives walk up to the station, they stare straight up at the clock at the top of the tower on the front of the building. Max holds the door open for her. There is another set of doors that are locked. To the right of the second set of doors is a button that has a sign above it that reads, *After 5 p.m. push button for assistance.* Max pushes the button and gets a buzz. Max sees a woman stand up from a cubicle and head over to the doors. He and Jesse both pull out their credentials. The woman is short and stocky with short hair and wears glasses.

She opens the door to the station. "Are you the detectives from Rockton? Chief Detective Abbott said you would be by tonight. Unfortunately, he can't help you himself this evening. He had a previous engagement that he could not get out of. I'm Officer Kimball. He instructed me to get you to the motel and get you settled. If there is time, I am supposed to take you over to the house where the murders took place. There is a new family living there and they remodeled the interior of the home, so going inside will do us no good. However, Abbott left us some photos that didn't appear in the report that we sent you. He took these photos himself and wants you guys to take a look at them. He thinks fresh eyes may find something he didn't." She hands Max a manila folder bearing the label *Cold Case # 24167.*

Knowing Max does not want to see the pictures, Jesse grabs the folder from him. "I'll take that," she says.

With a frown, Max thinks, *I guess I better look at these pictures now. I know I said I wouldn't, but I better so I can get a feel for what we are going to do here.* Max reaches over and takes the folder back. He opens it and begins flipping through the pictures as he follows Jesse and Officer Kimball out the door.

Officer Kimball walks toward her squad car; she turns around to Jesse and Max, and says "Follow me, please. The motel isn't far. We'll get you checked in and get over to that house."

Max hands the folder back to Jesse. "I'll look at them some more later, Jesse. Let's just get over there and take a look at the area." They both get into Max's car and begin following Officer Kimball. "Hey Jesse, is it just me or does this town seem pretty dark except for the police station and that movie theatre up ahead?"

"It sure does," Jesse says. "It seems like we have been here before. Clinton was a lot like this, too. That was only ten years ago, though. I would hate to think that this murder twenty-five years ago had a lot to do with the fall of this town, like it did with Clinton. I sure hope we can catch this guy soon, because I certainly don't want to see this happen to Rockton!"

Officer Kimball pulls into the motel parking lot, behind the motel. In the front of the lot, there's a house that's been converted into the main office. It has a flashing vacancy light in the front window. All three walk up the steps to the front door of the office. A light turns on in the upstairs window and they can hear someone coming down the stairs as Officer Kimball turns to Jesse. "Mr. Sampson, the guy that runs this place, is pretty strange. He built this house thirty years ago with his bare hands and then, about two years later, he decided to build the motel on the land that he had been farming. I guess he figured it would be more lucrative than farming. He was wrong and ever since then, he has had a chip on his shoulder. Just answer any questions he has with very short answers and don't get into too much detail—if you do, it will just upset him more. Most people just call him the grumpy guy of Merrillville."

The door opens. Mr. Sampson is standing at the door with a scowl on his face. An older man in his late sixties, it appears as if he has been working in the fields all day. In reality, he just doesn't care about his appearance. He has gray hair in a comb-over. "Can I help you?" he says in more of a snarl than a welcome.

"Hello Mr. Sampson. These are the out-of-town detectives that we called you about earlier. They will be here one night and the city will pick up the tab. Remember?"

Mr. Sampson talks under his breath the whole walk over to the counter. Jesse and Max each catch part of what he is muttering. "...*Damn out-of-towners will probably trash the place....*" As he reaches the counter, he puts his hand out to hold himself up. He turns around and faces the officers. "Can I see an ID, please?" he asks Max.

Max flashes his badge. "Okay, you guys get rooms 1 and 2. They are the cleanest," he says as he turns around and grabs a key off the peg board behind him.

There is a TV and the standard Bible in the nightstand. The room appears to be clean, but the smell of mothballs is a little strong. There is a door next to the bed that seems to lead into Jesse's room. He unlocks his side and knocks on it.

Jesse unlocks her side and opens the door. She is smiling. "Quaint, right?" she says with a chuckle. "You have to love the remote being screwed into the top of the nightstand. I'm glad he has given us complimentary toothbrushes in the bathroom. We left so fast that I didn't bring everything I needed."

Max laughs out loud. "So it is going to be two days with the same clothes for you? I dropped you off at home. What were you doing?"

Jesse sticks her tongue out at him. "I was taking care of my cat. I wanted to make sure she had enough food and water for the next two days, just in case," she says to him as she closes the door in his face.

Max opens the door back up and says, "Okay, let's get outside and wait for our fellow officer so we can go to the house. I really don't want to stay here any longer than we have to."

He walks into Jesse's room, still laughing a little bit at her lack of preparation for an overnight investigation. As they see the police car pulling up into the parking lot, they head for the door.

Once inside the back of the police car, Max starts to look at the file in earnest. He pulls each picture out this time and looks thoroughly at them one by one. As he finishes with them, he hands them to Jesse to look at. The fourth picture in the file seems to have caught his attention more than the first three. He stares at it for a minute before leaning over to Jesse. "See that?" he says and points to the picture. "There are dents on either side of the wife—just like Gwen Bjornson and Amber. Her stomach was stabbed multiple times. Not as precise and calculated as the other two women. This was very emotional. It was probably his first time doing this. He just stabbed randomly while he was kneeling over her."

He passes that picture to Jesse and stops again at the last picture. "Now this is interesting," he says. "Look at how he killed the husband. He cut his throat and forced the victim's car key into the esophagus. I know now why the chief detective didn't send these photos over to us. They never released that information to the public." The effect of the photos is electric to Max, as he sees a resemblance between these victims and the couple from his nightmare. *Or maybe I'm just superimposing their faces, trying to make sense of it all.*

Jesse agrees with Max as she takes the last photo from him. "You sure you are going to be okay after seeing this? It is pretty horrific," she whispers.

"I'll be fine," he answers. "Thanks for your concern, but I think I'd rather deal with nightmares than the knowledge I didn't do everything I possibly could to apprehend this guy."

The squad car comes to a stop in front of a very nice house. It is well-lit, with small spotlights pointed at every part of the brick exterior. The yard is very well maintained, with bushes that are sculpted in many different shapes. There are many windows in the front of the home.

"This is it," Officer Kimball says as she leans her head over her right shoulder into the back seat.

She lets them out of the backseat to look around.

"You mentioned that the people who own the house now did some renovations. Did they only do the inside?" Max asks Kimball.

"They only did the inside. This neighborhood has always been the *well-to-do area,*" she answers with an air quote. "All of these houses have been here for forty years plus. They added the lights on the outside for security, I am guessing. But other than that, it is exactly how it looked twenty-five years ago."

Jesse and Max look around the neighborhood and see a lot of houses that are very similar. All of them are brick with decent-sized yards. This is definitely a better part of town.

Max walks up and down the sidewalk in front of the car. "I've seen enough here. We need to get back to the motel and get some rest. Then, in the morning, we will meet with your chief detective and pick his brain," he says as he heads back to the police car.

Officer Kimball agrees that it is getting late and that they should head back.

Back at the motel, they wish Officer Kimball a good night and the two detectives go to their rooms. Max wants to watch a little TV before bed. It helps him relax and hopefully, will push the pictures he saw earlier out of his dreams.

Max lies in the bed flipping stations until he finds an old Hitchcock-themed movie. He watches the movie in its entirety and still cannot fall asleep. Worse yet, the images of the man and woman killed in this town twenty-five years ago are still in his mind's eye. He gets up from the bed and goes into the bathroom. Splashing some water on his face, he thinks, *I will give one more movie a shot. Hopefully that will help me sleep.* He climbs back into bed and flips stations again. This time he puts on an old sitcom repeat. This is one he has definitely seen before so he thinks it will bore him to sleep. About five minutes into the show, it starts to do just that. His eyelids start to feel very heavy and he drifts off to sleep.

Two hours later, Max is lying in bed, furiously thrashing around in a restless sleep. The comforter is on the floor, as are most of the pillows. Despite the lack of covering, Max is pouring sweat. "No! No! I can't!" he yells out from his sleep.

Jesse comes running into his room through the still unlocked adjoining door. She is wearing only a t-shirt and panties. Her legs are spectacular. While he is still screaming, she grabs him by the shoulders and holds him steady. She shakes him a little at first but he still isn't waking up. After she shakes him a little harder, his eyes pop open.

"What the heck are you doing here?" he says as he looks around his room. "Where am I?" He shakes his head, clearing his thoughts. "Oh, Jesse, it's you. Sorry about that. I had a weird dream. I was that boy again, only this time, I was looking at the Bjornson couple lying in bed, and here is the really weird part: not only were the Bjornsons lying in the bed murdered, but so were my parents. They were all asking me to help them, but I couldn't. I was just a little boy." Dropping his head into his hands, he murmured, "Jesse, we need to figure this out quick or I might totally lose it."

Jesse crawls into the bed and puts her arm around him. "I get it, Max. This is a tough case. It affects you and our whole town. You must be thinking this guy is going to come after your parents. I'm sure they're not even on his list. He only attacks people who waste his time. Go back to sleep, Max. I'll stay here the rest of the night and keep an eye on you. I can get some sleep tomorrow on the way home."

Jesse leaves the room and comes back wearing pants. She climbs into bed with Max, but stays above the covers. "Close your eyes. You'll be okay in the morning."

Max closes his eyes, feeling safer. "Thanks, Jesse. I don't know what has come over me. I feel like a little kid. I am glad you're here." He falls back asleep while Jesse turns on the TV and puts the sound way down so she doesn't disturb him.

Seven a.m. comes quickly for Max. The sun filters through the grungy orange drapes as he gets out of bed. Jesse is not in the room. He decides to take a hot shower to help him wake up. Enjoying the hot water flowing over him, he feels clean and somehow sanitized, as if the events of the night are washed down the drain with the water.

Max comes out of his bathroom wearing nothing but a towel over his mid-section. He looks around; Jesse is still not in his room. He breathes a sigh of relief, knowing that eventually he is going to have to talk about it. Feeling silly for needing someone to be with him while he slept, he knocks on the adjoining door and while still dressing yells, "Let's go, Jesse. We need to get over to meet the chief detective and get back home."

He hears a knock at his front door. Grabbing his gun, he pulls the dirty curtains back. It's Jesse. He opens the door. "What the heck? I was just yelling at you through the door to get ready," he says as he finishes buttoning his shirt. Max walks over to the bed to put his socks and shoes on.

"I left your room about an hour ago. I needed some coffee and I figured you could use some, too. You slept pretty well after I came in, but before that, I don't know how you did. I thought maybe you could use the extra boost," she says as she hands him a cup of steaming coffee.

Max smiles at her. In his whole life, he has never had anyone get him as much as she does. She thinks like him when it comes to crime and even comes up with the same theories. She complements him as a partner better than he ever expected. "You read my mind, partner." He takes a sip of the coffee and gets up from the bed. "Thanks for last night. You are a true friend. Of course, you will have the decency to not mention this to anyone at all, right?" he says with sarcasm in his voice, but seriousness in his eyes.

Jesse cracks a smile. "Tell them what? That the great Max Larkin is human, after all?" She puts both of her hands to her face and opens her mouth and eyes wide to mimic a shocked face. "What will people think?" she says as she rolls her eyes.

Max shakes his head. "Ha-ha. Now let's get going, shall we?" he says as he pushes her out the door. Making a joke about it makes him feel better, as that's how Max deals with stress. It is easier to make jokes than to acknowledge it.

Max remembers how to get to the police station from the motel. It is a straight shot down the main street of Merrillville. They pull into the police station parking lot and get their first look at the station in the daylight. It is just as big as it was at night, but without the bright lights shining from the windows, it seems less intimidating.

The inner door of the station is still locked, but there is someone sitting at the security window just to the right. Max walks up to the window. "Detectives Larkin and Fairlane to see Chief Detective Abbott. He is expecting us." Max shows his badge.

The officer picks up a phone and relays the message. After she hangs up the phone, she tells Max that Abbott will be right up front to meet them; they can have a seat in the front lounge area.

Max and Jesse sit down and wait for the chief detective. They take the time to look around at the large, modern lounge area. The walls have serene pictures hanging, and commendations for officers. The sun shines in the front door and window area, accenting the pictures to perfection.

Chief Detective Abbott comes through the door. He is a well-dressed

African American man, walking with a slight limp. His hair is graying throughout. He has silver and black glasses that accent his graying hair nicely. The glasses seem to blend into his hair, as if they are a part of him.

He reaches out his hand as he walks toward Max and Jesse. "I'm Chief Abbott, and you must be Detectives Larkin and Fairlane." Max and Jesse extend their hands for a handshake. "Nice to meet you both. I'm sorry it had to be under these circumstances. I know that Officer Kimball took you to the house and area last night. What else can I do for you today?"

"I need you to help us put some of the pieces together," Max says as he releases the Chief's hand. "You were the lead detective on this case twenty-five years ago." The chief nods. "I need to know more about that little boy. What did he see? What can he remember now? Where is he now? He might be the only witness who is willing to talk. We have one back in Rockton, but he is not very helpful. If this boy can give us anything right now, it might help us catch this guy."

Chief Abbott turns around and starts walking back toward his office, motioning for Max and Jesse to follow him past the detectives in the squad room. He holds his office door open and motions for them to sit.

Abbott begins, "I try not to talk about this case in front of anyone. I look at it as a failure. I had an eyewitness—granted, he was only three years old, but he still saw and spoke to the killer. Outside of that, I had nothing to go on. There was absolutely no physical evidence of any kind left behind by this guy. He used a knife that he got from their kitchen to cut the man's throat. He jammed the victim's keys into the opening and through the esophagus. The medical examiner couldn't determine which happened first—the man drowning in his own blood that flowed into his throat or the blood loss from the original cut. Either way, it was not a quick, painless death. The only thing that looked out of place was a single twenty dollar bill left next to the husband on the bed—like the killer gave it to him or something. We left the key facts out of the press. We didn't want any copycats out there, or fake confessions. Nobody knows about the keys in the throat. Nobody knows about the boy outside of law enforcement. Like I said, I look at this as a failure. The fact that you are even here right now reminds me of how badly I actually failed. He obviously struck again in your town and that makes me sick to my stomach, but I do not want to show that to my detectives. They need to know that I am solid."

Max and Jesse listen closely to every word that the chief says. Any insight or piece of evidence they didn't already have would make the trip worth their time. Max interrupts, "Chief Detective, do you have any theories on why the victim's keys were used as part of the murder?"

Abbott responds, "We were never sure if they had to do with the motive or were just close by. It made the most sense that they had something to do with the killer's reason behind choosing that family. We know they bought a new car that week, but nothing solid panned out from that part of the investigation."

"Is there any way possible that we can meet with this boy?" Max queries.

"Well, he is not a boy now. He would be what…twenty-eight or twenty-nine?" Jesse volunteers.

Abbott sits up in his chair, crosses his arms in front of him, and leans in a little bit toward the two detectives. "I would love to help you with that, but he was placed with his aunt and uncle in another state. That's all I really know about him. His name wasn't even listed in the report in order to keep his identity a secret. His records were sealed for his protection. It would take a court order to unseal them and truthfully, I really don't want to be the one that makes him remember that night. I think you are better off just going to the witness you have now and getting him to talk. I understand he is not cooperating, but you need to push him. Better him than this kid who went through hell twenty-five years ago."

Jesse can see Max tensing his shoulders and flexing his fist. She knows that he really wants to catch this guy but realizes that it would be better to leave this particular witness alone unless absolutely necessary. She reaches over to Max and touches the arm of his chair. "Max, I think Chief Abbott is right. This kid went through hell twenty-five years ago and bringing him back to that moment would not be right—at least not yet. If we need to get those records unsealed we will, but let's go back at Stephen Bjornson first. I still think he has more to tell. Not to mention, his ordeal is fresh in his mind. The kid was so young he probably doesn't remember any of it, anyway."

Max stands up and reaches out to shake Chief Abbott's hand as they smile, resigned to figuring out how to catch this crazy guy. "I get why you are protecting this boy, but we need to catch the killer. If I can save a lot of lives versus protecting a young man's feelings over his parents' murder,

I'll choose the lives. My partner doesn't agree with me on this and I will trust her judgment for now, but keep an eye out for me because the next time you see me, I will have that court order to open the kid's files. Good day to you, Chief." Starting to the door he says, "Let's go, Jesse. I want to talk to Bjornson again. I need more from him and it has been a couple days now. I am going to press him, and press him hard this time."

As Max walks out into the squad room, Jesse stays behind and quickly explains to Abbott how important this case is to her partner and about the killer's escalation. His willingness to push a witness from so long ago rather than a local witness from earlier this week has her thoroughly confused.

A car comes to a stop in front of Rosie's flower shop. Rosie's is known around Rockton as the place to go for your large floral arrangement needs. Rosie has personally designed the flowers for almost every wedding that has occurred in the Rockton area. She is the only person in the shop today, as her delivery person is out sick. Either way, this is her quiet time every day, when everyone else is out to lunch and she can create her beautiful arrangements in peace.

Rosie's Flower Shop sits next to the only other store on the block. Korry a Tune, a whimsically named music store, is attached by a brick wall. That store is owned by Korry, or Korrina, Giannopoulous. The closest building to these two stores is more than two blocks away. Surrounding the two stores on both sides are empty lots where cars park to catch the train to work or where summer carnivals are held. Litter blows in the wind across the lots and between cars.

A man in a suit steps out of the car and heads to the flower shop. His head is down, looking at the ground, shaking back and forth, and a quiet mumbling can be heard coming from his mouth. He pushes the door, ringing a bell that sounds to alert Rosie. Immediately, he looks up at Rosie as she stands behind the counter. She is arranging lilies in a vase. He thinks, *Rosie sure is beautiful. I wish I could still trust her.*

Rosie looks up, recognizes her visitor and raises her eyebrows. They exchange smiles. She is very excited to see her beau. "Hey baby, let me finish this arrangement. I'm going to need to deliver it today around five." Rosie puts some baby's breath inside the vase and continues to arrange the flowers. "I didn't expect to see you until tonight. I know you work until nine. To what do I owe this pleasure?" She continues fussing with the flowers and finally takes a step back, looking at her latest masterpiece.

81

She then takes off her work gloves, shoving them into her apron pocket, and placing the vase off to the side. "I thought you had to work today, sweetie."

Rosie approaches her man and embraces him in a warm, loving hug. Her head rests on his shoulder. Once she can't see his face, the smile drops from his lips and his eyes become cold. She gently pushes away from him and his face immediately reverts back to a smile, brightening the warm brown eyes. "Well, Rosie, is there any harm in a man coming to see his love and spending some time with her? Besides, I don't go into work until two o'clock today, so I thought why not come and see the woman I love?"

He grabs a piece of her hair and twirls it between his fingers. "I thought maybe you would want to have some *fun!* I know that Tim is out making deliveries so we have some time. What do you say?" He winks at her, raising his eyebrows a few times. "Come on; let's go into the cooler for some privacy. Do you mind if I switch the open sign to closed? I want you all to myself, with no interruptions."

Rosie nods her head, excited, and immediately begins to take off her apron as she heads back toward the cooler. "Tim needed to take a sick day. He isn't feeling very well at all. He must have caught a bug," Rosie says with great anticipation. Her boyfriend hears this and thinks of ways to take advantage of the fact that he has as much time as he needs to complete his work.

He walks over to the sign, flips it around to closed and locks the door. He starts whistling the same song he always whistles when he knows he is about to give someone what is coming to them. As he walks back toward the cooler, he punches one hand into the other and clenches them together, cracking his knuckles.

"Okay babe, I thought we could try something a little kinky today. What do you say, Rosie?" he asks her while rubbing his hands fiendishly together like he is washing them under a faucet.

"What do you have in mind? I love it when we get wild. I love you so much, Tom! I am the luckiest lady alive." Rosie's voice gets lower and sexier as she turns around and jumps right up on the counter in the cooler. She beckons Tom over with a come-hither look and curling of her finger.

Rosie watches as he closes the cooler door very slowly. "We don't want anyone to hear us in here. I plan on getting pretty wild," he says to her with a 'cat that ate the canary' grin on his face. "Where can I find something to tie you up with, my love?"

She points over to a cabinet of supplies with her right index finger. "Right over there, baby. Oooh, we have never done tie-up games before. You really do want to get kinky, don't you?" He nods his head at her, raising his eyebrows again. *Just too easy,* he thinks.

Tom grabs some twine and rope from the cabinet. "Come here, honey, right under these hooks. I want to tease you for a while. You know what they say. It isn't just the act of lovemaking; it's the anticipation of it. By the time I'm done with you, you will beg for it to be over, I promise."

Rosie saunters over to him under the hooks, twirling as she gets close. First, he ties her wrists and then her legs with the twine. He grabs the rope and wraps it a few times around her waist. Taking another piece of rope, he puts it on the floor next to her feet. He climbs up on the counter with rope in hand and runs it through five hooks in the ceiling, then climbs down and pulls the rope gently. He begins to lift Rosie up, but he stops just before her feet lift off the ground.

Tom loosens his tie and begins to take off his jacket as he reaches for one of Rosie's work aprons. He moves toward Rosie and begins to whistle again.

"What is that song, babe? It sounds so familiar," she says.

Tom keeps walking toward her, not saying a word. When he gets close enough, he puts his finger to her lips. "Shhh, just enjoy yourself." He grabs her dress and rips it open. The buttons fly all over the floor. Rosie gasps in excitement. She acts as if she is going to faint as he walks behind her, caressing her body as he moves around her. He leans into her neck, breathing heavily over her ear and hairline as he kisses her up and down. He begins to expose her shoulders as he kisses down her neck toward the shoulders.

"Are you getting excited, Rosie?" he whispers into her ear. She nods, her breath coming fast. "Do you want me to continue?" Again, she nods enthusiastically. "What do you want, Rosie? Tell me what you want," he whispers.

Rosie can hardly hold it in any longer. "Make love to me. Show me how you feel about me! Take me, take me now!" she exclaims breathily.

Tom steps back from her and grabs a stool from the corner and puts it in front of her. He sits in front of her for a moment, just scanning her from head to toe. Tom notices some roses on the floor near him. He gets up and grabs seven of them and places six on the floor at Rosie's feet and begins to caress her skin with the last one. "Do you know what I want, Rosie?" he whispers into her ear.

Gasping in excitement, Rosie squeaks out, "No, baby. Tell me what you want. I'll give you anything. I'm all yours." Tom cuts the stem short on the rose and places it behind her ear. He then reaches down and puts the remaining twine in his left hand.

Tom grabs Rosie's ponytail with his free right hand and pulls on it really hard. "I want you to pay for my time that you wasted. I cannot believe you betrayed me like that!" he screams suddenly into her ear. He lets go of her hair and wraps the rope around her neck, tying it in a loose slip knot. He then pulls the rope tightly and stretches it to the stool to sit down. He starts whistling the same song again, shaking his head over and over again.

Rosie has morphed from excited anticipation to a sobbing mess. She gasps for air as he loosens the rope from her neck just enough for her to answer him. "What are you talking about? Why are you doing this? I love you!"

"You love me? Are you serious? Love doesn't involve betrayal!" he screams at her while standing up with the end of the rope still in his hand. "You have betrayed me and therefore wasted my time and Rosie, my dear, time is money! I figure you owe me about $105,078 for all my time that you wasted. Do you have that kind of money?"

"You know I don't. How did I betray you? How did I waste your time? Please stop, you're hurting me!" Rosie's cries are getting louder and her gasping has increased.

"You're right, Rosie. I know you don't have that much money. However, when I'm done here, I'll take what you do have. I am going to give you three chances here, Rosie." Tom picks up three of the six roses at her feet. "Three chances to explain yourself. Three chances to convince me I am wrong about you." Tom is now pacing with the rope in one hand and the flowers in the other. He begins to wave the flowers at her, back and forth, simulating a metronome. "Just three chances. If you lie to me, there will be a consequence, so I suggest you tell me the truth. Got it?"

Rosie nods. She is now terrified. She begins to think about every time they were together, how he would shower her with compliments. *Your hair is so pretty. I truly love kissing your lips.* She continues running through the times he would take her out and always open the door for her, pull out her chair. He would even brush her hair back from her eyes when her bangs fell. "Tom, I do love you. I don't understand what's going on here."

Tom stops dead in his tracks. "Liar!" he cries. Tom drops the rope and heads to the supply cabinet to grab a stapler. He opens the stapler into a straight line.

He walks back to Rosie, holds one rose to her forehead and staples the stem to her forehead. Her screams are bloodcurdling, even to his ears. "Shut up! That is one lie. I told you there would be consequences, and you only have two chances left. So again, I suggest you start telling me the truth."

Rosie nods her head as blood trickles down into her eyes. Her body is trembling from the pain. Her lips are quivering as she tries to hold back her cries. "Okay, I won't lie to you, I promise. Please just tell me why you're doing this."

"I ask the questions here. You have no right to ask me anything," he calmly says to her. He seems at ease right now, as if he does not have a care in the world. "Now, let's start with my first question. Is it true you did the flowers for the Franklin and Smythe wedding last weekend?"

Rosie nods her head yes. "Good, you are finally telling me the truth. You see, I already knew that you did. I saw the flowers being done and the name on the order. I was just checking to make sure you weren't going to lie to me again. Now for question number two. Are you ready?"

Rosie again nods her head up and down. "Super! Did you know that Smythe was my ex-wife's maiden name?" Tom calmly asks her. Rosie freezes for a moment. She thinks hard about it and shakes her head no.

"Uh-oh! Someone is lying again. You know what that means." Tom reaches over to the opposite side of her forehead and staples another rose stem to her forehead. She cries out and winces repeatedly from the pain. "You see, Rosie, I know I told you that when we first started dating. I also reminded you when I saw my daughter's engagement announcement in the paper. You see, she was getting married last weekend and she actually dropped my last name and took her mother's maiden name. Do you remember that now, Rosie?"

Rosie nods her head again. The blood from the first rose has dried around her right eye now and she is continually blinking, trying to see.

"Here, let me get that for you," Tom says as he grabs a tissue from his pocket and wipes the blood away from her eye. "I want to see your eyes when you answer me. I will be able to tell if you are telling me the truth that way. So you do remember that story. Good! What you failed to tell me was that you were doing the flowers for my daughter's wedding, the wedding that I wasn't even invited to. I mean, I knew she wouldn't ask me to walk her down the aisle, but to not even invite me—that is unacceptable. She betrayed me, just like you did. She will get hers soon enough. Right now, let's just concentrate on you, shall we? This is how you betrayed me. You knew she was my daughter, yet you did her flowers anyway. You didn't even tell me that they contacted you about it. So you also hid it from me. Does that sound like a person who loves me? I don't think so." Every word has gotten louder, so his voice has gone from a whisper to a scream by the last word.

"Please stop, Tom! I'm sorry. It was just business. It has been super slow here lately and it was a large order. I need to make ends meet!" Rosie cries out to him.

"I do believe you when you say you're sorry. However, that's just the beginning. Now, based on the six months that we've been dating, I calculated that I spent an average of three hours per day wasting my time with you, and my time is valuable. On average, I make about $211 per hour at my job. If I had spent the time working rather than with you, I would have been much better off. So six months at three hours a day and $211 an hour comes to about $105,078 that you owe me. I gave you some credit for days that we didn't see each other, but I figured that was a good estimate," Tom says matter-of-factly. "I truly thought I loved you and could be with you for a very long time, but now I know you are more about yourself than you are about us. I'll tell you what, Rosie. I will tell you my whole story. Do you want to hear it?" he says to her, hoping she does, because he needs her to understand why he is doing this to her. Rosie lets out a moan that sounds close enough to a yes for Tom to continue.

"It was about thirty years ago that I met my ex-wife. Her name is Phoebe Smythe, but you already know that from the wedding announcements. We fell in love almost instantly. It was a whirlwind romance. We were both around twenty, but way beyond our years in maturity. I had a good-paying job and she was working nights at a security company. We spent almost all of our free time together for the next few months. When we weren't working, we were together. We enjoyed movies, dinners, dancing—heck, you name it, we did it together. After about four months, I figured it was about time we got engaged. I even asked her father's permission before I asked her. That is how much I respected her and her family.

"We got married and less than a year later, we had our daughter. I never thought I could love another human being as unconditionally as I did my little Amanda. She was so beautiful as a baby. I barely took my eyes off of my daughter because I loved her so much. I made sure I had her picture with me at all times if I couldn't be there with her—in my office, in my car, and especially in my wallet, so I could look at her any time I wanted. Well, of course, Amanda started growing—as kids do, you know—and before I knew it, she was five and heading off to school." Tom looks wistfully into the distance as he continues his story.

"Now, during the first few years after Amanda was born, my wife stayed home. Kids cost money and money was getting tight, so when Amanda went to school, my wife went back to work. After a few weeks of her working, I noticed some changes in her attitude toward me. Phoebe didn't understand how she could work normal hours and get paid, but I couldn't. She kept telling me I was working too much and that she barely saw me. She demanded that I should spend more time at home. I told her over and over again that I needed to work a lot because I was only on commission. If I wasn't there to sell, I missed out on money for all of us. It seemed like she didn't care what I had to say. All she cared about was her new job. She started drifting away from me. There was nothing I could do but work harder to try and convince her that I loved her and Amanda—that I was doing it for them."

Rosie opens her eyes a little wider, and from her facial expression, he feels like he can read her thoughts. *What is she thinking?* he wonders. *Is it that the time we have been together has been nothing but a lie? Whether I am the person she thought I was?*

She musters the strength to lift her head up and look right at him. "I don't understand. You get commission working for the government? How is that possible?"

Tom stopped talking and just sat there for a moment. "I just realized something. I never told you what I really do. I told you I am a government agent, didn't I? That is why I work so many hours and couldn't always be with you. That is how I explained driving a lot of different cars all the time. I wouldn't want anyone following us, would I?" Tom starts laughing at Rosie. "How could you be so gullible? I can't believe you fell for that. Now here is a shocker for you: I lied about that. I am just a car salesman. I work on commission. I couldn't have you coming into my dealership in Clinton anytime you wanted to see me, so it was better to say that I was out of town on a mission or something like that. Poor Rosie—so simple-minded."

Tom's eyes laser into her. He can see she is bleeding a little heavier now and her eyes are closed. He walks over to her. "Are you still with me, Rosie?" Tom slaps Rosie in the face a few times to wake her from the daze she is in. "Rosie, oh Rosie, are you listening?" he whispers softly into her ear.

Rosie musters a soft yes. She is weak from the pain and is suffering from shock. "Liar! Strike three! Now I have to hurt you more and hope this time you will actually listen!" Tom yells into her ear this time.

He takes the final rose from his hand and staples it to the middle of her forehead. This time, he hits a nerve ending—or Rosie just can't take it anymore. She lets out a scream that makes Tom's skin crawl. Her face is now covered in blood from the first three roses as they pull on her skin with their weight. The stems lie over her face like jail bars. Her eyes are wide open now and she is fully alert, struggling against the ropes.

"Shall I continue?" he asks her. She nods slowly. Rosie's lips move silently in prayer. "I'll tell you what, since I actually do care about you, Rosie, I will give you three more chances." He picks up the remaining three roses at her feet and goes back to his stool.

"Okay then. Where was I? Oh yeah. So my wife is working, I am working and Amanda is at school in the mornings and at daycare the rest of the day, until my wife gets off work. After a few months of this, my wife decides that she no longer wants to be married to me and takes our daughter away from me. She says that she is tired of waiting so long for me to get home and that she has found another man who can take care of Amanda and her better than I can. Can you believe that? After all I was doing for our family, she said I wasn't good enough to be a father and a husband. Granted, my income had gone down because of people like you, Rosie—people who wasted my time.

"You see, some people go into retail establishments to look at things and then start talking to a salesman. Deep down, they know they have no intention of buying the salesman's product, but they don't care that they are wasting his time. He is just there to amuse them and make them feel special. What most people do not realize is that most sales personnel are on commission only. So when someone spends hours of the salesman's time and does not buy anything, he gets nothing, while if he could have gotten a different customer, who was really interested in his product, he could have made a sale. So instead of making money, the salesman made nothing; therefore the people wasted his time. It was then and there that I decided people would not waste my time anymore. I told myself that if someone intentionally wasted my time, I would make it my goal to stop them from doing it again." He looks over at Rosie at this point to see that she is still awake and paying attention. He notices that her eyes have widened. "Don't get ahead of me now, Rosie. I don't want you to miss out on what I am saying to you. This is where the story gets good."

Rosie begins to cry again and Tom says, "Please stop interrupting me. This story is a good one. I'll tell you what. Are you thirsty? I know I am. I will go into the shop and get us some water. Now, while I am gone, please pull yourself together and stop interrupting. Unfortunately, I can't have you screaming while I open this door, so I am going to have to tape your mouth shut." He walks over to the cabinet and grabs some packing tape, putting it over her mouth.

Tom heads to the door of the cooler. He looks back and sees Rosie struggling with the twine on her wrists and ankles. "You need to stop that or you will not get any water. Now be a good girl and sit still and think about what you have done while I am gone. I will only be a few seconds. Even if you were strong enough to break the twine, you wouldn't be able to get past me. You might as well just stop trying and wasting your energy and time. After all, time is money." He starts to whistle yet again as he walks out into the flower shop.

Tom takes a look around at the shop. "A hundred and five thousand dollars is a lot of money she cost me," he says to himself. "I wonder what she has that can help me recover some of that loss. Hmm…what have we here? A lovely cash register." He pushes the no sale button and the drawer opens. Inside the cash register is quite a bit of money. "Hello there, gentlemen," he says to the money. "Let's see what we have here." Tom begins counting the money. "$2,954, to be exact. I guess she lied about business being slow right now. I think I will let her go on that lie for now.

She still owes me $102,124. At least I am going to get something from her. I hope I have enough time to get to her house when I am done here and see if there is anything there for me to take, as well." He shuts the drawer after removing the money.

Whistling yet again, he grabs two small cups next to the water cooler and fills both cups before returning. Tom opens the door ever so slightly and pokes his head inside. "Here's Tommy!" he says with a big, glib smile. "Did you miss me?" Tom re-enters the cooler, still whistling his favorite song. He walks toward Rosie and callously rips the tape from her mouth. As she sits there sobbing, she looks at him through the thorny rose stems and begs him one more time to please stop. "Here Rosie, drink up. We just have a little bit left of my story, I promise." With that statement, he places the cup to her lips and tips the cup forward to dump water into her parched mouth.

"We have gotten to my promise to myself to never let anyone waste my time without compensation again. I decided it was time for me to move. I couldn't be here anymore. There was nothing for me here. My wife had moved on to another man and she took my daughter with her. Sure, I got to visit my daughter, but seeing my wife all the time with her new man was too much to handle so I decided to leave Rockton. I moved to a small town in Indiana—Merrillville, to be exact—just over the state line. I promised Amanda I would come get her every summer for two weeks of vacation and that would be our daddy-daughter time." Tom shakes his head like he is shaking the cobwebs out. "Sorry, I got off on a tangent there."

He continues, "Anyway, I moved to Indiana and things were going great for awhile. Then, after being there about a month, I had some customers come into the car dealership I was working at. They wanted to look at a new car. After about four hours of my time, the husband and wife stood up and said they had to think about it and would let me know. They picked up their son and left. Four hours! I couldn't take it anymore. Every chance I got I watched these people. I had gotten their address from their driver's licenses and followed them around on my days off and lunch hours. They didn't have a care in the world. They didn't care that they cost me money, and they certainly didn't care about anyone else outside their little bubble. I had been following them for about three weeks before I knew it was time to teach them their much-needed lesson—after they bought a new car from some other dealership! They were usually home every night before 8 p.m. so they could get their kid to sleep. By 11 p.m., they were generally in bed and sound asleep. I got off work at 9 p.m. and drove to their house on the outskirts of Merrillville. I sat in my car for a few hours just to be absolutely sure that they were asleep. When midnight came around, it seemed the perfect time to go in. I put on a ski mask and walked up to their house. I saw a window slightly ajar so I opened it up and climbed in. Their house was very nice—too nice for such selfish people. My first stop was their son's room."

Rosie gets really flustered when Tom says he went to the son's room first. He sees Rosie struggle against her restraints. He can tell that she thinks he is going to harm her son. "Don't worry, Rosie. Your son Johnny is safe. He did nothing to me. He has nothing to do with this. Besides, if you had not interrupted me yet again, you would know the whole story by now. So let's just keep comments and questions to the end. Okay, sweetie?"

Rosie mumbles a small yes and Tom continues. "My first stop was the little boy's room. He was sound asleep, lying in his bed with his football sheets over him. I can still see his room if I close my eyes. Footballs, baseballs, and basketballs on the wall. I had walked into the room with the intention of taking his life, to save him the misery of living with his two selfish parents, but when I looked down at him I realized I couldn't do it. He reminded me so much of Amanda when she was that age. I just couldn't do it. I actually reached in and tucked him in a little bit. Even though he was sleeping, he got a little smile on his face as if to say thank you to me. I had to take care of the parents, though. They were the real reason I was there, anyway. I walked out of his room and closed the door quietly so he couldn't hear what I was about to do next. See, don't you wish you had waited to hear that part of the story before jumping to the conclusion that I killed the little boy?" he asks Rosie in a very sarcastic tone.

She nods and he continues. "I crept down the hall so I didn't wake the husband and wife before I got there. Their door was left ajar, which made my job easier. I could see they were asleep. I had brought some duct tape with me and some tranquilizers that I had stolen from my dog's vet earlier that day. To this day, I use one of my insulin needles filled with ketamine to subdue the people who waste my time before I end their time here with us. It is pretty effective and works well with a low dose.

"I injected the wife first because she was closest. Then it was hubby's turn. One milligram of ketamine will subdue them for about an hour and I can then tie them up so they are not a threat to me. While they were sleeping, I took the duct tape out and taped their mouths shut. I then proceeded to duct tape them to the bed. This really did take some time. I could soon see the husband start to fidget a little so I slapped him awake. I took off his tape gag and explained to him how they wasted my valuable time. I said I wanted my money back for that time. I wanted my $320 dollars. Back then I wasn't making nearly as much as I am now. I calculated it to be about $80 an hour, so $320 was what I wanted. He said he didn't have any cash on hand and that he wouldn't give it to me if he did. I couldn't take him anymore. I grabbed him around the throat and choked him until he died in my hands.

"The wife had woken up to this and even though her mouth was duct taped, I could sense she had something to say. I took the tape off her mouth and told her the same story. She never stopped crying the whole time so I put my hand over her mouth and said, 'If I do not get my money, you will wind up like your husband.' I took my hand away from her mouth and listened to her babble on about being cash poor and very much in debt. I leaned into her and told her that was not good enough. I left the room and went to the kitchen. I grabbed the biggest knife I could find and went back to her. I guess I hadn't perfected my technique yet because she managed to get one hand free and was working on the other when I walked back in. She immediately stopped what she was doing and stared at me. I stabbed her in the chest and stomach over and over. There was no way I was going to let her waste anymore of my time. Blood was now all over my suit and I still hadn't received my money from them. I looked over at the husband's night stand and saw a nice gold watch, so I took it. I still wear that watch to this day." He holds up his left hand and shows off his gold watch. "I figured I got my money's worth from them, after all. I will say this…I felt so much better knowing I rid the world of two time wasters. They would never hurt anyone ever again. I did the world a favor.

"But there still was the matter of the little boy. What to do with him? I couldn't bring myself to kill him, and I certainly wasn't going to leave him there all alone. I decided to teach him a lesson, so he wouldn't do what his parents did to me. I went back to his room and picked him up. I carried him to his parents' room and put him down on his feet. He started waking up at this point. He rubbed his eyes and looked up at me. He took one look at my mask and started to scream.

"I knelt down to him and said, 'Don't worry. I am not going to hurt you, but you need to remember this. The reason your dad and mom are not with you anymore is because they didn't care about other people. They wasted people's time, so please don't grow up and waste people's time or you could wind up like them.' I then grabbed their phone from the bedside table and dialed 911 for him. I put the phone to his ear and told him to tell them what happened so the police could come get him. He froze and couldn't speak. I had to yell at him to do it. He finally did and then he dropped the phone. I told him I was leaving now and to remember what I told him—not to waste people's time. For no apparent reason, I just started whistling. Whenever I am about to rid the world of time wasters, I whistle the same song. It has been stuck in my head now for 25 years. It's kind of annoying, but catchy at the same time. Maybe it's because I'm working hard to make this world a better place for everyone, so why shouldn't I enjoy a catchy tune while I am doing such a good job for humanity?" Tom starts whistling again.

"I felt like a giant weight was lifted from me after ridding the world of those horrible people. I didn't even do it again until about 10 years ago. Yes, it was 10 years ago. It was about the same time that my ex-wife told me that Amanda didn't want me coming around anymore. I was sad about that. I actually moved closer to her so we could spend more time together. I moved to Clinton, Wisconsin—about 20 minutes from here. I got offered a great job at a brand new car dealership. This place was huge. They built it right off the highway so people could see it as they drove by. We had a lot of people that would just stop and look around because it was so big. I really didn't mind those people because they let me know right away they were not there to buy a car at that point. They didn't waste my time at all. I would just let them wander around and they would leave.

"But the same day that I got the news about Amanda, another couple wasted my time. These people were almost as bad as the first. They took three of my precious hours from me. I am not going to bore you with their details, though. Truthfully, I can barely remember the night I killed them. After finding out about Amanda not wanting to see me and then having these people do this to me, I was so angry! I decided to crawl into a Jack Daniels bottle. I did still follow them awhile and watched them waste other people's time, but before I got to their house, I really tied one on at the tavern. The only thing I remembered was where the house was. Actually, a few days ago, I went back there just to see if I could remember anything from that night. I climbed up a ladder into the bedroom where it all took place. I sat on their bed and just stared at my artwork on the wall. You see, Rosie, I forgot to tell you whenever I rid the world of the time wasters, I leave a message in their own blood on the wall so people know not to follow in the dead person's footsteps and waste people's time. I figure if I can reach enough people, I will rid the world of these selfish people and my work will be done.

"So, after sitting in that room for what I am guessing was about two hours and not remembering a thing, I decided to just leave and chalk it up as a disappointment in my overall scheme of things. I did get the job done, but I do not remember the details of it. Thank you very much, Mr. Daniels." Tom starts laughing hysterically at the little joke he just made.

Tom slides the stool in close to Rosie. She is drifting again. He stands up and leans in close to her. "Can you hear me still, Rosie?" She nods her head. "In all honesty, Rosie, I need to tell you something. My name isn't Tom. It's Michael. Michael Hogan. Amanda did take her mother's maiden name, Smythe, when she decided that she would be better off not spending time with me anymore. I couldn't tell you my real name because of my past—and my present, for that matter. Couldn't have you poking around, asking about me in town."

Rosie gasps a little in fear and swallows some of the blood dripping from her forehead. She spits and chokes on it. He looks at her one last time and gives her a kiss on the lips, tasting her blood. He licks her blood from her lips and smiles like a man who just finished eating something very delicious.

Michael walks over to the supply cabinet again and grabs some pruning shears. He walks behind her and whispers into her ear. "I am truly sorry it has to come to this." He kneels down and grabs her right hand. She resists his touch. He pulls her fingers apart and begins to cut off Rosie's index finger on her right hand. He is having a hard time because the shears are not as strong as the bolt cutters he is accustomed to. It seems to take him four times as long to remove the finger and thumb with the shears. He has to keep moving the shears around the finger and thumb to get them to cut through the knuckles. Rosie is flailing uncontrollably as he cuts. The pain is unbearable and she passes out.

He walks back in front of her and pulls the rope hard and fast; it tightens around her neck. She opens her eyes as she starts to struggle to breathe. "I truly did love you, Rosie, but I cannot have you waste my time anymore. It just isn't fair to me." He pulls the rope even tighter until Rosie dies, strangled to death.

Michael picks up the finger he is finally able to remove and walks to the wall to write, *BITCH WASTED MY TIME.* He goes back to where the woman he once loved is now hanging from the ceiling, lifeless. She is bent over at the point where the rope meets her abdomen. He lifts her up, leans her back and picks up her thumb. He writes 'time waster' on her chest. When he lets go, she slumps forward again. He has to make sure his message gets across so he ties the rope from her neck to the same wall he tied her waist rope to. This gives Rosie the appearance of floating in mid-air.

One down, and now I think I have to finish Stephen off. He is wasting the doctor's time and the police officers' time as well, but how am I going to get to him in the hospital? Michael thinks. Then he laughs as a plan formulates in his devious mind.

Michael takes Rosie's van and drives off toward the hospital. He decides he has more important work to do today than sell cars. He grabs his phone from his hip holster and calls his boss while driving to the hospital. "Hey Rich, yeah it's me, Mike. My girlfriend isn't doing well. I am going to take care of her today. I'll be in tomorrow. I know we are short-handed, but her head is killing her. She said it feels like she has something sharp digging into her skull. I can't leave her alone like this. I did, too, tell you I had a girlfriend. No, I am not going to bring her into the dealership. You guys would eat her alive. That is why I haven't brought her in yet. Let's face it, you guys are pigs. Hey Rich, I will make up the sales next week. Okay? Fine. See you tomorrow, then."

The white Rosie's Flowers van pulls up to the Rockton hospital. Mike Hogan is wearing a shirt, tie, very nice dress pants, Rosie's delivery jacket, and her cap. Mike parks the van right in front so he can make a quick exit from the hospital. He exits the vehicle and grabs balloons and flowers from the side door of the van, keeping his head down and cap lowered enough to cover his entire forehead.

He enters the hospital and heads right to the visitor's desk. The receptionist notices the flowers and immediately asks if they are for a patient or an employee. She isn't able to see his face since his head is tilted down and the flowers and balloons are blocking most of his head. Mike says, "A patient—Stephen Bjornson. Could you please tell me what room he is in?" The receptionist gives him the information and smiles nicely at him.

Mike walks to the elevator, making sure to notice where the stairs are as well, just in case he has to leave quickly. He carefully scans the entire lobby of the hospital for cameras and security personnel. *Not much security here at all,* he thinks. *Should be easy to get out pretty quickly if need be.*

Mike gets off on Mr. Bjornson's floor and immediately heads over to the nurse's station. "I have flowers here for this station and balloons for a...Stephen Bjornson," Mike says as he puts the flowers down in front of the nurses.

The nurses act all giddy and excited, not taking their eyes off the flowers for a second. One nurse motions her hand toward the left hallway and says, "Bjornson is in room 405, down that hallway." She immediately goes back to the flowers and talking with her fellow nurses.

Mike thanks them and heads toward Bjornson's room, being sure to keep the balloons in front of his face and whistling the whole time. Mike notices the stairway exit is right near Bjornson's room and figures that he will be better off going down the stairs than to risk walking past the nurses again. Mike sees a nurse's cart next to the room and looks for a weapon to use on Stephen. *Scissors! Perfect!* he thinks.

He peeks into Stephen's room and notices he is asleep. Mike grabs some gauze and heads in with the balloons. Looking at his victim from a few days before, he can't help thinking, *I wish I had finished this earlier.* Stephen is still restrained. Mike takes some gauze, pushes down on Stephen's chin, and shoves it into his mouth.

Stephen wakes up and sees his worst nightmare has come true. The man is back. Even though he couldn't see his face the first time, he will never forget those eyes looking down on him as the man killed his Gwennie. Stephen can't get any words out. He tries screaming, but it is just muffled.

"Well, Stephen, you didn't listen to me. Now I have to finish what I started. All you had to do was tell everyone to not waste people's time. You couldn't do that, though. Instead, you just wasted doctors', nurses', and police officers' time. Now you have to die." The moment Mike stops speaking, Stephen starts squirming furiously, shaking as if he is having a seizure. "Well, goodbye Stephen." Mike thrusts the scissors into Stephen's chest. Blood starts to ooze from the new wound. Mike removes Stephen's left hand from his restraints, takes his left index finger, and puts it in the blood now pooling on Stephen's gown. He writes, *HE DIDN'T LISTEN* on Stephen's gown, below his stab wound.

Mike then grabs some of the balloons and leaves the room. He takes a quick glance at the nurse's station, where the women are still fawning over the roses. Rather than chance one of them looking up, he exits down the stairwell. Four flights of stairs later, he is back in the lobby and heading toward the door. He hears the receptionist behind him ask, "I thought you were delivering those balloons?"

Mike doesn't even turn around and just keeps walking, stating without missing a beat, "Nope, wrong hospital. Have a good day."

When he gets back to the van, he pushes the balloons through the side door and climbs in after them. He climbs to the front seat, starts the van, and starts to leave the parking lot. As he is heading toward the west exit of the parking lot, he notices a black Firebird pulling in the other entrance to the parking lot. He knows from news articles about the Rockton Police Department that it is Max Larkin, the town's top detective. Mike decides he should stop and verify that this is correct. He calmly pulls the van off to the side of the road and watches as Max and Jesse get out of the car.

Great! They have the best detective in town on me. How am I supposed to finish my work now? Mike thinks. *Maybe I should mess with his mind a little. Throw him off the scent. I'll give him a minute or so to find what I left him. Good luck, Max Larkin; you are going to need it.*

"**S**on of a bitch!!**"** Max yells as he looks at Stephen Bjornson lying in his hospital bed with a pair of scissors stuck into his chest. Written on his gown in blood is *HE DIDN'T LISTEN.*

Max bolts out of the room like a bullet and heads toward the nurse's station. "What the hell is going on here?" he blurts out to the nurses as they all sit there staring at a bouquet of roses. They are laughing and talking amongst themselves, oblivious to the fact that he is even there until he says something.

"Sorry, sir," a beautiful young nurse says to the very angry detective. "We were just wondering who sent these flowers and who they are for. All it says on the card is from a secret admirer. Now then, how may I help you?"

"Stephen Bjornson, the man down the hall from here. When was the last time one of you checked in on him?" Detective Larkin demands.

"I don't know, maybe twenty minutes or so ago. What's the big deal? He was fine then and he is fine now," the nurse spits back at him in a very defiant tone. "He is not going anywhere! What is your problem? Sheesh!"

"You are right about that, he definitely isn't going anywhere. He is dead—murdered! That is my problem, and maybe if you nurses were doing your job instead of sitting around here like a bunch of grade school girls with a crush, you would have been able to stop it from happening. Or at the very least, you could have seen who did it!" Max says as he leans in closer to her so she gets it.

All of the nurses stop dead in their tracks, gasping and dropping their jaws. They are completely still. Finally, the eldest of the nurses speaks up. "Okay, ladies, we need to call Security immediately, get a doctor up here right away, and then get that body out of here. Move, let's go, right away!"

"Don't you dare touch that room!" Detective Larkin snaps. "That is my crime scene now. I want Security up here with footage from this hallway and the entrance *right now!* Who here can tell me how many people have come up here to this floor in the last half hour or so? Also, who has seen Mr. Bjornson today?"

"The only person who has been up here besides us is the flower delivery man. He had flowers for us and balloons for…" The young nurse stops mid-sentence and blanches. "Oh my God, he brought up balloons for Mr. Bjornson. He even asked me what room Mr. Bjornson was in."

Max runs back to the room, with all of the nurses following frantically. No balloons are in sight. "Are you telling me that you got a look at the man bringing in the flowers?" he says as he grabs the younger nurse's arm. "You can identify this guy?"

The nurse is crying, shaking with fear and anxiety. "I can't remember ever seeing his face. It was behind the balloons. Besides, I was focusing on the flowers because I thought they were for me."

"We all were focused on the flowers. They are so beautiful!" the elder nurse states matter-of-factly. "Hey, wait a minute. I do remember the man wearing a baseball cap. It was pushed down pretty low and his head was leaning forward a little so I still wasn't able to see much. Between the balloons and the cap, there was no way to see his face at all. I am sure I am speaking for all four of us when I say we are very sorry about what happened, but there was no way for us to know what was going on. So you need to cut us some slack. We didn't do this on purpose."

Detective Larkin shakes his head in disbelief and heads back to his new crime scene. Detective Fairlane remains in the room, looking for evidence, while Larkin attacks the nurses. She dusts for fingerprints on the table in the room and the phone, but they are full of smudged prints. The scissors are probably medical scissors used for cutting tape for bandages and such. They are too small to get any prints off them. They must have been taken from somewhere inside the hospital, like the tray standing down the hall, covered in small tools. All Jesse can do is shake her head at Max when he walks in. He knows that, just like the other murders, there is nothing left behind by the killer to help them. The only thing they have now is some video from security that might be able to help them. No matter how brief a glimpse it might be, anything will help. At least they have confirmation that the suspect is male.

As the two detectives examine yet another dead body, the phone starts ringing. Detective Larkin picks up. Nobody answers his hello, but he can hear breathing. "This is Detective Max Larkin of the Rockton Police Department. Who is this?"

A very deep voice, sounding like a professional broadcaster, finally speaks up. "Well, well, Detective, it is nice to see that the police department actually put their best man on the job. I have read about you many times in the paper. You are the top cop around here. I feel honored to have you trying to find me. The only question I have is: who is the hot little number they assigned to the case with you?"

Max starts motioning to Jesse for a possible trace on the call. Jesse stares at him wide-eyed for a second and then leaves the room to call the station to get a dump of phone calls to the hospital extension. She thinks how bold this killer must be to call his own crime scene. And then she looks around to see if anyone is watching them or the room. How did he know they were there—or was it just luck?

Detective Larkin says in a very calm, soothing tone, "Why are you doing this? Talk to me. Maybe I can help you and stop any more people from being hurt. Nobody else needs to die. These are good people."

"You have no idea what you are talking about, Detective!" Mike yells. "I'm doing what needs to be done in this Podunk town! I am getting rid of the selfish people here. These people don't care about anyone but themselves. This guy's wife was having an affair, for God's sake. That doesn't sound like a good person to me. Her husband wasted three hours of my time alone. I am sure he has wasted a lot more people's time than mine. I gave him another chance and what did he do with it? I'll tell you what he did. He wasted your time and your partner's time. He needed to die. I am sick of people wasting my time! My time is very valuable—too valuable to be wasted on these selfish people anymore. I believe if you are not a part of the solution, then you are a part of the problem." His voice has started to calm and is nearly normal volume by his last statement. "Now I am going to be the solution and fix the problem."

"So how did Mr. Bjornson waste three hours of your time? I mean, come on, that is a lot of time to spend with someone. What did he do to waste your time?" Detective Larkin asks.

As the man laughs confidently, he says, "That is for me to know and you to find out, Max. You are the detective here. So let's see if you can do your job and find me. But until then, Detective, I will continue doing my work to rid this town of its selfish, time-wasting inhabitants! Good day to you, sir."

Max hears a click and dial tone. He puts the phone on the hook and turns to Jesse, who re-entered the room just before the call ended abruptly. "This guy is nuts. He actually thinks he is helping this town by getting rid of the 'selfish time wasters.' Please tell me you got a trace on that call!"

With her cell phone still at her ear, she shakes her head. "He wasn't on the phone long enough for the trace to be put in place. The station is working on getting a dump of the incoming and outgoing calls for this room and for the hospital in general. Maybe he called before, asking for Mr. Bjornson or his room number."

"This guy isn't done. He is going to kill again and *soon*!" Larkin mutters. "Let's get a good look at those video tapes, Jesse. Maybe they got a good view of this guy and we can nail him to the wall!"

The two detectives head down the hallway toward the elevator. They hear the nurses sobbing in the background. Uniforms have taken over the scene so no one can enter without showing police identification. The partners stand in the elevator watching the numbers go down as they descend toward the basement and the security room.

Tape after tape and angle after angle, all they can see is the man carrying the flowers wearing a baseball cap. Just as the nurses stated, his cap is lowered to cover his brow and part of his face. The parts that the cap doesn't cover are blocked by the dozen or so brightly colored balloons. They can faintly see some brown hair protruding from the cap. He looks pretty tall, with an average-to-heavy build.

"Pause the tape right there, Jesse," Max blurts out. "There is a name on the jacket. Can you make it out? Is that an 'R' at the beginning? Yep, it is. The only florist in town beginning with R is Rosie's Flower shop on Grand Avenue. We need to get there now." He grabs multiple tapes that they haven't viewed yet and bolts for the door. Jesse follows behind him, running to keep up.

As they run to the car, Jesse stops only one time to pick up a security tape Max has dropped in the parking lot. He doesn't even seem to notice in his haste. He jumps into his car and has it in gear before Jesse even has her door closed. He takes off like a bat out of hell and Jesse's door slams shut from the force of the take-off. "Good thing I have fast reflexes, Max.

You almost took my leg off with this door," she yells at him. Then she laughs at the exhilaration of a lead.

"Sorry, but we're in a hurry here. This guy might still be at Rosie's. He might be the regular driver. He may have made the mistake we are looking for. We need to get there right now," he says, turning to her with a smile.

Siren blaring, red light flashing, Max's car moves like a spaceship approaching warp speed. The car brakes to a screeching halt in front of the flower shop. They both jump out of the car, leaving both doors open and siren and lights still going.

"You take the back, Jesse, and I will go in the front. If he is in there, don't let him get past you, no matter what. Shoot if you must, but I want him alive," Max orders.

She immediately runs through the alley to get to the back door and wait for Max to enter the front. She screams "GO" at the top of her lungs. She hears the bells of the front door. Max must now be in the flower shop. She slowly opens the back door quietly. Let him think that it is just him and Max. She is hoping to surprise him with his back turned and attention focused on Max.

"Clear," Max yells. "There is nobody in the shop, Jesse."

She comes in from the back room and sees her partner standing there. He is clearly upset. They see a cash register on the counter. It is open and Max can tell there is no money in it. "Must have been a robbery here, Jesse. What do you think?" he asks her. Jesse can only shrug in disbelief. She knows this has to be more than a robbery if the killer took the van and killed Mr. Bjornson.

"Do you hear that?" she asks him. "That humming noise like a machine running. A generator maybe? No…not a generator. A compressor? Air compressor? Nope, the refrigerator compressor. That's what I hear!"

On the north wall is a steel door with a small handle on it. It looks like an old meat locker. They both look at each other and head toward it. Jesse positions herself so she will be the one to open the door while Max has his gun pointed at the opening.

She grabs the handle and pulls slightly, just until she can hear the latch give. Then she yanks the door open quickly. What Max sees isn't at all what he expects.

Hanging on the back wall is a woman that Max can only assume is

Rosie. She is suspended by ropes around her waist and neck from a set of hooks that are used for hanging plants. She has three roses stapled to her forehead, with the green stems covering part of her face. Dried blood is crusted on her forehead and down her face—almost like she had cried blood tears. Her dress reminds Max of the old-time diner waitress' dress—short with pockets on either side of the button-down front. The dress is ripped open so you can see the woman's bra and bare stomach. *TIME WASTER* is clearly written in blood across her stomach—etched into her skin. Her right finger and thumb are both removed. Written on the wall next to her in blood is *BITCH WASTED MY TIME*. The woman's bloody finger and thumb are laying on the floor under the writing. Laying next to the finger and thumb are a set of scissors—flower shears, to be exact. They also have blood on them.

"The killer used shears this time and not a bolt cutter, Jesse," Max says as he points to the bloody instrument. "This guy is getting worse and worse. It seems as though he wasn't planning on killing this woman. He wasn't prepared. He didn't have his weapon of choice with him. This one does not feel calculated like the others. He didn't lay her down. He didn't position himself over her like he did the other women. This was more personal. He knew her better than the other women. Look at the flowers. They are stapled to her head and there is blood dripping from them. That means she was still alive when he stapled them to her forehead. There is a pool of blood under her hand where the finger and thumb were cut off. She was still alive then, too—just like Mr. Bjornson. Only he didn't leave her alive after removing her fingers. He really wanted to torture her. This is very personal."

Jesse walks around the refrigerator looking for more clues, but just like the other scenes, nothing seems out of place other than the dead woman and her amputated appendages.

"Hey Max," Jesse calls and then hesitates suddenly in her search. "Do you see anything wrong here? Anything out of place?"

Max takes a step back and scans the room, shaking his head. "Nope, nothing out of place at all. That isn't unusual for this guy."

"No it isn't, partner," Jesse agrees. "However, the other people were drugged in bed. This woman was awake and yet there is no sign of a struggle. I agree with you that this is a personal attack. I believe she was willingly going along with the rope thing. This may have been her husband, boyfriend, or at the very least, a lover."

Jesse pauses for a moment to see the reaction she gets from Max. "Hear me out here, Max," she says in a strong voice. "Picture this: it's almost lunch time. Rosie is working at the counter and her lover walks in to give her a special treat. She is very excited to oblige and walks over to the door, changing the sign from open to closed." Max turns and looks out at the door to see that the sign does say open on the inside. "Her man takes her into the cooler and rips open her dress. See the buttons on the floor, Max?" Max nods in agreement. "He convinces her to let him tie her up; first, her hands behind her back with some twine, then her feet, followed by the rope around the stomach. Kinda kinky, but she agrees. After all, they are lovers and she has no reason to mistrust him. He runs the rope over the five hooks in the ceiling and ties her up around the waist. He pulls her up a little off the ground and ties off the rope on the hook on the wall behind her. At this point, she isn't elevated enough to be off the ground, but she does have the suspended feeling. Her feet are still on the ground, but just barely. He grabs another rope, and this is where he loses it. Coming up behind her, he wraps the new rope around her neck. He ties it tight enough she can barely breathe but still can hear and answer him. Then he comes around to the front and launches into a rant. He doesn't hear what he wants to hear from her and takes three roses from the nearby vase, stapling them to her head. At this point, she is screaming, but nobody can hear her because they are in a closed cooler. He is still going off on her and decides he has heard enough. He doesn't want to risk her screams coming out of the cooler if he opens the door to go get his favorite weapon, the bolt cutter, so he grabs the shears nearby. They don't cut as quickly as the bolt cutters do. I can tell that is the case because you can see extra cuts on the finger near the knuckle, like he missed a few times. He is now done, except she is still breathing. He grabs the rope around her neck and completes the job with an old-fashioned strangling." She lifts up the eyelid of the woman. "See the petechial hemorrhaging in the eyeball? That says she was strangled." Jesse steps back and looks at her partner and does a little curtsy as if to say 'ta-da.'

Max looks very impressed with the scenario that Jesse came up with, but he can't let her know that he is that impressed. After all, it is her first case and he doesn't want her to think she is better than he is. He looks for any mistake she might have made or something she may have missed in her synopsis. Unable to find anything wrong with her idea, he finally spits out, "Great observations, partner. You played it just like I thought it happened, as well. I just wanted to see if you were able to figure it all out or if I was going to have to point out some things you missed. I am glad to say that I don't think you missed a thing and I agree with you 100%." He walks toward Jesse and gives her a pat on the shoulder.

Max grabs his cell phone from his front pocket and hits a key. "Captain Perry? Yeah, it's Larkin. We have another one at Rosie's Flower Shop. Can you get a forensic team over here ASAP? Okay, thanks. I know, Captain… Fairlane? She is doing okay."

Jesse snaps her head around quickly at the word okay. She mouths, "Okay?" at him with an inquisitive expression on her face.

"All right, Captain, I'll tell her." Max hangs up his phone and begins walking out of the cooler without acknowledging Jesse at all.

Jesse comes running out after him. "Tell me what? What did the Captain say?" she pleads, sounding like a young kid begging for candy.

"What?" Max acts as if he has no clue what Jesse is referring to. "What did who say?"

Jesse slugs her partner in the shoulder. "First off, I am doing better than okay. And second of all, I know the Captain told you to tell me something so spit it out, you big jerk."

"Fine," Max says as he rubs his shoulder in real pain. "He said to pay close attention to me because I am the best. And that you will be best served to observe me with wide open eyes."

Jesse draws back her arm, getting to ready to punch him again. "Okay, okay, I'm just teasing. Damn girl, remind me to never really piss you off," Max says, laughing. "Captain Perry said keep up the good work and that your dad would be very proud of you right now. As for the 'okay' thing, I said that because I don't want to build up your ego up too much, or we will never be able to get your head through the doors of the station."

Max gives Jesse a little shove. He pushes her a little too hard and she bumps the cash register. As she looks down into the register, she notices the plastic drawer isn't fully in place. She lifts it with a glove and sees no money underneath.

Max and Jesse guess that he must have taken the money he thought Rosie owed him from the register. "We can't have any idea how much this guy thought Rosie owed him. If she keeps books of her cash, we may be able to determine how much money was in the register. Based on the $633 from Mr. Bjornson and the $53 from Amber, we can then determine the money that Rosie owed him. As soon as the forensic team gets here, let's visit Rosie's house and see if we can find any evidence of him being there. Maybe she has a picture of him somewhere. Hey Jesse, do you think you could interview the people in the music store next door to see if they saw or heard anything?"

Jesse nods her head and gets right over there to get as much information about Rosie and the most recent visitors to her store. Jesse barely enters before she is bombarded with questions by the little Greek woman behind the counter. She isn't more than five feet tall. Her hair is mostly gray, with some black mixed in. She has a gray mustache that seems rather thick for a woman.

"Are you a police officer? Is Rosie okay? What is going on?" the woman says in a deep Greek accent. She is trembling as she speaks.

"Ma'am, I am Detective Fairlane. I need to ask you a few questions about your shop neighbor, Rosie, but let's first start off with your name, address and date of birth. Then I need to know if you saw anyone go into the flower shop anytime in the past two or three hours." Jesse tries to sound official to calm down the woman.

"My name is Korrina Giannopoulous. Korrina is Greek for maiden," the woman says, still shaken from seeing a police car pull up so fast and watching the occupants fly into a friend's place of business. "The only people I saw going into Rosie's today are Rosie herself and her low-down boyfriend. Did he do something to her? I never really liked him at all."

Jesse's demeanor brightens when Korrina says she saw Rosie's boyfriend. If Korrina did in fact see him, then they will know exactly who they are looking for.

"Korrina—is it okay if I call you Korrina?" Jesse asks the music store owner.

Korrina says, "You can call me Korry."

"Korry, you said you knew Rosie had a boyfriend. What can you tell me about him?" Jesse asks.

Korrina stands still for a few moments and then leans into the counter. Her chest barely reaches the top of the counter. "I never really saw much of him. Rosie said his name was Tom and that he worked very odd hours. He would come by at 10 p.m. to pick her up from the shop, and my shop closes at 9 p.m. He would come take her out to lunch once a week, but I only saw him from behind because he would park right in front of Rosie's with his car facing the wrong way on the street and when he got out, his back was always to me. Whenever they left for lunch, they always took Rosie's van, so I rarely saw him leave and I never got a good look at his face because he always had his head down, like he was ashamed of himself or was hiding his face. That's why I never trusted him. He acted very suspicious. I told Rosie what I thought one day, but she just said I was overreacting and that she loved him and he treated her well. Once she said that, I let it go. After all, that is what I want for my friend—a man that treats her well. Now please, tell me what happened to Rosie!"

"Korry…" Jesse hesitates. "Rosie is dead. She was murdered in her cooler within the last two or three hours. Is there anything else you can tell me about Rosie or her boyfriend? Can you describe what you did see of him?"

Korrina is crying at this point. Her friend of fifteen years was just murdered right next door to her and she didn't help her. She shakes like a leaf in the wind, small and frail. She reaches under the counter and grabs a cup that has been used for many years to drink coffee from. There are rings of coffee stains circling the rim of the cup. There are even brown stains on the side. She takes a sip of the coffee to calm her down. "He is about six feet and has brown hair with a bald spot on the top of his head near the back. His head seems a little large for his body. He was always in a very nice suit. Oh, and it seemed like every so often, he would show up in a different car. Sometimes they were sporty and sometimes they were family vehicles. But I would have to say that I saw him in at least ten different cars over the six months or so that they were dating. I wish I had asked Rosie more about him. I didn't even know what he did for a living."

"Did you happen to get a license number on any of the cars?" Jesse interrupts Korrina.

"No I didn't really pay attention. I figured the farther away from him I was, the better I would be. And let's face the truth, dearie—I am getting older and my eyes are not what they used to be," Korrina says, very distraught.

Jesse reaches into her pocket and pulls out her card. She hands it to Korrina and says, "If you can think of anything else, please call me. No matter how big or how small a detail, it could be important. Thank you for your time and I'm sorry for your loss."

Jesse walks slowly back to Rosie's to meet Max and fill him in on the information that Korrina gave her. There is some new insight into the killer. He has many cars at his disposal. He works late hours. Other than that, it is same old story.

After Jesse fills in Max, they both decide to head over to Rosie's house. The fear and frustration builds inside Jesse so much that she has to say, "Hopefully we can find some more on this Tom guy there. If they have been together for six months, there have to be pictures of him. We have to find a way to get this guy off the street, Max. This town can't take any more of this and frankly, neither can I! He always seems to be one step ahead of us."

Max can tell Jesse is trying to figure this all out in her head. She has been on the job only a few days, but she has seen enough blood to last her a lifetime of being on the Rockton police force. The detective duo keeps staring out the window as street sign after street sign goes by them. Whenever Jesse looks at Max, he seems to look away, and she does the same when he looks at her. What was just sibling-like fooling around at the flower shop has turned back into a very serious situation. Neither detective knows how to act at this moment. Does Jesse continue with the hilarity and push Max's hand off the gearshift that he is continuously fiddling with, or does she just sit silently and let her partner's intuitive mind try to figure this mess out? Awkwardness is their passenger, and it is buckled in for the ride.

osie lived in Sleepy Hollow, a small secluded subdivision of Rockton. It is sequestered away from most of the town and the houses are very small on big lots. Each house seems to be farther away from the road than the other. Rosie's house is no exception. Her driveway has a small S shape to it as it winds up to the house. The driveway ends at the street with a very big lip at the end that feels like a mountain when Max drives the low-riding Firebird over it. Jesse almost hits her head on the ceiling because Max takes the bump a little too fast, not realizing how large a lip it is.

Jesse immediately snaps at him, "Hey, want to take it a little easy there? I would really like to not have a concussion from your driving."

Max chuckles a little bit at what he hopes is her attempt at humor as he continues driving just a little too fast up the driveway, making sure to swerve and hit every little bump or crack so that Jesse feels it. They both smile at each other as they reach the house. Even though the car ride was quiet and long, they both realize they need to lift the dark cloud.

Max is first out of the car. The house is small and has an attached two-car garage. There is a hum coming from the garage. Smoke is coming out from under the garage door. Max spots a door on the far side of the garage. Gun drawn, Max immediately kicks the door in. The delivery van is in the garage, still running. With their guns at the ready, they open the back door, hoping to find the killer inside after he decided to end it all with toxic fumes from the exhaust. No such luck.

"Damn, I thought he was going to be in here. That would have certainly been the best case scenario for us," Jesse yells across to Max, who drops his gun to his side. "Who am I kidding? We wouldn't be that lucky!"

Inside the van, the killer left behind the cap and jacket that he had worn in the hospital. After careful examination of the cap, Jesse notices some black and gray hairs inside. Knowing the killer had brown and gray hair, she realizes this hair is probably from Rosie herself and not the man who just killed her. "Nothing here that requires immediate attention, partner. I think we should go in to the house and see if we can find those pictures or anything that he might have left behind for us to help identify him," Jesse says as she moves her weapon into the ready position once again. She heads to the door that leads into the house. Max is already there waiting for her. His gun is pointed at the door, ready for whatever lurks behind it.

Jesse opens the door and takes a position where Max can see around her and to the opposite side of where her gun is pointed. She walks in slowly and heads to the left. Max heads right, moving just as slowly. If the killer is here, they want to make sure they get the drop on him before he gets it on them. Jesse is at the front door and notices it is slightly ajar. She opens it farther and, even though the sun is at the horizon, she still gets a glimpse of bright light as it passes through the stained glass screen door.

Jesse heads toward the dining room area, gun still at the ready position. She notices a small cabinet in the corner of the dining room. The cabinet is a black wood laminate and the doors are open. She can see dishes on the left, but it appears that there were things removed from the right side, as there is a vacant spot and some dishes have fallen onto the carpeted floor.

Jesse heads toward the kitchen now, gun still ready. The kitchen is painted a bright yellow. Even though it is getting darker outside, this room is very bright. She scans the room and can see many cabinets open, with things falling out of them. It seems as though someone was looking for something inside them. *I wonder if he found what he was looking for. He certainly made a big enough mess looking for whatever it is,* Jesse thinks.

Max goes around the corner of the one-floor ranch style house and moves into the main living room. The room is a pretty simple layout, with a loveseat on the left-hand wall and a medium-sized old tube television sitting on a wooden stand to his right. He hears Jesse say, "All clear," as she passes from the dining room to the attached kitchen and heads toward him. Straight ahead of Max is the hallway, where there are three doors. He motions to Jesse to take the left door and he will take the right. That would only leave the one door that is at the very end of the hall facing them.

Jesse opens the door to the bathroom and immediately pulls back the shower curtain to show nothing but shampoo and conditioner on the lip of the bathtub. "Clear," she says again. She does notice that the medicine cabinet is open and just like the kitchen cabinets, things are shuffled around, as if someone was rifling through the cabinet looking for something. Rosie's toothpaste tube and a bottle of perfume have fallen out of the cabinet into the sink.

Max has opened the door to a small sewing room. It could have been a bedroom earlier, but at this point, the only thing in it is a rather large sewing machine sitting on the far wall under a window. There is a bright yellow fabric that is currently in the sewing machine needle. It looks like it would be a dress. Next to the sewing machine is a fabric tree of sorts. It is a long pole with branches sticking out that have many different colors and textures of fabric hanging on each branch. The closet to the right has a single door on it that is wide open, and only empty clothes hangers are in there. The clothes that were in this closet were removed rather quickly and there are quite a few hangers on the floor of the closet. This time, it is Max's turn to yell "clear" to his partner.

They both come back into the hallway. Max motions his finger to the door at the end of the hall. The door is closed but not locked. Max opens the door slowly as Jesse kneels down in the ready position, with her gun aimed at the door. As the door opens, they cannot see anything; the room is very dark. There is a nauseating smell permeating the room—a smell that they are all too familiar with. It is the smell of fresh blood. Max turns to the wall and sees the light switch. He flicks on the lights. The first thing that he sees is a queen sized bed. Laying in the middle of the bed are the remains of a dog. The dog has been sliced open and its blood covers the bed almost entirely. The oddity of it all is that the pillows have been rubbed into the blood. Jesse reaches into her pocket, pulls out a latex glove and puts it on her right hand. She grabs each pillow and flips them over. The blood is on both sides of the pillows. Max opens the door to the closet while his partner inspects the bed. The inside of the closet is completely full of women's clothing, dresses, skirts, blouses, and of course, shoes. Not one empty hanger in the whole closet. Jesse goes to the dresser and opens the drawers full of more women's clothes and undergarments.

"So, Jesse, since you did such a good job of explaining the scene at Rosie's flower shop, do you want to take a crack at this?" Max says as he holsters his weapon.

"If I must," she jests back.

Max stares at Jesse for a millisecond and retorts back, "Oh, you must, you must."

Jesse just grins back at him. "Our guy brings the van straight here from the hospital. He leaves it running because he is in a hurry and just plain doesn't care. He does exactly what we hoped he wouldn't. He gets rid of all the evidence that he was ever here. He has taken every photograph from the entire house, removed all of his clothing from the sewing room closet, and he even took all of his toiletries out of the bathroom. He killed the dog on the bed intentionally. This way, the dog's blood can mix with any DNA he left behind from his time in bed with Rosie. Once that is mixed, there is not going to be any way for us to separate the sources of DNA, thus eliminating identifying him with the results of the tests. He made sure to smear the blood all over with gloved hands. Then, to make sure he got all the fluids and DNA mixed together, he grabbed both pillows and rubbed them on one side and then the other in the dog's blood. Miss anything, partner?"

"Yeah, I think you did," Max says in a told-you-so kind of way. "You missed how he left here with all that stuff. I mean, he didn't just walk down the street hitchhiking now, did he? And he certainly didn't take the vehicle he came in so tell me this, Miss Smarty Pants. How did he leave?"

Jesse looks at the bed, then her partner, back to the bed, and finally back to her partner. "That is easy. There are two stalls in the garage. He took Rosie's car. She must have left her car here today and just drove the van to the shop."

Max nods his head in agreement. "Very good. Very good indeed. I will let the chief know that you are learning a lot under my expert tutelage." The smile on his face can only be described as super cheesy, all teeth.

The phone next to Rosie's bloody bed rings. Both detectives look at each other and then the phone. Jesse takes a couple of steps toward the phone and it stops ringing. She shrugs her shoulders and starts walking out of the room. Just when it seems she is ready to say something to Max, the phone rings again. This time she reaches quickly for the phone and answers, "Yello?" like it is her own personal phone. She hears breathing, but no talking. She motions to Max to come over and listen. He leans in as Jesse tilts the phone so they can both hear. Max hears the same breathing as he heard earlier when he picked up Stephen Bjornson's hospital phone.

"'Yello'? Is that how you answer a phone, Detective?" the voice on the phone speaks finally. "I expect better from you. Maybe next time you should let Max answer the phone. At least he is professional. I knew you were not Rosie because I killed her earlier, so I had to assume you were the police. Good job, by the way, getting here after I left. Maybe someday you guys will only be one step behind me instead of the ten you are right now."

Jesse speaks before Max can. "I am pretty professional, buddy. You only think we are ten steps behind when in fact, we are right on your coattails."

The killer laughs, a deep throaty chuckle. "Maybe, just maybe, you are indeed closer than I think. But I need to ask you one question before I can believe you. Did you find the man I rid this world of for wasting people's time? Did you?"

Jesse looks at Max with inquisitive eyes. She puts her hand over the mouthpiece so she can speak to Max candidly. "Is this guy seriously losing it or what? He just called us at the hospital after he killed Mr. Bjornson."

"You know we did. Mr. Bjornson is dead, thanks to you. You called us in his hospital room earlier today. I think you are finally losing it, Tom. Yep, that's right. I know your name now," she says to him confidently. Again she hears laughing over the phone. "What is so damn funny, Tom? You know we are right behind you. You will slip up again and when you do, BAM! We will be there."

The laughing continues. "You are one man behind, my dear. You still haven't found the man who wasted my time the day after the Bjornson family left our world. He wasted my time that very next day, and it was so blatant that I couldn't wait. You see, with the Bjornsons, I watched them carefully. I wanted to make sure that they were as bad as I thought before I rid the world of their time-wasting abilities. I had to be sure that the kids were going to be as bad as the parents. I wasn't just going to take the kids' lives without being sure. I was very sure of this guy's time wasting in this world, so I took care of him that night, right before I rid the world of Amber's time wasting. This guy had wasted so much of my time that day he positively had to go. So once again, Detective, good luck being ten steps behind me."

Jesse and Max stare at each other, simultaneously mouthing to each other, "Someone else?"

Max interjects loudly, "Hey, Tom, you are wasting our time, so you should definitely rid this world of yourself right away." He takes his ear from the phone and looks at Jesse. He lifts both his eyebrows and gives her a smirk.

The man on the other end of the line starts laughing hysterically this time. "You are a real funny man, Detective Larkin. You should take that act on the road, since you have to be a better comedian than you are a detective. I will not stop ridding this world of time wasters until people stop wasting my time. I am only one man and I can't stop everyone, but I am going to keep doing my work until others stop wasting my time. Based on your performance so far, I think I will continue my work for a very long time." The next thing the detectives hear is a click, followed by a dial tone.

Max grabs Jesse by the arm and leads her out of Rosie's bedroom. "Jesse, I am going to call the Captain and see if anyone has been reported missing. You get some pictures of this room. I have no idea who this other dead man is, but we need to find him and hopefully this guy will give us some clues. I am sick of running around here like a chicken with my head cut off," Max snarls as he pulls his phone out.

"Hey, Captain, it's Larkin. Has anyone been reported missing lately? No? Damn! Our killer just called us at Rosie's house and told us we were ten steps behind him. He claims to have killed another man the day after he killed the Bjornson family. Let me know the minute you hear of any missing persons in Rockton or the surrounding areas. Ok, got it, Cap. I'll let her know." Max puts his cell phone back in his pocket. "Jesse, there hasn't been anybody reported missing in the last few days, but the Captain will let me know as soon as one is. He also said for me to tell you that Melissa called and asked for you to come over to her apartment as soon as you could. Isn't that the girl that witnessed our killer leaving that apartment? What was that girl's name again? Amber? Right?"

Max looks befuddled by a witness calling his partner instead of him. "I wonder why she is calling you and not me? Captain Perry said she specifically asked for you. Maybe your little extra-long hug did indeed help her feel more comfortable with you and she does have some information for us."

Jesse looks perplexed. "Yep, that victim's name was Amber—duh,

Tom just said it. Her neighbor across the hall is Melissa. Maybe she just feels more comfortable talking to a woman. Why don't you and I head over there right now and see what she has to say," Jesse says as she snaps her last picture.

Max takes one last look around Rosie's house as he walks toward the front door. Another forensic team has shown up to secure the scene. "I think I am going to call it a night, Jesse. There is not much more we can do right now," he says. "At least, not until someone is reported missing. There are tons of guys that are starting to lose their hair and drive different cars. I'll take you back to the station to get your car, and you can head over to Melissa's place on your own. I think you are ready for a solo shot. You are way better than I could have hoped for. Besides, I'm beat. I am going to head over to my parents' house in the morning before I come in. I need to say happy birthday to my dad. I won't be in until about 8:30 instead of 8. Okay?"

"Yeah, Max, that is fine by me," Jesse says as she walks behind him. She has a little extra spring in her step, thanks to the wonderful compliment Max just gave her. "If you think I am ready, then I must be ready. If she tells me anything new, I will give you a call."

Max and Jesse get into Max's car and he turns over the ignition. "Hey, Max, could you possibly take it a little slower down the driveway than you did going up it? This car is pretty low to the ground and I felt every little bump. Oh, and watch out for that lip at the end of the driveway. I wouldn't want you to mess up this nice ride!" Jesse intones with a wry grin.

Max looks at her closely. "Fine, you're no fun at all," he says, laughing. "I'll go slow for you. I wouldn't want you to break a nail or mess up your hair." His little chuckle has turned into a full belly laugh as he turns toward Jesse to see how she handled that comment. Her face is a shade of red. She is either upset or embarrassed. Either way, Max figures it can't be good for him.

"Come on, Jesse, that was funny. You know I'm just kidding you. In just the two days we have worked together, I have gained more respect for you than I have for McCarren or any of the other detectives at the station. And I've worked with them for years. So take a compliment when I give it and take some good natured ribbing with a grain of salt."

Jesse sits quietly in the passenger seat. Her face has lost most of the red. "I can take anything you dish out at me. Just be prepared for it to come back to you," Jesse says to Max as she punches him in the arm again. Max drives toward the station. "Max, do you think we will find his other victim? What if there are even more of them out there that he hasn't told us about and he just disposed of the bodies rather than leaving them for us to find? I can't get this guy's voice out of my head right now. The part he said about being ten steps behind is very disconcerting. I know we are not that far behind him, but even one step behind is one too many. This guy is going to keep doing this every single day until we stop him," Jesse says as her voice changes from childish giddiness to a very serious businesslike tone.

Max can say nothing. He just sits in the driver's seat and nods his head affirmatively. The time from Rosie's house to the station parking lot flies by. It is 7 p.m. and both detectives have been racking their brains trying to figure out if they have missed anything at all in the last two days that could give them some insight into how this guy picks his victims or why he picks them, outside of them wasting his time.

"See you at 8:30 a.m, Jesse. We'll check on the forensic team's progress then. Give me a call if that Melissa lady has anything we can use," Max says to his partner as she leaves his car and heads to her green Ford Taurus. There is so much rust on it that green could actually be considered the secondary color. "Hey, Jesse, you are a detective now. I think it's time you trade that piece of crap Ford in for a respectable car. You are no longer just a patrol officer. Time to show it."

Jesse turns to her partner and flips him off. "I love my car. It is only twelve years old and has only 150,000 miles on it. I think it will last a little longer!" she screams at Max over the wind.

Jesse climbs into her car and tries starting it. She hears a noise that is very unfamiliar to her. It certainly is not the car starting, that is for sure. She pauses for a moment and thinks, *Maybe he is right. It is time to get a new car. I just don't have time to do it right now. Not with this maniac on the loose.* Jesse caresses the dashboard of the car. "Come on, baby, I need you now. I just defended you and you pull this right now. Come on, baby." As she keeps caressing the dashboard, it finally starts. Just as it does, Max drives by her and honks his horn, laughing.

Jesse drives toward Melissa's apartment wondering why Melissa requested her and only her. *There must be something she remembers that she wouldn't be comfortable telling Max,* she thinks. The ride over gives Jesse time to think about the case as well. Her brain is a non-stop machine, running scenario after scenario of what may be motivating this killer. *What does he do for a living? Where does he live? How can he afford so many cars? After I get done at Melissa's apartment, I am going to go home and just take a nice hot bath. Hopefully, I can get this out of my head.*

Jesse's car sputters up to the apartment building she was just at yesterday. It looks a lot different at night. Only a few lights are on in the apartments above her. She looks around and sees how easy it would be for someone who had bad intentions to get into the building. There is no light at the front door and no buzzer system to let people in. Of course, in Rockton there is no need for super security systems. That is, until now.

Jesse walks in the door past a man coming out of the building. He is a short Asian man with close-cropped black hair and wearing a white t-shirt with stains on it. His pants are of the blue family, but the color is faded and stained with what appears to be food stains all along the front. He doesn't question Jesse at all, but looks her straight in the eyes and then puts his head down. Jesse shakes her head in disbelief. She approaches the stairwell—the very one that Melissa said she saw the killer go down after he murdered her neighbor. It seems to take a little longer than normal for her to go up the stairs. Stair by stair, she glances at the railing and the wall, hoping to catch a glimpse of something the forensics team could have missed in the poorly-lit hallway. The only thing that she gets from this stairwell trip is the beginning of a small headache from the smell and the dim light.

Jesse approaches Melissa's apartment and looks across the hall. The police tape is still over the door. She decides to go into Amber's apartment first to take another look around. This will put the scene fresh in her brain again for any details Melissa has to share. Jesse bends down and grabs the doorknob through the tape. It is still unlocked. The moment she enters the room, the all too familiar smell of blood permeates her nostrils. This time it is a little stronger after sitting for a day and a half. She can hardly breathe from the stench. She powers through the smell for a few moments to take a look around. A few seconds is all she needs to refresh her memory and about all of the smell that she can handle. In fact, it's making her headache worse.

Once she is out, Jesse takes a deep breath through her mouth, gulping in fresher air. She then takes another deep breath using her nose. A smile crosses her face as she breathes in the freshness of the hallway. She knocks on Melissa's door. "Who is it?" the voice inside calls.

"Detective Fairlane, Rockton PD. Here is my badge and identification," Jesse says as she holds up her credentials. "You called my captain and asked me to come see you as soon as possible, so here I am." Jesse can hear the door unlock.

Melissa is standing at the door in very short white shorts and a white tank top t-shirt. Jesse can see through the white tank top and notices she is not wearing anything under it. Her hair is wet and hanging loosely off her shoulders. Her feet are bare and it looks like she is just settling in for a nice, relaxing night at home. "Sorry about my appearance, Detective. I just got out of the shower and was going to have a glass of wine. Would you like one, providing you are off duty right now? I wouldn't want to get you into any trouble with your boss or that grumpy partner of yours," Melissa says as she sits down on her loveseat and grabs a bottle of red wine, pouring two glasses. She then tucks one leg under her and wriggles herself comfortable as only a woman can do.

Jesse realizes that Melissa has two glasses readily at hand. "Were you expecting me to come this quickly?"

With a sheepish smile Melissa says, "I asked your captain to send you over so, of course, I expected you to come eventually. I haven't left the apartment since yesterday. When I told my boss exactly what was going on, he gave me a week off and told me to just sit back, relax, and take care of myself. So I took his advice. I have been sitting here with my door locked, trying to forget what I saw and move on with my life, but honestly it is hard. That is why I asked for you to come over."

Jesse is standing by the loveseat, looking at a very beautiful, scared young woman. She is having a hard time following what Melissa is saying. "Why did you ask me to come over? Do you have any more information that can help us find the guy who did this to your neighbor? We can use all the help we can get," Jesse says as she grabs her notebook and pen from her back pocket.

"I asked you to come over because before you left, you made me feel safe. I trust you and right now, I am just a little bit scared still. Earlier today, my cat jumped up on this loveseat while I was taking a nap and I freaked out because I thought that man was here to kill me," Melissa says with some fear in her voice as she hugs herself. Jesse sees her fear and sits by her on the loveseat.

Snuggling an arm around her, she gives her a squeeze. "It will be okay. If that man wanted to hurt you, he would have done so when you saw him. He didn't hurt you because you didn't do anything to him. He has killed several people in the past and even one today, but all of them had done something to him. He felt they had wasted his time and that they had to pay him back for his time." Jesse starts getting frustrated as she speaks. "You know what, Melissa, I am off duty and I really do need that wine. This case has really gotten me flustered. I could use a night of relaxation. I need some time to clear my head. You truly don't mind me being here?" Melissa shakes her head no as she pours wine into the second glass.

"I'm sorry, Detective, if you thought I had more information for you. I just wanted company and, like I said, you make me feel safe. I really need that now," Melissa says as she hands the glass of wine to Jesse.

Jesse takes the glass, but stops short of sipping. "Before I start drinking and I put my notebook away, are you sure that there is nothing else you can tell me that can help me with this case? I just want to be sure before my judgment gets clouded. And stop calling me Detective. You can call me Jesse," she says with a laugh.

"I am sorry, Detec…I mean Jesse. I'm sorry I have nothing more than I told you yesterday. I just needed some company and some girl time. Please forgive me for making you believe that I did have more information for you. Thank you for staying with me, even if it is just for a little while."

Jesse puts her notebook and pen away, and slouches into the loveseat, her wine glass in one hand and the other hand on the back of the loveseat behind Melissa's head. She is getting very comfortable and takes a long drink from her glass. By the time she puts her glass down, half of the wine is gone. "You know what, Melissa? This is exactly what I needed. Thank you so much for inviting me over. I don't have a lot of friends right now. I got out of the academy and busted my butt to get to detective. I felt like I always had to do things better than most because I was getting compared to my dad. He was killed in the line of duty for our beloved town of Rockton. Oh, sorry, I just ramble sometimes when I drink. I didn't mean to bring my personal life into this."

Melissa is sitting up on the loveseat now. Her legs are crossed Indian-style and she is facing Jesse. She is paying very close attention to every word that Jesse is saying. "No, no, Jesse. I want to hear all that you are willing to share about yourself with me. You and I are very alike. I don't have a lot of friends either. I, too, have been working real hard at my job. My career is my life. I have no significant other and really, outside of my cat, I really don't have any friends. I'd like us to be friends. I think we can be great friends. It is really cruddy how we met, but I am glad we did. You seem like someone I can talk to about anything, and I need that in my life now more than ever."

Jesse reaches out and gently squeezes Melissa's hand.

Melissa smiles at Jesse, but her smile fades almost as fast as it appeared, giving way to tears. She pulls her hand from Jesse's grip and puts both hands over her face and starts sobbing uncontrollably. "I'm sorry. I have been crying off and on all day. Things look great and I cry. Thinks look bad and I cry. I just can't control it today." Melissa pulls her hands away from her face and shakes her head, trying to clear the tearful thoughts away. "More wine, Jesse?"

Melissa stops crying long enough to pour herself and Jesse another full glass of wine. As she puts the bottle down, Jesse grabs her arm and pulls her close. She wraps her arms around Melissa in a loving hug. "It's okay, Melissa. You've been through a lot the last couple of days. There isn't a person alive that wouldn't break down occasionally after seeing what you've seen. Nobody should have to see that. I am here for you. Just let it out."

Melissa, feeling safe and secure, starts crying again. Her head is buried in Jesse's neck and shoulder, and Jesse is caressing her hair. It seems to be calming Melissa down. Melissa slows her crying and looks up from Jesse's shoulder directly into her eyes. Her eyes are red from the tears and her makeup is running down her cheeks. She bats her eyelashes a few times to clear the tears away. She is still looking intently into Jesse's eyes as she leans in and puts her lips to Jesse's.

Jesse's eyes widen as she puts her hands on Melissa's shoulders to push away but oddly, she cannot build up the strength to resist. Her mind is saying *no*, but her body is saying *don't fight it*. She slides her hands down to Melissa's sides and around her back as she begins to kiss back. She hasn't felt this warm inside for a very long time. Jesse always knew that she was attracted to both men and women but never really pursued it. Her last boyfriend couldn't make her feel like this. Melissa is so soft and gentle. It just feels so right to be kissing her. Their tongues swimming madly back and forth, Melissa's hands begin caressing her back. Jesse feels tingly all over, her passion rising, when Melissa stops kissing her. A slight moan escapes Melissa as she pulls away from Jesse.

"Oh my!" Melissa says as she fans herself with her hand. "I was hoping that was okay. I have wanted to do that ever since you hugged me yesterday. Most times I can tell, but I didn't know if you liked women or not. But once you sat down and we started talking, I could tell you wanted me. And oh boy, am I ever glad that I did! That was sensational!"

Now that the moment has passed Jesse looks ambivalent, but at the same time, excited and happy. "Melissa, I agree—that was awesome! I did want you to kiss me, but I don't think we should go any further than this—at least, not right now. I am sure you have heard this or said this before to someone, but hear me out before passing judgment on me. Okay? " Melissa nods her head reluctantly as Jesse continues. "It isn't you, Melissa. It's me."

Melissa's gaze is expectant. She can tell that Jesse enjoyed kissing her but every time 'it's me' has ever been said to her, it always was *really* about her and not the other person. "I don't understand what's wrong. Didn't you enjoy that?

Jesse interrupts her. "Like I said, let me explain. I want you more than I could have possibly imagined. It isn't you at all, Melissa, and here is the weird part. It isn't me, either. It is my partner, Max."

Once Melissa hears Max's name, she pulls away. "Whoa, are you two an item?"

Jesse grabs Melissa's hand while shaking her head no. "No, not at all, Melissa. He and I are just partners at work—nothing more. However, his last partner had an affair with a suspect and even though the suspect was eventually cleared, Max didn't think it was right. He forced his old partner to leave Rockton by threatening to report him for an ethics violation. Max never told his bosses why his old partner left, but he regrets not going to them. I just don't want him to have a reason to not trust me. I truly do think you and I can be good friends and much more, but after this case is over. Right now, we need to just be friends and let things progress slowly."

Melissa smiles briefly, like a bright white flash bulb going off. "I totally understand, Jesse, but I don't know that I can wait that long. I'm not sure I can just be friends with you. Can't we just date secretly for now?" Melissa gently plays with Jesse's hair, tickling her neck and giving her goose bumps.

Jesse grabs Melissa's hand away, kissing it gently, unable to concentrate while her heart is racing. "While this guy is out there, I need to concentrate on catching him. We can spend some time getting to know each other for now. I suppose it sounds old-fashioned, but it will give us time to become friends and see what develops once this case is over. I need Max's trust. He has to have my back in any work situation, and I'm learning a lot from him."

Melissa gushes, "You are so beautiful and so hard to resist, Jesse! I understand, though, and will try to keep my hands to myself." Melissa squeezes Jesse's hand a little bit tighter, and leans in and kisses here on the cheek. "Let's have some wine, watch a movie and just have a good time as friends tonight. Please stay with me a while. I am still shaken up after what happened to Amber. I feel safe with you around, and now I feel better knowing that you and I are going to be good friends, and maybe more."

Jesse leans in close and kisses her on the forehead. "Of course I'll stay. There's no place I would rather be." She wraps her arm around Melissa and cuddles up to her. Melissa puts her head on Jesse's shoulder and smiles. She is content and happy again. They fall asleep cuddling. In their sleep Melissa's hand goes to Jessie's breast and Jessie waits a few minutes before gently removing it. But she is smiling.

Meanwhile, Max is just settling into a beer and movie at home and trying to forget about what he saw today. He typically does this with beer and either a movie or a sports game. The type of sport is never important to him—baseball, basketball, or football. The competition is enough to help him forget the day's events. Movie-wise he stays away from heavy dramas and murder mysteries. His favorite movies are comedies, as they just make him think of a life that he wants, where seriousness is not a part of life every day and where everything always works out for the best.

Max's cell phone buzzes and rouses him from enjoying the most recent rom com that he rented. It's a text message from Jesse. "Nothing new with Melissa. She was just scared and needed someone to talk to. See you in the a.m."

"No problem. See you tomorrow. Good job today."

Outside of trying to find the guy that was killed yesterday, I think it should be a slow night. Hopefully it will be, anyway, Max thinks. He turns back to his television and starts to drift off to sleep in his armchair. His half-finished beer and pizza are still on the table in front of him. In the glow of the TV set, his nightmares do not come.

After a few hours, Max wakes up and shuts the screen off. As he drifts back off to sleep, he starts to jerk erratically in his recliner. After about ten minutes of this, he sits straight up in his chair wide awake. "AAAAAHHHH!" His eyes are like saucers. He saw the man wearing a mask and pulling on him by the arm. Although he couldn't see his own body and face in his dream, he could tell he was a small child, based on the angle of the man pulling on him and the size of the man. He kept seeing the man pulling and tugging at his arm. The man dragged him into another room and showed him two people lying in bed. They were both dead. The masked man started yelling at him, and that is when he woke up. *That story from 25 years ago has really gotten to me. I feel for that poor kid. He lost both his parents in one night,* Max thinks. *Looking at those pictures from back then has really affected me. I saw those pictures of the kid's parents lying in the bed and now, I see them clear as day in my dreams. I need to find this guy. I wonder why he left that kid alone, but killed the Bjornson kids. I have to stop thinking about this guy.* Max looks at the clock. 5:35 in the morning. *Earlier than I wanted to, but I better get up and get in the shower to head over to Dad's to wish him a happy 60th today. Even though I'll have to go to the party tomorrow, I did promise Mom I would be there at 7:30 for breakfast to wish him happy birthday today. Ugh!*

Max gets up from his recliner and does a big stretch, followed by a yawn. He trudges toward his bathroom, stopping at the kitchen first. He truly is living the bachelor life. The sink is filled with dishes and pizza boxes line the counter. He opens the fridge to find nothing in it but mustard and some mystery Chinese food, obviously aged. He opens the Chinese food container and smells it. "Whoa!!" He shakes his head to try and get the smell out of his nostrils and puts it back in the fridge. He continues toward the bathroom again, dropping clothes on the floor as he goes. They still need to be sorted and washed, depending on their relative gaminess.

His bathroom is in similar condition—piles of towels on the floor in the corner and toothpaste tubes left open with crusty toothpaste stuck to the top. A musty, mildewy smell lingers in the room. Most people would be overpowered by the smell, but Max's nose is desensitized to it. The old pipes in his apartment take a long time to produce hot water. Max waits until the steam fills the bathroom before he climbs into the shower. As usual he begins thinking. *Is our murderer at work? What does he do that makes $211 an hour and requires a suit? Lawyer? Judge? CEO? This guy is really getting to me.*

The warmth of the shower doesn't stay with Max very long after he towels off, anxious to get over to his dad's house. As he looks into the mirror to brush his teeth, there appears to be something written in the condensation. It's beginning to fade now that the shower is off. Max turns on the hot water in the sink so the steam can rise directly to the mirror. He steps back to read the message. *QUIT WASTING TIME; LET ME DO MY WORK.*

Max runs over to his phone, dropping the towel as he stumbles over his dirty clothes, grabs his cell phone from his coffee table and calls Captain Perry. "Hey, Captain, it's Larkin. That bastard was in my house… No, I don't know when. He left a message on my bathroom mirror. It said to quit wasting his time and to let him do his work. No, nothing else has been disturbed. No need to send a team over here; I can already tell you there won't be fingerprints on the mirror. He used gloves, as usual… I'll be in at 8:30 and we can discuss it then. I just wanted to let you know. I am still going to my dad's place this morning for his birthday breakfast. It is important to him and I need some normalcy in my life right now." Max ends the call, walks back to the bathroom and takes a picture of the message with his cell so it can be added to the case file.

Max starts getting dressed, smelling each individual article of clothing before he puts it on. He has to admit to himself that he mostly said no to the team in his apartment because he doesn't want to clean up for them. He is unsure if the mess keeps him from bringing women home or would make him more sympathetic to the opposite sex.

He goes back to his bathroom to brush his teeth and finds himself staring at the mirror for minutes on end. *I can't believe he got in here. How did he know where I live? I hope he tries to make me his next victim. That will be the very last thing he ever does.* Max grins at himself in the mirror.

He feels compelled to look over his car before unlocking the door to ensure no one tampered with it. He gets down on his knees to check underneath for anything that might stick out like a bomb or any other type of tampering. He walks around, looking for any sign that it was opened by anyone other than himself. Satisfied after a few moments that his beautiful car has not been touched, he gets in. He lowers his head and inserts the key into the ignition, takes a deep breath, and turns the key. The car starts. Max breathes a sigh of relief.

Max's parents live only about five minutes from him and he should be right on time for his dad's birthday breakfast. He drives along Park Street and heads toward Commonwealth Avenue, where his parents live. It's a two-mile street lined with mostly one- and two-story modest houses that remind Max of his childhood. The streets are breaking apart because of the lack of maintenance. He understands that Rockton can only afford to do so much road repair but wishes they would eventually get around to this part of town. The bumps are very hard on his vintage car and jar his bones when he can't avoid them. He turns right onto Commonwealth and sees his mom's minivan in the driveway just a half block away. He turns left and parks directly behind it.

Before he can get out of the car, he can see his mom at the front door, like she has been waiting for him. He really likes to go over to his parents whenever he finishes a case. It helps him to remember why he became a policeman in the first place: to protect his family and the community. It also gives him a sense of normalcy after chasing liars, thieves, psychopaths, and junkies.

The front porch area, enclosed by many windows, is filled with brightly colored balloons. Max remembers many times when he would have friends spend the night and they would always sleep in that front porch area with the windows opened. Some of his friends would get scared because of the openness of the room. However, nothing happened in the residential areas back then.

"Come on, Maxie, your eggs will get cold," Max's mom yells out to him as he digs around the junk in his backseat for a pen to fill out his dad's card.

Max looks up at his mom and raises his arms. "Mom, I'm fifteen minutes earlier than we agreed on. So if I showed up on time, they would be cold for sure. Is that what you are saying?" Max embraces her in a hug. He leaves one arm around her as they walk into the foyer. He can see his dad sitting at the dining room table, already eating his breakfast.

At six feet three inches, Max's father is a tall man who has lost most of his hair. He has a paunch that has developed over the years from the usual reasons. He has a weekly vow to eat better and get to the gym more often. Max is happy that his dad has lasted this long, considering how poorly he takes care of himself. His father looks up from his pile of scrambled eggs, bacon, and toast long enough to chastise him. "You know your mother, Max. She likes to have everything done early so we don't have to wait. So cut her some slack, and sit here and enjoy a meal with your old man, would you, Mr. Big Shot Detective?" Max's dad never really wanted him to go into law enforcement. He always envisioned Max as a pro athlete or a corporate type. While he is very proud of Max, he still wanted so much more for his only child.

"Happy birthday, Dad," Max says as he walks up to his father and gives him a hug from the side. "I can't believe you're sixty years old today!"

Max lets go of his father and moves to the other side of the table "I can't stay long today, but I will be back tomorrow for the party. I may not be able to stay long then either, but I'll be here."

Max's mom starts scooping eggs onto his plate and stops when he says he won't be able to stay long tomorrow. "Maxie, it's Saturday. What is more important than your father's birthday party?"

"I know it's Saturday and I usually don't have a problem taking Saturdays off, but this is different. I have a new partner and we are on the biggest case this town has ever seen," Max tells his mom.

"You have a partner? What's his name? You can bring him with you tomorrow night as well, you know. Is this that case all over the news—the guy that is killing all those people and leaving messages in their own blood on the walls?" she says as she continues to put bacon on Max's plate.

His mouth full of eggs, Max simply nods. If he does talk with food in his mouth, he is likely to get hit with a utensil by one of his parents. His dad used to smack him just hard enough on the back of his head to show he was serious and called the licks brain dusters. Max swallows his food so he can speak. "First off, Mom, **her** name is Jesse. Secondly, yes Mom, it is that case. I really shouldn't get to into it, but we found cases from years ago that we think are the same guy. The one that happened ten years ago was right near here in Clinton. The one 25 years ago was in a town in the southern part of Indiana. He made a three-year-old kid talk to the 911 operator then." He looks at both his parents.

They have been staring at each other with apprehensive looks while he spoke. "Mom, Dad, I have been wondering why you didn't tell me about the one in Clinton when it happened. It was just over the border in Wisconsin. Literally thirty minutes away from you, and yet you didn't tell me about a big homicide just thirty minutes from your front door. That has been eating at me ever since I found out about it a couple of days ago. It's just not like you to hold back something like that."

Max's parents sit quietly for a few moments. Something foreboding hangs in the air. Max's father looks up from his plate and stares directly into his son's eyes. "Max, there are some things I think you should leave alone in this world, and this is one of those things."

"Dad, if you know anything about this guy, you need to tell me. He broke into my apartment at some point in the last day and left me a message. So you need to help me if you can," Max says. He suddenly feels very uncomfortable, like he needs to interrogate his parents.

Max's mom sits down at the table, wringing her hands together. "Harold, if our son is in danger because of this secret, we need to tell him. Please, we can't let him hurt our boy."

Max straightens up in his chair and gawks at his parents, befuddled. He can't believe that they kept a secret from him. "Secret? What secret? You guys always told me that there shouldn't be any secrets between us, and now you are saying you have been keeping something from me. What is it? Please tell me! I need to know."

Harold sighs and begins to sob a little bit. "Your mother and I had to keep this secret for your own good, son. Since you have been threatened, I better tell you." The atmosphere the room is thick enough to touch. "Twenty-seven years ago, your mother and I found out that we could not have children. Your mother has a problem with her body that prevents her from carrying a baby to full term. We had a few pregnancies that didn't go full term and lost all hope of ever having a child. We never considered adoption because it wouldn't be a part of us. Not our blood—you know what I mean?" Max nods a bit hesitantly. "Then one day, we received a call from an attorney in Merrillville, Indiana. He told us about my dad, your grandfather, having another family. He had another wife and a daughter, Sidney, at the same time he was married to Grandma Tina. Sidney was about the same age as me. Although Sidney and I had never met, we were the only children that your Grandpa George had. The attorney told us about Sidney and her life as a banker in Indiana. She was married and had one son. One night, after Sidney and her husband put their son to bed, a man broke into their home and killed them. The worst part is that the man forced Sidney's son to make the 911 call. The son, Max, was only three years old at the time. I was your only blood relative. They asked us to be your guardians. It didn't take long, but after some thought, we decided to raise you as our own son."

Max is sitting still at the table, staring at his parents, his mind whirling. "I don't know what to say right now. I cannot believe you kept this from me all of these years."

Max's mom, still crying, walks over to him, trying to get a hug from him. He is reluctant at first, but finally stands up and hugs her. She sobs into his chest as she speaks. "Maxie, sweetheart, I want you to understand that we did it for your own good. You saw your parents dead at the age of three. We figured it would be better to not bring up that horrible memory unless you did. Your whole life, you never said one word about anything that happened to you that night. Your mind must have blocked it out. We were so happy that it did block it out because we didn't want to see you hurt by that tragic night. Please forgive us, son. We love you and we couldn't love you any more if you were our own."

Max slowly pulls his mom back to arm's length. He stares into her blue eyes that comforted him every time something wrong happened. He remembers first learning how to ride a bike with his dad and falling down the first time he was let go. He fell, skinning his knee, and she was there to make everything all better. These people were there for him when things were good or bad. Memories flood back. When he graduated high school and college, they were in the front row. Max realizes that no matter how he came into their lives, they will always be his parents and he will always be their son. "Of course I do, Mom. I love both of you, and I understand why you did what you did. If anything, I think I have even more love and respect for you guys. You took a kid in that you didn't know from a long-lost sister that you didn't know even existed. Having raised him as your own son, you protected him from the bad thing that brought him into your lives. Both of you are the most wonderful people on this planet and I am the luckiest son on the planet."

The old man gets up from his seat and hugs both Max and his wife. "You make us so proud, Max. We are the lucky ones here."

"That certainly does explain why I wasn't in any of the pictures of the car before I was three years old," Max says with a great big smile on his face.

All three start to laugh. They all feel the years of stress from this gigantic secret floating away like a cool fog on a fresh spring morning. Max steps back and flushes all of a sudden. He sits back down in his chair and puts his hands over his face. His mother and father stop laughing. Their faces go from joy to fear. His mother speaks up. "What is it, son? What's wrong?"

Max pulls his hands away from his face and looks at his mother. "I have had some dreams recently about that night. In the dreams, I am talking to the 911 operator and looking at the people lying in the bed. They are not moving. The man that made me do it is yelling at me because

I was too scared to speak to the operator. I think reading about that murder the other day triggered the memory in my brain. I really thought it was just me putting myself in that boy's shoes. I would have never guessed that the boy was me."

Harold sits down in the chair next to Max. He turns the chair so he is facing him. He grabs his son's hand gently. "Max, I know that these are bad memories, but you need to look past them and figure out how to catch this guy. If anyone is going to be able to catch him, it is going to be you. I may not have liked the fact that you became a police officer, but now that you are, I know you are the best there is. You have always been great at everything you have done. Now, this is going to be tough, son, but I need you to close your eyes and try and remember that day when he killed your birth parents. Picture his face, his eyes, his teeth—anything at all that may help you catch him."

Max closes his eyes and prompts his memory to reveal something to him. He reaches deep through the fog of time and tries to bring that whole night back. He was only three years old when it happened, but there obviously were some memories there or he wouldn't be able to dream about them repeatedly from the boy's perspective. "All I can see is his black ski mask, his gray suit with a white shirt, and gray tie. He is wearing black leather gloves and wait—I see something: a bracelet—no, a watch. Yes, I see a watch. A gold watch, to be exact. It has a black face with a crown where the 12 position is on the face. It's a Rolex watch. He was wearing a gold Rolex on his left wrist. That is the hand that he was pulling me with from my room to their room. The watch showed right between the cuff of his shirt and the glove. That is all I can remember about him."

Harold and Ellen can tell that their son is exhausted. He slouches in the chair and opens his eyes. He takes a deep breath and lets it out. Ellen leans into him and gives him a kiss on the cheek. "My brave boy. Remember we love you, no matter what. Maybe you should stay here with us while you work on this case."

Max gets up from his chair and smiles. While he is anything but positive and happy, he feels he has to pretend for his parents' sake. He gives his dad a hug and says, "I'll be fine, Mom. Happy birthday, Dad. I am sorry that this came up. I love you and will see you tomorrow for your party."

His parents look happy and relieved, yet there is anxiety behind

Ellen's smile. They both sit down at the table and resume eating as Max leaves the house through the front door. He walks to the car and turns around to stare at his childhood home. All of his great memories flood his mind. He smiles and opens the door to his car. *8:10. Have to get to the station and fill in Jesse. I can't tell the Captain or he will take me off the case— conflict of interest and all that crap.* He takes one last look at his parents' house before he heads to the police station, feeling the difference in his life. The house and his memories have changed, somehow becoming shadowed by his dark past. He doesn't want to upset these people who raised him with such love, but he needs some time to think through all of this.

Max and Jesse both arrive only seconds apart from each other at the station, parking next to each other. Jesse struggles with her squeaky door as she forces it open. Max stifles a giggle as she finally gets out of the old rust bucket. "Really?" he teases her. "I'm worried about you making it out of that car without requiring a tetanus shot."

Jesse stifles her response, veiling a grin. "All right already, I will get a new-ish car tomorrow. It is Saturday, and I think there's a sale. Would that make you happy?"

At this point, she has caught up to him near the side entrance to the station. He glances at her and says, "Yes, it would. That would be one less thing for me to worry about. You would not believe the morning I've had. First, our killer leaves a message on my bathroom mirror and then I get some weird information at my parents' house."

Jesse stops in her tracks. She grabs Max by the arm and pulls at him until he stops walking. "What do you mean, he left you a message on your bathroom mirror? What did it say? When did he do it? Why didn't you call me? What the hell? I'm your partner and I need to know these things!"

Max stops and looks at her. He has never really had to answer to anyone before. He just thought it was his problem and only his problem. "Sorry, I am not used to having a partner. I called the Captain, but obviously he didn't tell you, so I do apologize. I'll remember the next time it happens, okay?" he says with the beginning of a smirk forming.

Jesse shakes her head and laughs a little. "You damn well better tell me next time a killer breaks into your house. Mind you, I hope it isn't any time soon that it happens, but if it does, you better tell me. Got it?"

"Got it."

"What did the message say?" Jesse asks.

"It said to stop wasting time and let him do his work. He did it with a leather glove, I'm assuming. There were no fingerprints on the mirror, but there was moisture and the only way it showed up on my mirror was from the steam of the shower. I guess you didn't get the same message at your place, huh?" Max asks as they walk through the front door. She shakes her head no.

The police station seems extremely dark to Jesse after the sunny ride to the station. Some of the hallway lights are burnt out or flickering. The lights in their squad room are much brighter. Jesse looks at it as a metaphor: there is light at the end of the tunnel. It seems to fit with the case they are facing. They know deep down they will catch this guy, but they don't know when. There is hope, but it seems distant.

Jesse decides she better be honest with Max about where she was last night. "I wouldn't know if Crazy Killer left a message, as I didn't go home last night. Melissa was scared at her place, and I stayed with her."

Max looks at Jesse. "I thought those clothes looked familiar. Let's see, you said she had nothing more to say about the man she saw, yet you stayed all night. Hmmm… I grow more curious by the second on this, but it will have to wait. We need to find out from Captain Perry if anything else has come up. I'll tell you what, you can tell me about your night at lunch, and I will tell you about my morning. No matter, we are both sworn to secrecy on both subjects. Agreed?" Max extends his hand for a handshake agreement.

She realizes that her partner has a secret about the last 24 hours, just like she does. She thinks her story might push him over the edge, but he promises to keep it a secret so she feels better. Even though they have only been partners for a few days, she knows she can trust him with her life. If she does tell him the whole story about Melissa, that is exactly what she will be doing. He will have her career in his hands. She suddenly feels a lump in her throat at just the thought of losing her new promotion from one night of indiscretion.

At the squad room they see that all of the other detectives are missing. It's a ghost town except for Captain Perry sitting in his office. They look around the room, trying to find any clue as to where the other four detectives are. Jesse glances at McCarren's desk and sees a note that says Rockton Hospital.

"Hey Max, McCarren wrote a note that just says Rockton Hospital. Maybe they all went there," Jesse says with a shrug.

Max knocks on the Captain's door, pushing it open without waiting for an invitation, Jesse in tow. Captain Perry is on the phone yelling at someone. "Never mind, they are right here." He slams the phone down. "Where the hell have you two been? You are the lead detectives on these cases and we can't get hold of you at all!"

Jesse and Max both pull their cell phones out of their pockets and look at them sheepishly. "Mine is dead. Sorry, Captain, I didn't notice that it didn't charge last night," Jesse mutters.

"And what is your lame excuse, Larkin? I've never not been able to get you on your cell!"

"Sorry, Cap, I put mine on silent while I was with my parents. I told you I was going to my dad's for his birthday. I forgot to switch it back. What's all the hostility about? And where is everyone?"

Captain Perry stands up and puts both hands on his desk. "Where is everyone, you ask? Everyone is out doing your job. Rockton Hospital called and reported one of their residents didn't show up for work the last two days. He has never missed a day, let alone two. So I sent McCarren and Johnson to the hospital, and I sent Phillips and Salvo to the doctor's house. Maybe if you both didn't have your heads up your butts, I wouldn't have to send all of my detectives out on *your* case. Now McCarren and Johnson have already finished at the hospital and they are on their way back, but Phillips and Salvo haven't checked in yet so get over to the doc's house and find out the hell is going on." Captain Perry hands Max a piece of paper with the name Hanush Patel and his address written on it. "Why are you two still here? Get going!" he yells at them.

Jesse leaves immediately, glad to be out of the boss's sight. Max, on the other hand, slowly strolls out of the Captain's office and says, "Lighten up. She made a mistake."

"Get out of here now, Larkin!" the Captain yells back at Max.

Max, with Jesse in the passenger seat, is racing to the doctor's apartment. Siren going and lights flashing, he puts the pedal to the floor, weaving in and out of traffic. Jesse finally says, "You don't think they caught the guy in the act and he did something to them, do you?"

Max glances over at his partner and with pursed lips, shakes his head negatively. "Let's just get there and find out."

Max pulls the car into the parking lot of the doctor's apartment building. He sees Phillips and Salvo's car parked near the door, but they are not in the car. Max and Jesse both leap from the car, leaving the doors open, siren still going and lights flashing. They both run toward the basement apartment with guns drawn and in the ready position, proceeding cautiously down the stairs now. If the killer is still there, he surely knows they are coming, but they don't want to alert him to where they are coming from so they use hand signals to communicate. Max moves his hand toward the door, telling Jesse she is first in this time. She moves toward the door and sees it is open a crack.

Max positions himself outside the door, facing inward, and waits for Jesse to open the door. She pushes the door open and walks in, slowly at first and then quickly as she sees Salvo duct-taped to a chair, his eyes wide open and his mouth taped shut. Salvo is facing what appears to be a murdered Indian man. The dead man's thumb has been cut off and is lying in a pool of blood that has congealed from sitting so long. Flies are swarming over the body and the blood. Jesse puts her hand over her mouth to keep from gagging.

Max looks around for Phillips, finding him behind the door, passed out cold. He checks him for a pulse. "He's alive," he yells to Jesse.

Jesse says, "So is Salvo. What happened here, Salvo?" she asks, as she slowly removes the tape from his mouth.

Dave Salvo is a decorated officer with almost thirty years on the force. He has been a detective for ten of those years. The entire squad loves him. He has never had to pull his gun out in any situation. He is a decent cop, but ever since he turned fifty, he has slowed down, riding out his time until he retires. He has put on some weight because of his lack of enthusiasm and energy for the job.

Dave doesn't answer Jesse at first. His eyes are glossed over. Jesse snaps her fingers in front of Dave and he seems to shake himself out of his daze. "He came out of nowhere. He hit Phillips over the head with bolt cutters and, then in one swoop, got me right across the face with the same bolt cutters. I was knocked out for a short time and, when I came to, I was in this chair tied up just like you found me. I got a look at him for maybe a second. He was wearing a mask and had a dark blue suit on. His shirt was white and his tie was a dark blue as well. He was just about to stick a needle into my neck when he heard my cell phone go off. It spooked him a little, but then he stopped in his tracks when he heard sirens in the distance. He picked up the bolt cutters, leaned in and whispered, 'I only came back for my bolt cutters. I left them here after I finished my work with the good doctor. I already lost two of these recently. I can't afford to keep buying new ones. Sorry for the inconvenience, Officer. You were just in the wrong place at the wrong time. You didn't waste my time.'

"Then he left. What about Phillips? Is he all right?"

Phillips is sitting up now, propped against the wall. Blood flows from the back of his head where the bolt cutters struck him. Phillips is a little bit younger than Salvo. He's in his forties and is still working hard. That is why Captain Perry put them together. He figured they would offset each other. Phillips is still in good shape for a detective in his forties and really does a decent job. Outside of Max, he is the most competent detective on the squad. Phillips' speech is slurred a little at first. "I'm okay. He came out of nowhere. I had no idea he was here. The door to the apartment was unlocked, but we didn't hear anything when we announced we were police officers. We entered the room and then bam, right in the back of my head. I was out instantly and the next thing I remember is you, Larkin, looking down at me."

Max reaches in his pocket and pulls out his phone, calling 911. "Help is on the way, guys. Just don't move too much."

While they wait for the ambulance, Larkin and Fairlane look around the apartment for any clues. They know deep down that the killer left none.

Max walks around, looking for anything out of place, while Jesse tends to the injured officers. He notices blood droplets that lead from the body toward the kitchen area. Following the blood trail to the kitchen, he notices some blood on the counter just in front of the sink. He looks around the sink for a weapon, but finds nothing other than more blood in the sink itself. "Jesse, I think the killer brought a knife with him this time because there are blood drops but no weapon. Maybe he cleaned it off in the sink so he could take it with him. The weird thing here is that he didn't leave any sign of money being taken from the victim. No money laying around as change. Check the victim's wallet and see if there is any money in there."

Jesse searches the doctor's pants for a wallet, but it is not there. "This is weird, Max. He doesn't have a wallet on him. I'll check the bedroom and see if it is in there." Jesse starts toward the bedroom, looking carefully as she steps for any evidence to avoid. She enters the bedroom and sees cut duct tape strewn across the bed. "Max, get in here. This looks like he had Hanush taped down like the Bjornsons and then he moved him before he killed him."

"Why would he bother to tape him up and then take him into another room to kill him? That's not his style. He tapes them up, talks to them, gets the money they supposedly owe him, and then he kills them. This is strange."

Max scans the room and notices a spot of black that doesn't look like tape on the bed. "There's his wallet—on the bed." Max goes through it. "Let's see, no cash at all; just cards. There are a few credit cards, but no ATM/debit card. Everyone nowadays has an ATM card or debit card, yet the doc doesn't? You don't think this guy tortured the pin out of him and stole the card to get his money, do you?"

Jesse asks Max for his phone so she can call the Captain. "Way ahead of you, partner," she says to Max while dialing. She impatiently tells him about what they found when they entered Hanush's apartment and then gets to the real reason she called. "Can you get someone to get us the financials on Doctor Hanush Patel and see what bank he deals with? We think the killer has his ATM card and is going to use it, if he hasn't already. Really? Great! Which one? Okay we will get over there as soon as the ambulance gets here for Salvo and Phillips."

Jesse cannot hide her happiness. "McCarren and Johnson already know which bank because the hospital does direct deposit. It is the First Bank of Rockton. They are already getting the warrant for his financials and they are going to meet us at the bank in fifteen minutes."

The ambulance siren can be heard right outside of Doctor Patel's apartment. They are cautioned that they are entering a double crime scene and to tread lightly. Jesse walks up to Phillips and puts her hand on his shoulder. "Max and I are leaving. We have to meet the guys at Doctor Patel's bank. You guys will be okay. Just relax and enjoy everybody waiting on you hand and foot at the hospital," she says with a smile to Phillips. Max isn't sure if her comment is meant as sympathy or a crack, which they richly deserve.

Max and Jesse drive toward the bank. "Could you imagine if this guy uses or used this ATM card? We would have him on camera finally. This could be the screw-up we have been waiting for." Once he finishes that statement, he switches on the lights and siren. He pushes the gas pedal down as far as it will go. "I want to get there now. Hang on! This is what this car is built for!" he whoops.

They arrive at the First Bank of Rockton. McCarren and Johnson are in the parking lot, standing outside of their vehicle. McCarren is holding a white piece of paper. He waves the paper at them as they enter the lot. Max barely gets the car in park before he shuts off the engine. He runs over to McCarren and yanks the piece of paper out of his hand. "It's about time you got something right, McCarren. Now go back to the station before you get lost out here doing real police work," he says as he jogs toward the bank. He sees Johnson flip him the middle finger out of the corner of his eye.

Jesse calmly walks up to the two detectives. She pats McCarren on the shoulder. "Don't pay any attention to him. You guys did a great job. He is just excited to think that this guy may have screwed up finally. See you guys back at the station." Jesse gives them a thumbs-up as she walks toward the bank.

Max is already at the front desk with the bank manager when Jesse enters. Max is leaning over the man, staring at his computer screen. She makes her way over to them and sits in the chair in front of the desk. "Max, give the man some time. He is going as fast as he can." The man shoots her a look, as he resents the invasion of his space.

The bank manager is staring at the screen and moving his finger down the screen. "Okay, Doctor Patel's last transaction was at 2 a.m. Thursday morning right here at the drive up ATM machine. It is going to take a minute, but I can pull up the video for you if you would like me to."

Max leans closer and sees that the transaction at that time was for a withdrawal of $520. "Hell yes, I want you to get me that video," Max says as he looks at Jesse. "We got him. He withdrew his money from the doctor's account right after he killed him. That would fit the timeline the evidence indicates. That would mean Mr. Patel was killed a day and a half ago."

The manager is feverishly typing away. "Here comes the video now, detectives." He turns the screen so both detectives can view the video. "Buffering, buffering, and still buffering…sorry, detectives. This network is good for transactions, but when it comes to video, it takes longer than normal. Okay, here we go."

Jesse and Max both lean forward. Jesse squints a little bit to see the grainy image better. "Wait, who is that? It's Doctor Patel! He withdrew the money himself. Our guy had nothing to do with the transaction. Damn it!" She stands up and throws her arms in the air.

Max starts to pull himself away but stops. "Wait! Rewind that a second or two, would you?" he asks the manager. "Who is that in the passenger seat? Can you zoom in?"

The manager plays with the video controls. Jesse leans in close again. "Is that a person next to him? Pause it," she says. The manager pauses the video. "Is the passenger wearing a mask? He is! Good catch, Max! That's our guy. That explains why he moved him from the bed to the dining room. He forced him to withdraw what he owed him. This guy is either really good or just plain crazy. Heck—maybe he is good and crazy. That makes for a lethal combination."

"Ok make a copy of that video, please," he says to the manager.

The manager reaches down into the desk drawer and pulls out a blank CD. A few moments go by and he pulls the burned CD out of the computer. "Sorry it didn't have what you wanted to see, Detective," he says as he hands the CD to Max. "There is something I don't understand, though. This guy forced Doctor Patel to take out only $520 when he has thousands in his account. Why is that?"

Jesse pats the manager on the shoulder. "That is a long story and we can't get into it during an ongoing investigation. Sorry."

Max has already stormed out of the bank. Jesse follows behind, running after him to catch up. "Max, sorry this wasn't the break we were looking for. I think we should go back to the station and watch the video again. Maybe we can see something on one of the lab computers."

Max agrees with her and they start to drive back to the station. Max is silent except for his heavy, angry breathing. Jesse stays calm and quiet.

Max suddenly pulls the car over into a parking lot not too far from the police station. "Jesse, there is something I have to tell you," he says to her with a very strange expression on his face. It looks as if he is carrying a heavy weight. "This morning, I found out that my parents are not my real parents. They are actually my aunt and uncle. They have been raising me as their own son since I was three."

Jesse's eyes widen as she gasps, "I am so sorry, Max. I know that had to be a shock to you. Between that and this case, how are you even functioning today?" She pauses for a moment. "Wait a minute. Your parents are actually your aunt and uncle? And they have been raising you since you were three? That sounds an awful lot like…" Jesse puts her hand over her mouth and gasps again. She pulls her hand away from her mouth. "That's why you are having these vivid dreams! *You* were that little boy twenty-five years ago. He made you call 911 after he killed your parents. Why didn't you figure out the people twenty-five years ago were your family? Didn't you recognize the names?"

Max shuts off the engine and explains the entire story. Sharing it with someone else makes it more real for him. After hearing the entire story, Jesse sits in the passenger seat, not moving. She looks blank. "Can you remember anything more from that night twenty-five years ago, Max? Maybe we should take you to a hypnotist and see if he can draw more out?"

Max closes his eyes and tried to remember his dreams. "I see him standing over me, telling me that I need to tell everyone to stop wasting other people's time. He said I needed to learn from my parents' mistakes. I truly can't remember seeing his face at all. It was dark in the room except for the moonlight spilling in through the blinds. His voice was deep and authoritative." Max opens his eyes and looks emotionally drained. "I can't remember any more, and I'm not going to see a hypnotist unless that is absolutely the last option. I'm always afraid I'll awake from my trance and think I'm a chicken later in life when someone rings a bell or says a weird phrase." They both laugh a little at his attempt at humor.

Max turns his head to the right and waits for Jesse to look him in the eyes. "You can't tell anyone about this until we catch this guy. If the Captain finds out, he will take me off the case because of conflict of interest and probably put McCarren on it. McCarren is a terrible detective. He can't figure out the case of the missing bologna sandwich from his own plate, five minutes after he ate the damn thing himself. You and I are the only hope this town has of catching this guy, so promise me you won't say a word." He holds her gaze as best he can in an effort to read her.

Jesse fights holding his gaze, but is also worried about how guilty that makes her seem. "I will keep your secret until we get him. I swear as long as you can keep my secret as well. I hate to add more to your plate, but remember how I said I had something to tell you? Well, here goes: I spent the night with Melissa."

Max guffaws, "Pshaw, I knew that. You told me that yesterday morning."

Jesse lowers her eyes. "Yes, but I didn't tell you that we kissed." Max snaps back from her as if he had been snake-bitten. "Wait. Just wait a minute. I remember the story you told me about your old partner. I swear to you, it was just a kiss. I stopped it before it became more. Don't get me wrong! I wanted it to become more, but I knew that wouldn't be right. Melissa and I promised each other that we would just be friends until this case is over, and I am going to keep that promise. See, we both have something that has to stay a secret until we catch this guy. I will keep your secret if you keep mine. Agreed?" Jesse extends her hand out to Max, looking for a handshake agreement.

Max thinks about it for a moment. He suddenly feels less sure of his trust in her, but he also knows he can't trust anyone else right now. His trust in his parents is a bit shaky since his childhood has been turned upside down. He really doesn't have anyone else to lean on and she has proven to be there for him time and again.

Jesse waits anxiously while Max is thinking. He has a perplexed look on his face while he stares out the windshield. Suddenly, he extends his hand toward her and they shake. Her lip biting turns to a smile of gratitude as she shakes his hand vigorously. She feels like hugging him but waits. Between the tightness of the car and his hesitation, she decides to wait until later.

Max pulls out of the parking lot and heads to the station. It's only three blocks away. He is still trying to comprehend what she told him. *Is she telling me she's gay? Bi? What?* He starts to wonder what else she may be keeping from him.

He pulls into the police station parking lot, parking in his usual spot. He shuts off the car and grabs Jesse's hand as she undoes her seatbelt. "I need to know if there is anything else you're hiding from me. I know what you did with Melissa is not the same thing as what my old partner did, but it could have been. I also had no idea that you liked women. So if there is more that you're hiding from me, now is the time to spit it out. I'm not happy with you right now but I'm willing to give you a chance to come clean about anything else you think might come back at you. I suggest you take this opportunity because if I find out something else I will go to Perry."

Jesse shifts in the seat, very uncomfortable. "Max, first off, I really didn't know I liked women like that either until she kissed me. I always was curious about it, but never really followed through. Secondly, I understand where you're coming from, but my sex life is not going to affect my job—not now and not ever. With that in mind, I will not hide anything that pertains to my job and our partnership from you, but you need to understand that there are some things that you don't need to know. I think you and I will be great partners and great friends. Please don't hold this against me."

Max stays still for a moment. *What did Jesse really do that was so wrong? She spent time with a scared witness and wound up kissing her. Can I trust her? She didn't hide it from me. She told me because obviously she trusts me. She is a great detective and a good person.* "Jesse, I'll try not to hold this against you. You didn't do anything wrong. I appreciate you telling me this and I am glad we can trust one another. Sorry if I overreacted, but the last few days have been rough on me."

Jesse breathes a sigh of relief. She feels she can trust her partner with anything and he will trust her as she continues to be honest with him. "Okay, enough of this wishy-washy stuff. Let's get inside and take another look at that video from the bank to see if we can see any more."

It's been a long Friday and the sun has set. The station is an island of light in a dark sea. The two detectives sit at Max's desk watching the video from the bank, slowing it down and rewinding when necessary. Jesse stops Max when she sees a slight glimmer between the masked man and Doctor Patel. "Max, pause it right there. What is that between them? Zoom in, please." Max zooms in on the spot she is referring to. "We need to clear that up a little." Max types feverishly on the keyboard as the screen begins to clear up. "That looks like a syringe possibly, based on the way he is holding it. See his finger over the top of the object like he is ready to push the plunger in? He has a needle stuck in the doctor's arm, probably to control him. I wondered why he just sat in the car and didn't try to escape."

They continue to watch the video. Jesse points. "Wait, pan down a little. Is that something binding Mr. Patel to the gear shift? Notice he never uses his right hand for anything. I bet he was bound to the gearshift to keep him from escaping. Okay, so he taped his hand to the gearshift and put a needle into his arm. This guy thought of everything."

Max rubs his eyes. "I'm getting tired again. This case is physically and emotionally draining. I need to get some rest. Let's call it a night, Jesse." Jesse agrees with a stretch and a yawn. "After what happened at my apartment with my mirror, I'm going to spend the next few days at my parents' house. That sounds kind of weird saying my parents' house, knowing what I know, but they will always be Mom and Dad to me. Tomorrow is Saturday, and we technically do not *have* to clock in, but I am going to be here about 10 a.m. What about you, Jesse?"

"I am going to be here about noon. I am taking your advice and buying a new car tomorrow morning. Well, new to me anyway. I am going to go to that dealership in Clinton, as we don't have any dealerships here. I didn't like hearing the story of how our murderer killed that town so my business may help. If I can help even a little bit, I will feel better."

"Sounds good to me, Jesse. I'll see you tomorrow about noon. Maybe I'll have some new information by then. Hopefully this guy takes a night off so we don't have another murder to work on. Oh and after we are done here, why don't you come with me to my dad's birthday party? Just some old friends of the family will be there and I could use some support from my generation. Besides, my mom invited you."

Jesse slips into her coat and starts for the door. She turns around at the invitation, with a skeptical look. "I'd love to go to your dad's party if that's really okay with you. Hanging out with new people sounds better than just thinking about this case."

Max shuts his computer down, gets up from his desk, and walks toward the door. He stops and turns around to stare at the desks that should be occupied by Salvo and Phillips. "I am going to get him for you guys!" he says out loud. "Nobody does this to my team and gets away with it." He turns out the lights and heads over to his parents' house.

14

ike Hogan is walking around the Clinton Car Emporium showroom on Saturday morning. Sales haven't been good lately. They haven't been good for almost ten years. *I really have nobody to blame but myself,* he thinks. Mike moved to Clinton for two reasons: to be closer to his daughter and to make a lot of money at the brand new dealership. Unfortunately, shortly after he moved to Clinton, his daughter, Amanda, didn't want to be around him anymore. He firmly believes it was his ex-wife's doing more than his. He believes his ex, Phoebe, told her a lot of lies about him and why they were not together anymore. She passed the blame onto him for everything that went wrong with their marriage, and poor Amanda got the worst part of it. That pushed Mike into a deep depression that he knew only one way to get out of. He had to rid the world of people who wasted his time.

Twenty-five years earlier his wife left him for another man and he went into a depression. His cure at that time was to kill a family that came into the dealership he was working at who took too much of his time and bought nothing. Once he finished ridding the world of their time wasting, he felt better. He went on with his life and didn't have to kill again until that fateful day that his daughter dropped the bomb on him ten years ago about not wanting to be around him anymore. He again found a time-wasting couple to cure him of his anger. The problem he faces now is that the Ostrowski murder killed his new job. Although sales decreased over the past ten years, he stuck it out in Clinton because he was physically close to his daughter. He never gave up hope that their relationship would get better.

Mike today finds himself in the same place he was those two previous times. His daughter was married last week and didn't invite him to the wedding. He thought about crashing it anyway, but he loves her too much to make her big day about him. Instead, he had to cure his depression again. He identified the perfect family. They wasted his time the day after he heard about Amanda's wedding. He followed them for awhile because he wanted to make sure it was the perfect scenario to rid him of his anger and depression.

There was a problem, however. Once he ended their lives, his negative feelings didn't subside. They grew stronger. He needed to continue his work on the time-wasting community to help cure him. After ridding the world of two more people he should have felt better.

Mike then found that the only woman he has loved since his wife left him had betrayed him. He needed to rid the world of her as well. Having done that, he should finally feel like himself again, but he still feels like nothing will make him feel good again.

Mike finds himself pacing back and forth in the showroom, not because of the lack of sales, but because of his own pain and suffering. He just needs to get rid of time wasters and then he'll feel better, but he can't seem to kill enough of them. One more seems to be the only answer that he comes up with after each and every kill. Maybe the next one will get rid of the depression and anger. The only problem is that it hasn't yet.

As Mike paces the showroom floor, his boss, Rich, is on the phone with the dealership's owner. He says, "I can't figure it, John. My best salesman is struggling. Even when sales are slow, Mike has always been the top sales producer for the dealership. He's the only one left of the original group of superstars. He outlasted them all and still made more money each year than the last. But for the past seven days, Mike has not sold a car. He also called in because his girlfriend was sick earlier in the week. When Mike does show up at work, he is often late and looks like he was up all night."

John says, "Just stick with him. Even the best salespeople have slumps."

Rich walks up to Mike and puts his hand on his shoulder. "What is going on with you, Mike? You're in a slump lately—that includes when we were shut down ten years ago because of the murders. Even that week you sold more cars than you have this week, and we were closed for three days. So what gives? Do you need a vacation?"

Mike is shocked by his boss and longtime friend's comments. He knows he is not doing a great job, but didn't realize how bad it looked to his boss. "Sorry Rich, my daughter got married last week and I wasn't invited to the wedding. I have been doing my usual cure for my depression, but it just never seems to be enough. I'll get out of it today. I promise you, the next person that comes here will leave in one of our cars."

Rich pats Mike on the back. "I hope you're right. I'm getting pressure from the owner to put you on notice for not producing. You know this business isn't about what you did for me in the past; it is about what have you done for me lately. All they see is you taking up space and driving one of their cars for free. Don't forget you are the only salesperson that still has a demo." Rich starts walking away and sees a beat-up old green car pull in. "Well, Mike, here is your chance. Go grab that person and get them out of that piece of crap and into one of our cars."

Mike sees the green car and hopes he can sell that person a car to save his job. As he is walking toward the door, he recognizes the person getting out of the car. It is Max Larkin's partner. He stops in his tracks, turns around and walks back toward the service center, hoping someone else approaches her before Rich sees him leaving the area.

"Hey Mike, where are you going? I told you to take that customer and sell them a car!" Rich yells from his office. "Sell like your job depends on it, because it just might."

Mike's face flushes. He has to sell a car to the person who is trying to find him and lock him away for the rest of his life or lose his job. *At least she thinks my name is Tom. So I have that going for me. I better give it my best and hope she doesn't recognize my voice.* Mike walks up to Jesse. "Welcome to Clinton Car Emporium. My name is Mike. How can I be of service today?" he asks her, extending his hand for a handshake. He is trying to sound different than he does on the phone.

"Hello Mike, I'm Jesse and I need a new car, as you can plainly see. My partner is giving me a hard time about not driving something nicer. I am looking at used cars, but in a few years, if I keep working hard, I will probably get a new car and would like to come back here and to you if you treat me well," Jesse says, shaking his hand.

"Great, I can definitely help you there. You said your partner put you up to this? Is that right? Will they be helping in the decision?"

Jesse takes a step back from Mike and starts to giggle a little bit. "No, no, not that kind of partner. I'm a detective in Rockton, Illinois and my fellow detective gave me a hard time because he drives a nice car and I don't. He has a classic 1982 Firebird in mint condition that his dad gave him, and you see what I pulled up in. I figured he was right about getting a new car, so here I am."

Mike heads for the lot and asks Jesse to follow him. "You are looking for a used car, correct?" Jesse agrees. "Two doors or four doors?"

"I never really thought about it. I guess I would prefer a two-door for now. I have been driving a four-door for too long. I think I want something sporty and fun," Jesse says, getting into the mood.

Walking the lot, they come across a nice, sporty red Scion TC. It is exactly what she is looking for, but she keeps her enthusiasm private. "Hey, what about that little red car? Is that a good car? Can I take it for a drive?" she asks Mike, turning her face away from him, trying to hold back her excitement.

Mike leaves her to get the keys to the car. Jesse walks around the car and gets very excited now. She loves the look of this car and really wants it, but she will control her emotions. Mike returns in a minute with the keys and dealer license plate in hand. "Let's go, Detective." He opens the driver door for Jesse to get inside, joining her on the passenger side. As she looks around the interior, he outlines the main features of the car and Jesse feels her heart beating faster in excitement. He can tell she likes the car a lot and he can smell a sale.

Jesse drives the car much farther than most other customers. She tells Mike that she has to test it in different situations due to her job. She takes the car onto the highway, through light Clinton traffic, and over bumpy and smooth roads. On her way back to the dealership, Jesse accelerates suddenly and then pushes the brake pedal hard, coming to a screeching halt. She can tell that Mike is getting really upset. "Sorry about that, Mike, but being a police officer, I sometimes have to accelerate quickly and stop almost as quickly. I wanted to make sure that this car could handle it," she shrugs, and with a wry grin pulls back into the dealership parking lot.

Mike is a little flustered, but doesn't want to show his temper, considering Jesse may recognize his voice. "No problem at all, Detective, I completely understand. Did she pass the test?" he asks, hoping to get her to show a strong interest in the car.

"Oh yeah, she did great," Jesse says enthusiastically, unable to conceal her glee any longer. "How much is she?" she says, worrying that there is no way she can afford this car. It is just too good to be in her range.

Mike tells her to follow him inside and he will work it all out for her. "Don't worry, Detective. You didn't waste your time looking at this car. I will find a way to make it fit into your budget." Mike stops after that statement. *Damn, I hope she didn't catch that slip-up. She hasn't recognized my voice yet so hopefully she didn't realize what I just said.*

Two hours go by and Jesse is the new owner of a used Scion TC. She shakes Mike's hand and struts out of the dealership toward her new car. "Thanks, Mike, for all your help. I am glad I didn't waste your time. I truly didn't think I would find anything today and I was afraid I would have to come back over and over until I did. Thank you so much!"

Mike is stunned that she used those particular words. "No problem, Detective. I am glad I could help you. Tell your partner he has to keep quiet about your car now. Have a great weekend!" Mike turns around and walks back to his desk. He sits down heavily and breathes a deep sigh of relief. He made it out of that situation, making a sale and even adding a few dollars to his pocket. *I still got it. If I can sell her a car, I can do anything. Why do I still feel like I have to continue with the time wasters? I think it is time that I rid the world of the biggest time waster of them all—Phoebe. She is the reason this all started. If I get rid of her time-wasting ways, I think I will be okay again,* he reasons with himself, cracking his knuckles.

Jesse is so excited about her new car that she can't wait to show Max. She hurries to the police station just so she can take him for a ride. Maybe now he will let her drive her car instead of him driving all the time.

She arrives at the station. The only car parked out front is Max's. On most days, there are a few more cars, but today his is the only one in the lot. She doesn't park her car in one spot like she normally would. Instead, she takes advantage of the semi-empty lot and parks it at an angle right in front of the door. She wants it to be the first thing he sees when she brings him outside.

She runs into the squad room, her excitement evident to everyone she passes. This is the first car she has ever purchased. Her green car was a hand-me-down from her grandmother and before that, her mom just showed up with a bigger piece of junk than the green car for her to drive for a first vehicle. She had said, "If you wreck it, who cares? It isn't worth much. But if you can show me that you can take care of a car, then we can upgrade soon." That seemed logical to her so she didn't complain.

"Max, Max, you have to come see her. She is gorgeous!" she yells as she runs into the squad room.

Max is more than happy to join her outside. He has been staring at files and the bank video for three hours. Just before Jesse arrived he had stopped and was staring at something and shifting from one document to the next. There were several of the victims' financials in a pile.

But she distracted him and he is happy to take a break. He walks behind Jesse as she runs to the door. She opens the door for Max as he walks outside and sees the red car sitting in the direct path out to the parking lot. "You do know you parked illegally. You can get a ticket for that here in Rockton," he says, chuckling. "It is cute, but does it do everything you need it to do? Did you get a good deal? Was the salesman nice and did he let you drive it before you bought it?"

Jesse stands there in awe of both the car and Max. She loves her new car, but he has to be the person that brings her back to reality a little. She is coming down from her new car euphoria as she answers him. "Yes, this is what I need and want, all in one car. I got a great deal and I'm very happy. The salesman was super nice. I think you would have liked him. He was straightforward and honest. It took less time than I thought to buy the car. It was like he was in just as much of a hurry as I was. His name was Mike something—I have his card somewhere in the car."

She smiles again, thinking about owning her first car on her own. "Our guy didn't strike last night, so let's go in and put all the files away for now. We can come back to it Monday with fresh minds and spirits. Killing ourselves over this will not help catch him. Hopefully, he takes the weekend off," she says to Max in a giddy way that makes him think hard about taking some much-needed time away from the case. "Besides, I really want to take you for a spin in my beautiful new car!" She winks at Max and skips back into the station.

Max waves his hand and says, "Fine, I give up. We can look at this stuff again tomorrow —not Monday, tomorrow. One night off is all we need to be fresh, okay?" Jesse waves him off as she enters the front doors, motioning him to follow her.

They walk out together and she gets into her car, thinking Max is going to go with her. He walks past it. She rolls down the window and yells to him, "Hey, I thought you were going to come along for a ride."

Max stops and turns back toward her. "Follow me to my parents' house and I'll drop off my car. Then we can go for a spin." He turns back around, gets in his car and takes off really fast. He wants to see if Jesse's new car can keep up with his sports car. He looks in the rear view mirror and sees Jesse doing a pretty good job of keeping up. He decides to slow down. He had his fun and now it is time to be an adult again.

Max pulls into his parents' driveway and parks the car. His mother is standing at the door again. It is almost like she sits at the window, waiting for him to come home. They put their whole lives on hold for Max when he was dropped on their doorstep. This is the time they should be enjoying life, but she would rather wait for her little boy than enjoy the time she has. As soon as Max shuts off the car, his mom opens the door for him to come in. He motions to Jesse that he will be a minute as he walks up to the house.

"Hey, Mom, I will be staying here a few more nights, if that is okay." He sees a gleam in her eye that hasn't been there for a very long time. "I am going to go for a ride in my partner's new car right now, though. We will be back in an hour or so for Dad's party. Is it okay if she comes to the party?" Max's mom's eyes light up. Like moms everywhere, she suspects a romantic link. "Sorry, Mom, we are not dating. We are just partners and truthfully, in the short time we have worked together, I trust her more than I ever trusted any partner. So I am not even going to try to date her. I don't want to screw up the great partnership we already have."

Ellen's face morphs from hope to acceptance. "A mother can dream, can't she?"

Yeah, a mother can, but honestly, you are my aunt, not my mother. It just seems weird thinking of you any other way than my mom, but you aren't really my mom. I have to keep up this charade of being okay with this for their sake. It isn't their fault that they couldn't have kids and got stuck with me. They took care of me and I really can't complain, Max muses. "Of course you can, Mom. Don't worry! Someday, I will find the right girl and you will be a grandmother. I promise." *I know that is her dream so I will feed it for as long as I can. I just see all the detectives get divorces, and Captain Perry has two divorces under his belt. I don't want to have that happen to me.*

Max gives Ellen a hug and kisses her on the cheek before he walks over to Jesse's car and gets in the passenger seat. They speed off down the street and Ellen waves as they leave.

Max is looking around the car, checking everything to make sure it works properly. He opens the glove compartment and inside is one of Jesse's handguns. "Really? You already have a gun in your car? Feel paranoid much?"

Jesse cracks a smile and slows down her car. "A girl can never be too careful. I figure I better put one in here just in case I come across a real nut job." Max laughs at this and shakes his head.

The detectives drive around a while and decide that it has been a good test run of Jesse's new car. They start back to Max's parents' house. Max is quiet most of the ride. "You've been pretty quiet, Max. What's up?" she queries.

Max rests his head in his hand and takes a deep breath. "It's my parents. I know they did what they had to do and they are actually great people, but I feel like they betrayed me a little by not telling me that I wasn't their real son. I feel weird around them now. I feel like I have to keep up a facade of happiness around them. Part of me wants to yell my head off at them and part of me wants to hug them for taking such good care of me all those years, even though I wasn't their own son. I mean, not once did they make me feel like anything but their son. I even know the reason they didn't tell me was for my own safety and my sanity. It's a lot to handle. I'm in charge of hunting down a man that killed my real parents twenty-five years ago. This is all pretty crazy even for me. When we bring this guy down, I am definitely taking a vacation from Rockton."

"I get it, Max. I truly do. There will be a time soon that you can reflect on all of this, but right now, there are two things more pressing. Number one: your father's birthday party. Number two: catching the guy that took your birth parents away. Tonight, you can take care of the first. After tonight, we will take care of the second one as a team." Jesse smiles at her partner and punches his arm.

They pull the car up to his parents' house and see a few cars parked in the driveway and the street. Jesse is apprehensive about parking her new car in the street. Max convinces her that it will be perfectly safe. "This is Rockton. Outside of these recent murders, it's probably the safest city in the country. Thanks mostly to me, of course," Max jests as he looks at the clock in the car. "It's 6:37. The party started at 6. I guess we owe my mom an apology for being late. Maybe we will be lucky and she didn't even notice."

Max and Jesse walk toward the house, unable to cease with the adolescent horseplay they have come to like. Maybe it has something to do with countering the adversity they face every day. Max opens the door and sees all of his parents' friends sitting around having beer and wine. They seem to be having a good time. Max is just there for his parents' benefit. He has no real attachment to any of these people, and now he is questioning his attachment to his parents as well.

Ellen meets Max and Jesse at the door. She has a glass of wine in her right hand and Max notices this probably isn't her first glass of the evening. She hugs Max and asks him to introduce her to his partner. "Mom, this is Jesse. She is my new partner. Thanks for letting her come tonight."

Jesse extends her hand toward Ellen and Ellen shakes her hand. "Nice to meet you, Jesse. I'm glad to see my son has a partner again. It helps me think he is safer since you have his back." Ellen pulls Jesse in close for a hug. Jesse is stunned by this, but hugs her anyway. Ellen whispers into Jesse's ear, "You are the first partner Max has ever brought to meet us in all of his years on the force. He must really trust you." She squeezes Jesse just a little bit harder before releasing her. They walk into the party and begin mingling right away with old family friends that Max hasn't seen in years. Jesse holds back for a few minutes, digesting what Ellen shared. She is realizing how closed off Max really keeps his personal life from work and wonders why he let her in.

Jesse leaves the party around 11 p.m. in order to get some rest before they start back in on the case. Max and Jesse agree that Jesse will drive on Sunday. She is to pick him up from his parents' house around 10 a.m. They plan on getting to work on finding more clues from Hanush's and Amber's apartments, and hopefully the Bjornson home. They feel they have to be missing something at their primary scenes. Nobody can be as ruthless and as covered in blood as this guy is and not be seen by someone. They believe he had to have made a mistake somewhere. His going from killing two couples in twenty-five years to killing seven people and a dog in five days is worrying them. They feel he had to have made some mistakes. They just have to look harder.

The wind is blowing hard through the town of Rockton, Illinois. Phoebe Smythe-Newman awakes from her sleep to the sound of the wind slamming the gate on her deck. Her thoughts are fuzzy, like she is drunk, but she had nothing to drink earlier that evening. She thinks, *Damn it! I forgot to close the gate after I got out of the pool last night. I won't get any sleep unless I close it now.* She tries to get out of her bed and cannot move. She struggles to move her head and feels tape pulling on her hair. Able to tilt her head forward from the bed just enough, she sees she is bound to her bed.

She moves her eyes toward where her husband should be, but he's not lying in the bed next to her. "Mark, where are you? What is going on?" she yells with fear in her voice. She sees a figure move from the shadows on the far wall. "Mark, is that you? Don't you think this is a little bit kinky for a man your age?" She continues to struggle against the tape. The figure comes out from the shadows and she can now see it is not Mark at all. It is a man in a dark suit, wearing a mask and black leather gloves. She screams at the top of her lungs.

"Scream all you want; nobody will hear you. You almost made this too easy for me. You built this house so far from your nearest neighbors that it would take a miracle for them to hear even cannons go off inside this room. So you should probably save your energy, because you're going to need it. As for your husband, Mark, he will join us later, but for now, he is busy—tied up, if you will." The suited man sits on the bed and runs the back of his gloved hand across Phoebe's face. She tries to pull away, but her tape prison prevents her from moving her head far enough away. He stands up angrily. "You know, you should be nice to me. You have already wasted enough of my time. Maybe I should just rid the world of you now, you heartless bitch!" he screams at her.

Phoebe freezes as he yells. A thought is forming at the back of her mind, like a word she cannot quite remember. "Please, just take whatever you want and leave us. Don't hurt us!" she begs her captor.

"Phoebe, we are going to play a little game. It is called 'guess who.' Are you ready to play?" he says as he glowers into her eyes. She flinches a little bit. The eyes seem eerily familiar to her, but she cannot seem to figure out why. She doesn't answer him but lets out another scream. "Now, now, Phoebe, even though your neighbors can't hear doesn't mean that I should have to hear that. This is your last warning before I tape your mouth shut or worse, got it? Now I am going to ask again: are you ready to play?"

Phoebe is able to muster up enough strength to resignedly agree. "Yes."

"Good! Now let's begin. My first question to you is pretty easy. Guess who is going to have a baby in about eight months." After he asks the question, he begins humming the *Jeopardy* theme song.

"My daughter, Amanda—she is going to have a baby in eight months," she says, her voice quivering. "Please don't harm her! She has done nothing to you—or anybody, for that matter. Please do what you want to me, but leave her alone."

"Amanda is safe for now; it all depends on how the game goes tonight, though. I do suggest you play within the rules, or Amanda's safety could be in jeopardy as well. Now let's get on to question number two. Shall we?" the suited man says as he stands towering over Phoebe. "Guess who is lying dead in this house somewhere?" He begins humming *Jeopardy* again.

Phoebe's face turns pale. "Mark is dead, isn't he? Why did you kill him?" she blurts out at him.

The masked man makes a noise that sounds like a game show buzzer. "Sorry, wrong answer." He pulls out a knife and walks toward Phoebe. "I forgot to tell you that if you get an answer wrong, you have a punishment. Today's punishment is you get cut." He puts the knife to Phoebe's face. She begins to squirm erratically as he moves the knife across her face toward her chest. "Now I just have to decide where it is going to be. Your face? No, too early in the game for that. I think the appropriate spot for this particular punishment is the legs. Yes, the legs it is." He takes the knife and slices across both of her legs right below the knee. Blood begins flowing from the cuts immediately.

Phoebe lets out a very loud, agonized scream. "Oh Phoebe, I know that hurt, but it won't kill you. I promise. It is way too early in the game for you to be screaming that loud. By the way, the correct answer is your mom and dad in the downstairs guest room. I knew that your daughter got married last week and they were here for that. They were going to get in the way of our game, so they had to go. So sad, but let's face it—they were not good people anyway. I mean they did raise you, the biggest time waster in the world, didn't they? If it makes you feel any better, they died quietly in their sleep. I smothered them. However, in the afterlife, they might have a hard time pointing at things or giving a thumbs-up to people because I cut theirs off." He reaches into his jacket pocket and pulls out Phoebe's parents' thumbs and index fingers from their right hands and drops them on her stomach.

She screams louder than the first time. He takes the pillow from the opposite side of the bed and pushes it hard against her face until she stops screaming. "I figure if I tape your mouth shut like I suggested earlier, I will have to remove the tape every time I want you to answer. So I can either suffocate you right now or you will have to stop that infernal screaming." She tries to fight against the pillow, but to no avail. Her screaming has stopped so he throws the pillow next to her on the taped-up bed.

The suited man leans up against the wall closest to Phoebe so she can still see him. "Time for our next question. Guess who is going to die next?" He again hums *Jeopardy*.

Phoebe lies rigid in her bed. The pain is unbearable from the cuts on her legs. She is crying uncontrollably. "Phoebe, oh Phoebe, I asked you a question. Guess who is going to die next? I'll give you a clue. You have three choices: Mark, you, or me. That narrows it down for you. You have a thirty-three percent chance of getting it right. So what's your answer?" He holds the knife up. Her blood is still dripping from the blade. He takes his right finger, touches the blade, and wipes some of the blood off. He puts the blood to his tongue and licks it off his finger sensuously. "I can taste your fear!" he says with a grin, flashing all of his teeth at her. It may be the drugs, but Phoebe thinks of a jackal smiling at her.

Phoebe is still crying, but answers in a very shallow voice, "Me. I am going to die next."

He paces back and forth for a second. He makes the game show buzzing noise again. "Sorry, wrong again. Now, where should we apply the punishment this time? Your feet? Nah, how about your hands? Nope—too early for that, too, although I do have only two more questions for you, so maybe it isn't too early for the face or hands. I vote face—what do you think?" He looks down at Phoebe for a moment. She is sobbing and doesn't answer him. "No opinion either way, huh? I guess I get to choose."

He places the knife up to her face. Using the blood already on the knife he draws a blood beard on her chin as she squirms under the knife. He looks at his artwork and laughs. "You would look funny with a beard, Phoebe."

He takes the knife to her forehead and slices it from left to right, cutting through the duct tape holding her head down to the bed. Phoebe lets out a scream as the suited man jumps back from her. He learned earlier from Rosie that the forehead bleeds a lot when it is cut open, and Phoebe's is no exception. Her blood is flowing pretty fast down the sides of her head and is pooling on the bed and her pillow. He leaves her side and goes into the attached bathroom whistling his favorite song. She hears water running shortly after he enters the bathroom.

He reappears, still whistling. A few moments later, he reappears dragging something from a rope behind him. Whatever he is dragging is very heavy, and he is struggling to pull it toward her. He drops the rope that he was pulling and walks toward Phoebe. He has a damp towel in his hand and places it on her forehead. "This might slow down the bleeding." He grabs the roll of duct tape that he brought with him and tapes it to her head. "Question number three: guess who I just dragged in here?"

Phoebe is still recovering from the painful cut on her forehead, but she knows the only other person in this house is her husband so she blurts out, "Mark. Mark is the person that you dragged in here."

The suited man claps his gloved hands together. The claps are very muffled from the leather gloves. "Hey, you got one right! That is good for you. So to backtrack a little bit to question number two, the answer is Mark."

The suited man walks over to Mark and looks down at him. His mouth is duct taped. He is lying in the fetal position with his hands wrapped around his knees and duct taped together. The suited man picks up the rope tied around Mark's wrists and legs and pulls it as hard as he can toward Phoebe's side of the bed. He takes the knife and puts it between Phoebe's head and the tape holding it in place. He makes one quick move and cuts the tape that is holding her head in place on the bed so she can turn her head toward Mark. "Have you anything to say to your husband before I take his life?" he asks her as he looks between her and Mark.

Phoebe decides to try to play the game. "Since I got the correct answer, shouldn't I win something?"

The suited man laughs so hard he bends over, holding his side. "I suppose you would be right if we were on some game show, but I was never one to follow the rules. At least I'm letting you say something to him, so consider that your prize—to be able to say farewell."

Phoebe turns her head toward Mark. "I love you, baby. I'm so sorry that this is happening. I just want you to know I never loved another man like I love you!"

That statement infuriates the suited man. He immediately thrusts the knife into Mark's side, right under his armpit. He hears Mark's ribs crack as he twists the knife back and forth. Mark is choking on his own blood filling his lung and bubbling up into his mouth. "Wow! I thought that would have killed you. I guess you are stronger than I thought." The suited man lifts up his right foot and stomps on Mark's head until he hears the skull cracking from the pressure. "That should do it."

Phoebe can no longer scream or cry. She is in complete shock from what she just saw. Her husband is lying on the floor in the fetal position with the knife still in his side and blood oozing out of his ear and nose from the crushed skull.

"I commend you for not screaming that time, Phoebe," he says as he wipes his shoe on the carpet, trying to get the blood off the sole. "Time for the final question, and this one could save your life. Guess who I am?"

Phoebe closes her eyes. Tears still flow from the corners of her eyes down the side of her face, mixing with the blood that has slowed down, thanks to the towel taped to her forehead. *Who is this guy? He obviously knows who I am. He knows my entire family and our history. Why is he doing this to me? I have seen those eyes before. Where? Think Phoebe, think. Oh my God.* She finally understands the unformed thought that has been tickling her brain since she first heard the man speak.

She gasps, "Mike. It's you, isn't it? Mike Hogan. My ex-husband from over twenty years ago." Her fear has changed to anger. She is yelling at him as if they are still married. "What the hell are you doing? Why are you killing my family? You bastard! I knew you were crazy, but I could have never dreamed of *this*."

"Congratulations, Phoebe! You won the big prize. I actually thought I was going to kill you without you knowing who it was that did it. You get to die knowing that the man that loved you and is the father of your child will get to watch your grandchild grow up while you will miss every minute of it."

His laugh is dry and cruel, like a hyena. She fights the tape, which opens up the wound on her forehead again. "Amanda hates you! She wants nothing to do with you. You will never see that child! So the joke's on you." she yells spitefully at him as the blood begins to run down her forehead into her eyes.

He starts pacing back and forth, mumbling the whole time, "You wasted my time. You wasted my time," over and over and over again.

"I wasted your time? Ha, ha. Don't make me laugh. You wasted my time. You were nothing and you still are. You have to kill people to make yourself feel good. You are nothing more than a pimple on the face of life. The person you should be killing is yourself. But you never could admit your own faults. Amanda knows the truth about you." Fueled by anger and remorse, she screams, "I shouldn't have married you in the first place."

Mike stops pacing. He moves quickly to her side and puts his face right next to hers. He sticks his tongue out and licks the blood from her cheek as she cringes. "You don't get it. I know that you lied to Amanda about me. I know you turned her against me. That is why you are going to die. Once you are dead, she will learn the truth from me. She will say she always loved me but didn't want to hurt your feelings by spending time with me over you. Without you around to stop her from seeing me, we will be happy again, spending time together and not having to worry about her bitch of a mother standing in our way. Then I get to see my grandchild every day if I want to, and there will be nobody around to lie to that child about me like you did to Amanda," he whispers directly into her ear.

Phoebe turns her head and laughs right into his face. "She will never agree to see you again. You will get caught and she will know the monster that you are and always were. You're pathetic. You're nothing."

Mike snaps up from his crouching position. He is so angry that he cannot stop mumbling. "You wasted my time. You wasted my time, and time is money," he yells, pacing back and forth, raising his arms and dropping them just as fast. He stops pacing and looks at his ex-wife. "You don't even know the best part. Remember twenty-seven years ago when we first got married? We took out a life insurance policy for both of us. Well, I have been paying on it all of these years, and I am the sole beneficiary in the event of your death. I will be able to stop working and spend all of my time with Amanda and her new family. I always say time is money, and the time you took from me is going to pay off big. So I guess I should thank you for that, but I won't because you deserve nothing more from me."

"Michael, Michael, Michael, it is you that doesn't understand. The police are going to know it was you. You just said yourself that you are the sole beneficiary of a life insurance policy on your ex-wife that you were divorced from for twenty-plus years. You are numero uno on the suspect list." She again starts laughing.

Mike yells, "Shut up!" so loudly that Phoebe eyes widen in fear and she recoils into the bed. "Phoebe, you never did pay much attention to what is happening in your own back yard. I have been killing people all week that have wasted my time. The cops are nowhere near finding me. They are going to think that you and your whole family are just another random murder, like the others. You will be nothing more than one of the many I've killed. The good news is that you will be my last ever. I don't want to push my luck after I'm rich." He steps back and smiles at her as he reaches into the inside pocket of his suit and pulls out a knife with a pearl handle. "Remember this?" he says to Phoebe as he waves the knife in front of her.

"Is that the knife we used to cut the cake at our wedding?"

Mike is laughing again as he climbs on top of Phoebe, straddling her. "Yep, the life insurance wasn't the only thing I kept up all of these years. I sharpened it, though, just for tonight. You see, I think it is fitting to stab you in the heart with it, just like you stabbed me in the heart all those years ago. Pretty ironic, isn't it?" He is now laughing uncontrollably. "Between the life insurance that you and Mark have, and all of the money that you undoubtedly left to Amanda, she will live a pretty good life. And both she and her child will be better off without you! Goodbye, Phoebe," he says as he stabs Phoebe through the heart. He feels the weight of twenty-five years of stress on his body lift from him like a kite on a windy day, just floating away. He looks one last time at the woman he loved so long ago and begins to whistle his song again.

He stands up and grabs the bolt cutters that he had set beside the bed earlier and cuts off her right index finger and thumb. He then looks down at Mark and does the same to him. He takes Mark's finger and thumb and writes *TIME WASTERS* on the wall above Phoebe's head. He walks toward the bedroom door and leaves. He is whistling the whole way out of the house.

4 A.M. SUNDAY MORNING.

Max Larkin is lying in the bed he had as a child at his parents' house. They left his room just like he left it seven years ago. It still has the Chicago Bears posters, along with the Chicago White Sox pictures all over the wall. He doesn't understand his mother's need to keep his room exactly as he left it, but he doesn't feel right taking anything down, like it really isn't his anymore. He wakes up suddenly to his cell phone ringing. He sees that it is Captain Perry. "Hello Captain, why are you calling me so early on a Sunday?…Damn it! Again?" There is a long pause as Max listens to Captain Perry explain the details to him. "I'll call Jesse and get over there. Text me the address." He ends the call and immediately dials Jesse's number.

Sleepily Jesse answers the phone.

"Hey, it's Max. Our guy killed again. He left the scene of the crime so fast that he didn't see a coyote crossing the street. He hit it in front of our victims' neighbor's house. When they went out to see what was going on, they saw a car driving away. They didn't get a license plate number because it was going so fast. However, they didn't recognize it as their neighbors' car so they went over to check on them and found two dead bodies and 'time wasters' written on the walls. Come and pick me up. Captain Perry is texting me the address as we speak."

He looks up from the phone and sees his mother standing in the doorway. "Is everything okay, sweetie?" You didn't have another nightmare, did you?" Ellen says, worry wrinkling her brow.

"No Mom, there is another murder. I have to get over there right away. Jesse is on her way to get me. Sorry I woke you up." He gets out of bed and walks past his mom on the way to the bathroom to brush his teeth. His mom is still standing in the hallway, watching him with great concern on her face. "I'll be okay, Mom. I promise. Now get some sleep before you wake up Dad." He walks back into his room and kisses her on the cheek as he passes her.

Jesse is in front of the house within minutes of him getting dressed and walking out the door with a cup of coffee he hastily made. He tells her the directions as he buckles himself in. "I hope we find something to help us this time," he says. "This is getting ridiculous. Nobody is this good at not leaving evidence. If we can't solve this soon, we may have to call in the feds."

Suddenly he slaps his forehead. "Hey just before you surprised me with your new car the other day, I was getting on to something. Then I forgot about it. It's about several of the victims. Guess what they had in common besides the obvious murder scene?"

Jesse shrugs. "What?"

"The doctor, the Bjornsons and my father all had just bought new cars just before their deaths."

Jessie's mouth opened in a silent scream. "My car salesman, Mike. He actually fit the description of our killer, which was kind of creepy at first. He has the same build, same hair color, and same color eyes. I really thought he might be at first by the way he was acting, so I slipped in a little comment during the test drive that I thought would trip him up, but he didn't even notice. I said I didn't want to waste time and he just kept right on showing me the car and its features. Not to mention, the salesman's name was Mike and our killer's name is Tom. But like I said, it was kind of creepy at first. I was ready to forget about him as a suspect. But think about it: a car salesman would have access to a lot of cars to drive. He also would make a good income if he was any good at his job. $211 an hour isn't much when you are talking about sales. It almost made sense, but then I figured he would have never talked to me because he has seen me and he would never take that risk. He would have pawned me off on another salesman and avoided me at all costs. It just didn't make sense, so I just let it go and kept thinking about getting my baby."

Max says, "He just made the hit parade. We have to visit him right after this murder scene investigation."

Jesse turns her head to her partner. He sees that she is ready to go after this guy. He is too, but rather than being adrenaline-fueled, he seems exhausted. *At the rate this killer is going, he could have the whole town killed within the month,* he thinks sarcastically to himself, feeling the thought is too morbid to share this early in the morning.

Max and Jesse arrive at the Newman home around 5:30 a.m. The coroner, ambulance, and patrol officers are already on the scene. Two patrol officers are interviewing the neighbor who witnessed the car driving away and also found the murder scene. According to Captain Perry's text, the male neighbor only saw the older couple's murder scene. He immediately called the police at that point and did not go farther into the house. When the patrol officers arrived, they discovered the brutal murder scene of the owners of the home, Mark and Phoebe Newman, as well. As Max and Jesse approach the home, they determine that the Newmans were very well-to-do. The killer doesn't seem to discriminate based on financial status. "The porch alone is bigger than my whole apartment. These people were definitely rich," Max says to Jesse as he opens the door to the Newman home.

Max and Jesse look around the front foyer area. It is loaded with crystal everywhere, from the chandelier to the crystal light fixtures lighting the hallways. A patrol officer sees them standing in the foyer and motions for them to come down the left hallway. They notice many paintings adorning the walls, each one with a plaque, similar to a gallery.

They enter the first murder scene. An older couple lies in the bed as if they are sleeping. The only reason to believe otherwise is the fact that both of them are missing a finger and a thumb. There is a small pool of blood under each of their missing fingers. "The fingers and thumbs were removed post mortem. It looks like they were smothered by their pillows," Max states. "Jesse, tell me what you see."

Jesse takes a moment and looks around the room. She pauses for a moment, "I see that these people do not live here. This seems to be a guest bedroom. There are not many amenities except for a small dresser and night stand. The whole house is very well decorated, yet this room seems to be plain in comparison. That tells me that the owners do not frequent this room very often. There are two suitcases in the corner of the room that are open with clothes still in them, indicating further that these people are just visiting." Jesse opens the closet and sees a very nice dress and nice dark suit hanging in the closet. "There are a suit and nice dress hanging in here, along with nice shoes on the floor. The garments seem to be the approximate sizes of our victims. I am thinking they are here for a special occasion, possibly a wedding or anniversary. The suit and dress seem a bit wrinkled so I would say that the event has already happened and they were just planning to stay through this weekend." Jesse puts her hands on her hips and smiles at her partner because she knows that she has gotten everything out of this scene that they can.

"Excellent job, Jesse! Now let's go to the other scene." Summoning a uniformed officer, he says, "Excuse me, could you lead us through this mansion to the other murders? I don't want to get lost in here," he jokes. The officer takes them up the stairs to the master bedroom.

They pass many other rooms. Max looks in a few of them. They pass a billiards room with a bright blue pool table. He also looks into a workout room with a treadmill, elliptical, and workout bench. They get to the master bedroom, with its French doors that open inward to a luxurious room. The bed sits along the back wall—a four-poster with curtains hanging off either side. Both sides of the bed have nightstands that are made of a dark wood, with silver lamps on each. Mrs. Newman lies on the side farthest from the door. She has been duct taped to the bed just like the previous murders. There is a knife sticking out of her chest. The knife has a pearl handle that has some blood on it. Next to her on the floor lies what the detectives can only assume is Mr. Newman. As the two detectives look over her body, they notice that her right index finger has been removed, as well as her thumb. Blood has started to soak through a towel that has been taped to her head. There are many blood pools on the bed, one under her head no doubt coming from the head wound under the towel. They also see blood stains by her legs that must have come from the cuts just under her kneecaps. A small blood pool from the finger and thumb is still growing. "Now, this is different. There seem to be extra fingers laying around. Hers are by her side. Her husband's are on the pillow and appear to be the ones used to write *TIME WASTERS* on the wall above the headboard of the bed. I don't remember seeing the other victim's digits laying around that room. Did you see them, Jesse?" She shakes her head no and sends the patrol officer to the other room to find them.

Jesse interjects, "I am betting those other people are her parents and the murderer wanted her to see that he had already killed them."

No words are spoken between the detectives as they turn their attention to the man lying on the floor next to the bed. His entire body is almost covered with duct tape. He was positioned in the fetal position and taped together to make sure he stayed that way. There is a rope around his wrists and legs. They can see drag marks in the deep shag carpet coming from the attached bathroom. Max points out the drag marks to Jesse. "It appears he was not in the room the whole time. He must have been duct taped in the bathroom and dragged back out here. I am thinking that our killer wanted his wife to see him kill her husband. Look at this," Max says as he points to the knife stuck into the man's side, with blood stains on his pajamas leading to a blood pool under him. "He stabbed him and appears to have twisted the knife to make sure that it killed him. However, take a look at this. He has blood coming from his ears." Max takes a close look at the man's head. "This appears to be a footprint on the side of his head. He was stepped on, repeatedly. The killer took this one personally. He wanted to make sure he suffered."

Max and Jesse decide they have seen enough of the murder scenes and want to let the coroner take the bodies. They leave the forensic team to do their thing. As they are walking toward the front door, they look throughout the house for signs of anything else that is out of place. In the formal living room next to the foyer, they see a slew of photos lying on the coffee table. There is also a black photo album next to the pictures. They walk into the room and see that the pictures are of a wedding. Based on the family pictures on the walls, it looks like it is their daughter's wedding. The date stamp in the lower left corner of all of the pictures is Saturday of last week. "This is the special event that the older couple came into town for, Max," Jesse tells her partner. "I'm willing to bet my whole paycheck on the fact that the girl in this picture is the daughter of the couple upstairs and the granddaughter of the couple downstairs."

Max stares at the pictures and agrees with Jesse. "We need to find out who she is, because I want to be the one to tell her about her parents. I feel a little kinship with her. We both lost our parents to this madman and I may be able to help her. Who knows, maybe sharing my story with a fellow survivor will help me as well."

Max picks up a few of the pictures and puts them in his pocket. He wants to be able to recognize the woman getting married and there is no better way than having a recent picture at his disposal. "Let's get back to the station and see if we can find a wedding announcement or anything else in the local papers to help identify her. That should be faster than looking through birth records for the Newmans. I don't want to wait until Monday," Max tells her as walks toward the door.

While most people in Rockton are coming home from church with their families or just waking up to enjoy the day off, Max and Jesse sit at the Rockton Police Station going through pictures and comparing them to local wedding announcements. "Max, I think I found her. Amanda Smythe of Rockton, daughter of Mark Newman and Phoebe Smythe-Newman, to marry Anthony Whitgrove of South Beloit on Saturday 3 p.m. at Christ Community Church of Rockton. That's our girl. It says here that they planned on honeymooning later in the year and will be residing in Rockton. We need to look up the address."

Max starts typing feverishly on his computer. "Way ahead of you, Jesse. Her house is about two minutes from here on Chicago Street." He stands up and grabs his jacket, walking briskly to the door, with Jesse trailing him.

Max looks uncomfortable in the passenger seat as they take the short trip from the police station to the Whitgroves. Jesse asks, "What's wrong, Max? You look uncomfortable."

"I know I volunteered to talk to her about her parents being killed, but I am a little nervous. I don't know what to say," Max says, fidgeting in his seat. "I think I will be okay once I start talking, but I need to do this, no matter what. Not to mention, I miss my car. I really like to drive and riding in the passenger seat is bugging me. I know you got a new car and it makes sense to let you drive, but I miss my baby." Max laughs, trying to lighten the mood in the car a little bit.

As they pull into the driveway of the Whitgrove home, they notice it is a pretty decent-sized home for a couple just starting out. It seems as though Amanda's parents may have bought it for them, either as a gift or just because they could afford it. The house is two–story, with a wrap-around front porch. There is a porch swing on the far side of the home.

Jesse grabs Max's arm. "Are you sure you can handle telling her this? If not, I will do it," she tells Max, knowing that this might be the most difficult thing Max has ever done in his life. "Telling someone that his or her parent has been murdered is hard enough, but knowing that the same person murdered your own parents has to be the ultimate worst thing to go through."

Max yanks his arm away from Jesse angrily. "I got this! Please stop treating me like a baby. I'll be fine. I'm just a little nervous, but like I said in the car, I'll be fine once I get going."

Max pushes the doorbell. The chime can be heard echoing through the house. There is a dog barking inside and the detectives hear the dog running across a wood floor. "Down Rusty, down," a woman's voice says to the dog as it jumps onto the front door. The door opens and a young woman is standing in the doorway holding the choke collar of what appears to be a black Labrador puppy. The dog is very excited to have visitors. His tail is going a mile a minute as he pants. "Hello, can I help you?" the lady says.

Max and Jesse pull out their badges and credentials, showing them to Amanda. "Are you Amanda Whitgrove?" Jesse asks before Max because he hesitates just a little too long. Max looks at Jesse angrily, telling her to be quiet without actually saying the words.

Amanda calls for her husband. "Tony, can you please come get the dog and chain him up outside? There are two police officers at the door." A man appears, grabbing the dog from Amanda. He is a tall black-haired man with a goatee. He is in pretty good shape; his t-shirt clings to his muscular body. "Yes, I am Amanda Whitgrove. How can I help you, officers?"

"Mrs. Whitgrove, may we come in please?" Max asks before Jesse can say anything.

Amanda opens the door and waves her arm to invite them in. Amanda takes them into a room with a sofa, loveseat, and reclining chair. She sits in the loveseat and tells the detectives to sit on the sofa.

Her expression shows great concern as to why they are there. Thoughts race through her mind of all of the worst-case scenarios she can come up with. "What is it? Has something happened to my mom?" She folds her hands together and puts them in her lap.

Her husband, Anthony, enters the room and sits next to her on the loveseat. He places his hand on top of her folded hands. "Is everything okay, sweetheart?" he asks his new bride.

"The officers were just about to tell me why they are here." She squeezes his hand tightly to brace for the news.

Max takes in a deep breath and Jesse notices that he swallows like a gulp of courage is going down his throat to help him deal with this bad situation. "I'm sorry, Mrs. Whitgrove. It's your mom. She was murdered last night, along with your father and another older couple that we have not identified yet. I am so sorry for your loss." Max feels an eerie déjà vu, like he is telling three-year-old Max that he is sorry for his loss, as well.

Amanda starts to cry uncontrollably. She throws her arms in the air and immediately puts them back down to her side. She drops her face into her hands and sobs, her shoulders heaving mightily. "You are wrong. This can't be happening! I just got married last week, and I found out I am pregnant last month. I can't do this without my mom. You must have made a mistake. Please tell me that you made a mistake!" she screams at the detectives from behind her hands.

"I'm truly sorry, Mrs. Whitgrove, but we don't believe we made a mistake." Max takes out one of her wedding pictures that has her mother, father, and her in it, handing it to her. "Is that your mom and dad with you in the picture?"

Amanda looks at the picture and caresses her mother's figure in the picture with her fingers. "Yes, that is my mom and stepfather—Mark and Phoebe Newman."

"Again, I must say I am sorry for your loss, Mrs. Whitgrove. Those are the two people that we found at their home on Wing Street. That is where their house is located. Correct?" Max asks to double check with her. She nods. "Can you tell us who the other couple is that was staying with your parents?" Max reaches into his pocket again to pull out a picture of the older couple. He hands her the picture.

She begins to cry harder. She starts hyperventilating a little, but Anthony calms her down by stroking her hair. "Nana? Pop-pop? They killed my grandparents, too?" she collapses into her husband's arms limply as she sobs into his shirt.

Jesse has been writing notes the whole time that Max spoke. "Okay, Jesse, you have that down: she identified her mom and dad."

Before Max can go any further Amanda interrupts him. "He is not my dad. He is my stepdad. My mom and dad got divorced when I was very young, so Mark pretty much raised me since I was six. He is more my dad than my actual father is. I haven't seen my real father in about ten years." She returns her head to her husband's chest to cry again.

"I am sorry to ask this of you, Mrs. Whitgrove, but can you tell me your grandparents' names besides Nana and Pop-pop? We need it for the file." Max pauses for a moment. "Also, can you give us your birth father's name? And if you know how to get hold of him, we would like to inform him also."

Amanda pulls her head away from her husband, trying to contain her tears. "He is all I have left of my family. My mom gave me his number a couple of years ago in case I wanted to talk to him again. I was the one who stopped wanting to see him ten years ago. I think I still have it stored in my cell phone." She reaches into her front pocket and pulls it out. She scrolls through the contacts and stops. She hands the phone to Max, who in turn hands the phone to Jesse.

Jesse looks at the phone and sees the name Mike with a phone number listed under the name. "You have your dad stored in your phone by his first name?" she asks Amanda.

Amanda nods her head. "Yes, like I said, I never wanted to see him again because of how he hurt my mother. But now I guess he is all I have left." She starts crying again.

"I understand completely, Mrs. Whitgrove." Jesse says as she continues to write the information. "His name is Mike Smythe, then, and do you know where your dad lives?"

Amanda stops crying and blows her nose in a tissue that her husband hands her. "His name is Mike Hogan. The last place I knew of was in Wisconsin somewhere. Reagan? No, it was another president's name. Lincoln? No, that isn't it. Clinton, that's it—Clinton, Wisconsin."

Jesse stops writing suddenly. She stops and pulls open her purse, fishing a moment and then retrieving a card. She stares at it and turns to Max and whispers, "It's him."

"Mr. and Mrs. Whitgrove, can you excuse us for a moment?" Jesse asks them as she grabs Max's arm and pulls him off the couch and into the dining room that is attached to the living room they were just sitting in. "Mike Hogan is the guy who sold me my car yesterday. Remember, I told you that he fit the description of our killer's body and hair, but he didn't sound like him or have the same name?"

Max stands perfectly still, pondering what Jesse just said. "Are you thinking what I am thinking?" Jesse nods her head. "Do you really think the killer of her mom and stepdad, her grandparents, my parents, and all the rest is a car salesman in Wisconsin? Do you think that he actually would sell a car to one of the detectives who has been hunting him down for almost a week?" His eyebrows arch. "If you want to talk coincidence, not only is all that probably true, but he is the same man who murdered your dad twenty-five years ago."

Jesse thinks it through. "I know it is farfetched, but it makes sense. He has cars available, he works odd hours, and he wears a suit for his job. Amanda just said they had a falling out ten years ago, and I will give you ten-to-one odds that her parents divorced twenty-five years ago. I say let's get him here to see his daughter in her time of need. While he is here, we can bring him in to identify the body or something, and then start questioning him. I may be wrong, but what else do we have right now?"

Max gives her a smile and they both go back to the living room. Max remains standing as Jesse sits back down on the loveseat. "Mrs. Whitgrove, I think it's best that you call your dad, Mike, and ask him to come here so we can tell him about your mom. Would that be okay with you?" Max asks Amanda.

Amanda's face is scrunched up like she is thinking really hard about the request. "I guess so. Like I said, he is all I have now, so I probably should mend the fence." She pulls her phone from her pocket and looks up his number again in her contacts. She sits there with a tissue to her nose while she waits for the connection.

Max interjects, "Please don't tell him we're here. We don't want him to be upset on his way here. It is best we tell him when he gets here." Amanda nods her head in agreement.

Right after Max stops speaking, Mike answers his phone. "Hello, Daddy?" Amanda says into the phone, sounding like a little girl. "It's me, Amanda. I need to see you. I'm sorry, too, Daddy. Can you please come to my house in Rockton? I miss you, too. My address is 440 Chicago Street. See you soon, Daddy. I love you, too." She ends the call. "He is on his way. Detective, can you tell him, please? I don't think I can."

"Of course I can, Mrs. Whitgrove. Anything I can do to help," Max says. "My partner and I are going to step outside for awhile. We will be back in a few minutes. Again, I am sorry for your loss." Max holds out his hand to help Jesse get up from the cushy loveseat. She refuses it and gets out of it on her own.

On the front porch, Max grabs her by the arm and spins her toward him. "Okay Jesse, this is your show. How do you want to handle it?"

Jesse considers all of the options. "First thing I am going to do is move my car down the street a little bit. He will definitely recognize it, considering he just sold it to me yesterday. I think we should call Captain Perry and let him know what's going on. We'll go back into the house and wait. When he arrives, we'll tell him about his ex-wife, her husband, and his ex-in-laws. After that, we will give them both the song and dance about actually identifying the bodies. We should have a patrol car standing by so we can take them both in the patrol car, saying it is best they don't drive in their emotional state. We will follow them in the patrol car back to the station, taking them both to the morgue and have them identify the body of Phoebe Newman. We need to watch his facial expression when he sees the body. Maybe he will give us something that might help us during the interrogation. After that, we take him to an interview room and we both go after him *hard*. I truly think he is our guy. We just need to get a confession because other than speculation, we have absolutely nothing. Agreed?"

Max has a smirk on his face. "I think that's an excellent plan. I'll call the Captain while you move your car down the street."

Max calls Perry and explains what they are doing, including why they need the car waiting. Jesse moves her car around the corner. She runs back to Max on the porch at the Whitgrove house. "Okay Jesse, Captain Perry is up to speed and he will meet us at the station. The patrol car is on standby and will be just around the corner. Now we just have to wait. He should be here in about ten minutes. I think we should stay out here and let the newlyweds have some time together before this all goes down. They have to be going through mental and emotional hell right now."

Five minutes pass before the two detectives go back into the Whitgrove house. Amanda Whitgrove is crying uncontrollably into her husband's chest. He is trying to console her as best he can, but he is not succeeding. She hears the door to the house open and she looks up at the detectives hopefully. "Sorry, I thought you might be my father," she says, her face falling back into sadness.

Max puts his hand on Amanda's shoulder. "Mrs. Whitgrove, we are going to wait for your father in the other room. It is best that he doesn't see us right away, because we don't want him to be upset before he sees you. It has been a long time since you two have seen each other, and we don't want his first time seeing you to be with two police officers standing over you both. Is that okay? I promise I will only wait a minute or two, so you won't have to tell him what has happened."

Max and Jesse go through the dining room toward the kitchen to wait for Mike. Within a few minutes, the doorbell rings. Max looks out and sees it is a man wearing a University of Wisconsin sweatshirt and jeans. He thinks, *Must be his day off. He isn't wearing a suit.*

"Hey Jesse, is that your salesman?" he asks his partner.

Jesse looks around him and sees the man standing in the front room talking to Amanda and Anthony Whitgrove. She nods silently. Max can't help but notice how he does indeed fit the description that Melissa and Korrina gave them. Their descriptions were vague, but what they did say matches Mike Hogan to a tee. The officers walk out of the kitchen toward the living room where the united family is sitting.

Amanda has not told her father anything, but they are both crying from the emotional reunion. Mike looks up and sees the detectives coming toward them. "What are you doing here, Ms. Fairlane? Is something wrong?"

Jesse and Max enter the living room. Max positions himself between the front door and Mike, while Jesse remains in the entranceway to the living room from the dining room and kitchen, essentially blocking the rear exit. They have to make sure he doesn't leave suddenly.

Jesse takes a step forward and puts her hand on Amanda's shoulder. "Mr. Hogan, Amanda asked us to be the ones to tell you that something has happened to her mother. She and her husband were murdered last night. Her grandparents were visiting from out of town, and they were also murdered." Jesse pauses to watch how Mike reacts to this news. She is hoping he makes some kind of move that will help her determine if he is indeed the killer. "I am truly sorry for your loss."

Mike breaks down crying. He drops to his knees as if he is going to pray. Throwing his arms into the air, he yells, "No! I will always love you, Phoebe." He continues to cry as he reaches up for his daughter's hand. She grabs his hand and cries with him

Amanda, still crying, pulls her head away from his hand long enough to say, "I'm so sorry, Daddy. I wish I didn't do what I did ten years ago. I love you and now that Mom is gone, I need you more than ever."

Jesse notices a smile growing on Mike's face, even though his head is turned downward. She wonders how a man who just heard a woman he still loved was dead could smile. His smile quickly morphs back to an expression of sadness.

Max now takes a step forward from where he was observing all that has transpired over the last few moments. He places a hand on Mike's shoulder. "I'm sorry for your loss, sir. Please be strong for your daughter. She needs you now more than ever." Max pats him on the back. "I am so sorry I have to ask you this, but we need you both to come to the station with us. I need you to identify the bodies. I know this is a hard time, but we need to verify identity before we can release the bodies for a funeral."

Amanda breaks down in a flurry of tears as she puts her head into her husband's chest. Anthony tells Max they will come down right away. Max pulls ever so gently on Mike's shoulder so he can see his face. "If it's all right with everyone, I will have a patrol car come right over and pick you up. I think it's safer that we take care of the driving, given the news you have just received. Is that okay with you, sir?" Max looks down at Mike. He's been keeping his face covered or down, but he does nod affirmatively to Max.

Max grabs his cell phone from his pocket and dials Captain Perry. "Hello, Captain. It's Larkin. We found the family of the Newmans. We are going to need a car to pick them up. Okay, we'll keep an eye out for it." He ends the call. "Captain said there is a patrol car doing his rounds only a few blocks from here and he will pull him off that detail to come right over."

It is only a matter of moments before the patrol car arrives. Max leads everyone out the door to go identify the remains of their fallen family. The patrol officer secures the family in the back seat and drives off toward the police station. Max waits for Jesse to bring her car around so they can follow. As he stands there, he notices the car that Mike is driving has some damage to the front end. Just under the license plate, the plastic is broken and there appears to be fur stuck in the crack. Max walks up to the car and pulls out some of the fur. He pulls out a tissue from his back pocket and places the fur inside the tissue. He takes a picture with his cell phone, making sure to get the license plate in the picture.

The little red sports coupe pulls up to the curb and Max rushes in. "Check this out." Max opens the tissue to reveal the fur. "It was stuck in the front plastic of Mike's dealer car. Looks like he hit something—say an animal? What did you think of his performance in there? Believe him?"

Jesse guffaws. "The Newmans' neighbor said they heard a car hit an animal as it sped down the street. And the patrol officers confirmed that they found a coyote that was hit by a car. As for believing him, are you kidding me? He is not *that* good a salesman. When his daughter told him she needed him, he tried to hide it but he *smiled*. Who smiles at a time like this?" She shrugs. "Do you have a plan of attack, Max? Remember, we need a confession because we have no evidence putting him at these crime scenes yet— at least, not in the houses."

Max thinks for a moment while Jesse drives. He doesn't have long because the station is in sight and they can see the family exiting the patrol car. "I was thinking that after they identify the Newmans' bodies, we separate them. Put him in one room and the daughter and her husband in another room. We can let McCarren question the daughter because I don't believe she had anything to do with it. As for Mike, since he has such a problem with women, we both will go in there and I will let you do the talking. I think a woman showing power over him might actually make him crack. Sound good to you?"

Jesse smiles. She cannot help but think, *I cannot believe that he is going to let me take the lead on the questioning. It is not only my first murder case; it is my first case as a detective, period. Please Lord, do not let me screw this up!*

"Sounds good to me, partner. As long you think I'm ready." She takes a deep breath as butterflies the size of pterodactyls bounce around in her stomach.

Max and Jesse arrive at the morgue in the basement of the station. Mike, Amanda, Anthony, and a patrol officer are all standing at a window, waiting for the bodies to be shown. They can see them covered with sheets.

Patrol Officer James Royter walks from the window toward the detectives. "I'm Officer Royter. I was the first responding officer on the Bjornson case. Are these murders by the same guy?" he quietly asks the detectives.

Max reaches out and shakes his hand. "Thanks for such great notes on that scene. It has helped our investigation so much. Yes Officer Royter, we do believe this is the act of the same man."

Officer Royter shakes his head slightly. "I hope you catch this guy soon. We waited for you guys before uncovering the bodies of the family, per Captain Perry's instructions. Let me know if you need anything else." Officer Royter excuses himself.

Max and Jesse walk up to the grieving family. Jesse reaches out and touches Amanda's shoulder. "Amanda, are you ready for this? I must warn you all that the bodies and faces have cuts and blood. You must look past that to identify your family members. We'll try to make this as quick as possible."

Amanda looks at her husband and then her father. Mike gives Jesse a nod and Max knocks on the window so the coroner can pull back the sheets one by one. The first two bodies are the grandparents. Amanda confirms that they were indeed her Grandmother and Grandfather Smythe. The next body is Mark Newman. His face and head are horribly mutilated. Amanda puts her head into her husband's chest and begins to cry. Anthony confirms that it is indeed Mark Newman.

Jesse knocks on the window and when the coroner looks up, she puts up her index finger to signal him to give them a minute. She puts her hand back on Amanda's shoulder. "Amanda, do you want to continue? I know this is hard, but it needs to be done. Is it okay if he continues?"

Amanda pulls away from her husband. She reaches out for her father's hand and he reciprocates. As they hold hands, he pulls her in close to him. He releases her hand and puts his arm around her. He squeezes her tight and gives a nod to Jesse. Jesse knocks on the window and the coroner removes the sheet from the next gurney.

Amanda collapses in her father's arms at the sight of her mother's mutilation. Mike holds her up and covers her eyes as he pulls her in close to him. "That's her. That is my ex-wife, Amanda's mother, Phoebe Newman. Can I take my daughter home now? I think she has been through enough," Mike pleads with the detectives.

Max can feel the sorrow coming from Amanda and Anthony. Mike puts on a show that he is sad and he sheds a few tears, but Max sees through that façade. There is a sense of victory and power emanating from Mike. The tears are there, but not the true grief he is trying to pass off. "Unfortunately, sir, we have some questions for you and your daughter. Please follow us. We'll make it as quick as possible."

Amanda lifts her head. "It's okay, Daddy. I need to do this for Mom. If there is anything I can do, Detectives, please ask me. I will be okay."

Amanda, Anthony, and Mike follow Max as he leads them upstairs, with Jesse following behind. Captain Perry is waiting in the squad room. He signals McCarren over to the empty desk, where he is perched near the interrogation rooms. "Mr. and Mrs. Whitgrove, I am Captain Perry and this is Detective McCarren. We are very sorry for your loss." He extends his hand to Anthony. They shake hands. "Could you please go with Detective McCarren? He wants to get some basic information from you and to ask you a few questions. Detectives Larkin and Fairlane, please take Mr. Hogan into room two to get his information, as well."

Mike stops in his tracks. "Can I please stay with my daughter?"

Captain Perry gestures for the Whitgroves to continue down the hall with McCarren and turns to Mike. "Sorry, sir, we need to find out where each of you were last night and we need to do that separately. It's standard procedure. Don't worry—it won't take long and then you can take your daughter home and help her get through this tough time."

Mike reluctantly follows Jesse and Max into room two.

'18

The dreary gray color of the room is a mute contrast to the detectives' moods. Mike walks over to the window covered in wire mesh and bars on the far wall. He positions himself facing away from the mirrored wall, behind which someone might be watching him. There is a table with one chair on either side of it in the middle of the room. On the table sits a yellow note pad and a pen on top of that. Max looks up at the camera in the room to make sure the red light is flashing. If they get a confession, he wants to make sure it is recorded. "Have a seat, Mr. Hogan." He pulls out the chair facing the mirror for Mike to sit, while Jesse takes the opposite chair. Max stands behind Mike and leans against the wall while Jesse starts her questions.

Jesse writes the date on the paper in the top right corner. "Your name is Mike Hogan and you live in Clinton, Wisconsin—is that correct, sir?" He nods. "You are the ex-husband of Phoebe Newman and the father of Amanda Whitgrove. Is that correct?" Again, Mike agrees with her. She writes his answers on the paper. "Can you please tell me where you were this past Saturday night into early Sunday morning?"

Mike is fidgeting in his chair. "As you know, I work at the Clinton Auto Emporium and I was there until we closed at 7 p.m. Actually, I had a customer who bought a car late so I was there until about 8 p.m. I can't leave until my customer does, and our finance manager really took his time with these people. After that, I went out for a beer with Brandon Witfield. He is a salesman at my dealership. We went to Magilicutty's Bar in Clinton. We stayed there until they closed the bar. That was around 1 a.m.; after that I went home. I was a little buzzed so I went right to bed and woke up when my daughter called. I went over to her house and now I am here. Can I go now?"

Jesse is writing nearly as fast as Mike is talking. "We are almost done here—just a few more questions. Were you alone at your place after the beer you had with…" Jesse looks down at her notes, "Brandon Witfield?"

"Yes, I went home alone. I was there all alone until Amanda called. I like sleeping in on Sundays and, normally right now, I'd be watching football. But you have me here wasting my time." Both detectives silently flinch at the comment. Mike is now starting to squirm and look impatient.

Max motions to Jesse to keep going by putting his hands together and pulling them apart slowly. He then walks over toward the mirror so he can see Mike's face.

Jesse gets Max's signal. "You drive a dealer car. Correct?"

"I am a car salesman so yes, I do get a demo to drive. You saw it in Amanda's driveway today. I need to get it back home because I shouldn't take it out of state." Mike's feelings are starting to show a lot in his face. He is getting angrier as the questions keep coming.

Jesse puts down the pen. "Oh, so that is your car that we saw with the cracked plastic front and animal fur in the crack? How did that happen exactly?" she asks as she leans back in the chair.

"Oh, that—it must have happened last night when I was driving home from the bar. I told you, I was little buzzed." He leans in toward Jesse, "Good thing you are not a cop in Clinton or you would have to bust me for driving under the influence." He winks at her and sits back with his arms crossed.

Jesse does not show any fear at all and stands up so she can lean in to Mike's face. "What would you say if I told you that the Newmans' neighbors reported a car speeding from their house and said that same car hit a coyote as it was flying down the street?"

Mike pulls back away from her. "First of all, stay out of my face, lady. Second, I was nowhere near that bitch's house." Mike's anger is now bubbling to the surface. His face is turning red and a vein is pulsating on his forehead.

Jesse pulls back and puts an inquisitive look on her face, "Bitch? You were just saying how much you loved her at Amanda's house. Now that your daughter isn't around, Phoebe is a bitch? Interesting…"

Mike forces himself to calm down a little. "That's not what I meant. Yes, I still love her, but she left me twenty-five years ago and I never really forgave her. That is what I meant. Stop twisting my words."

The door to the interrogation room opens. Captain Perry peeks his head inside the door. "Detective Larkin, can I see you for a second?" He holds the door open for Max.

Max walks out, very upset. "What is it, Captain? I think she is about to get him to crack and you pull me out here for what?"

Captain Perry hands Max a piece of paper, the lab report saying that the fur on the car did indeed belong to a coyote, but without the coyote that was killed by the Newman's house to compare it to, they can't confirm that it came from that coyote. The officers had left the dead coyote by the side of the road and it was not there when they went to pick it up later.

"McCarren has taken Amanda and Anthony home. I also sent a copy of a warrant that I have gotten to search Mike's apartment to the Clinton Police department. They are going to search his place for any blood evidence and get right back to me." He hands a copy of the warrant to Max. "She's doing well, but make sure if she starts to slip that you jump in, okay? We can't lose this guy because of a rookie mistake."

Max agrees and takes the report and warrant into the room with him. He enters the room and hands them both to Jesse. He whispers into her ear, "Use these."

Jesse looks down at the papers. "Tsk, tsk, Mike, this report shows that the fur on your car is from a coyote."

Mike jumps from his seat. "That means nothing. I told you, I probably hit the coyote on the way home from the bar—nothing illegal about that."

Max puts his hand on Mike's shoulder. "Sit down, sir, before I make you sit down. Are we clear?"

Mike sits down calmly. "Sorry, Detective, it won't happen again." Mike is now calmly breathing in and out, trying to get his wits about him. *I can't let her get to me. Stay calm, Mike; they have nothing on you,* he thinks.

Jesse looks at the other piece of paper. "Oh, what do we have here? It's a search warrant for your place in Clinton. What do you think we will find there, Mike? Some bloody clothes maybe, or maybe even a bloody set of bolt cutters?"

Max chuckles a little bit by the far wall, and Mike jerks his head around to stare him down. "Want to make it easier on us all, Mike, and just tell us what happened?" Jesse says confidently.

Mike leans in close to Jesse. He is very calm for a man who has just been told his home is being searched for evidence against him. "You won't find anything at my apartment because I didn't do anything. You have nothing on me and soon you'll see that. Now quit wasting my time, bitch. I don't know how much you make, but it can't be much. To me, time is money."

Jesse starts to look flustered. She is flipping through the note pad and the papers Max handed to her. The Captain opens the door and asks Jesse and Max to come out for a second. They both leave the room and stand in front of the two way mirror, watching Mike. Mike gets up and walks over to the mirror, fixing his hair. He is very calm. Captain Perry looks at Max. "I told you to jump in if she struggles. Now he thinks he has her flustered. Jesse, you stay here. Max, get in there and close this guy."

An officer hands Perry a fax from Clinton PD. "Great! There is absolutely nothing bloody at his apartment. The only things of importance are the three bolt cutters that are the same make and model as the one we found at the Bjornson house. No blood on them, though. Max, it is time for you to go do what you do best."

Max grabs Jesse by the arm. "Okay, but she is coming with me. She got him flustered and he has a problem with women. We can use her to get to him some more."

Captain Perry rolls his eyes. "Fine, but get it done! He knows we've got nothing on him. Pull that confession out."

As Captain Perry finishes talking, McCarren walks up to listen. "I took the daughter home. She wondered why we still have her dad. I told her that we just wanted to ask him a few more questions and that he will be brought back to her soon. It seemed to appease her. Hey Captain, can I listen in on the great Max Larkin and his flunky?"

Jesse sticks her tongue out at McCarren before she follows Max back into the room. Max sits down at the table, this time directly across from Mike. Mike still looks pretty confident. "Let me guess—your Captain just told you that they didn't find a thing at my apartment, which proves I didn't do anything that you are saying I did."

Max puts his hands on the table and stands up. He moves over to where Mike is sitting. He grabs the back of his chair and spins it away from the table. He jams his face about two inches from Mike's face and glares into his eyes for a second or two. "You're right. They didn't find anything at your apartment except for some bolt cutters that match the ones we found at another murder scene last week. But I do have some bad news for you. We do have an eyewitness that puts you at a murder scene."

Mike pulls away from Max and spins his chair back toward the table, glowering at the mirror. "I read the papers about those murders. There were no witnesses that saw the killer's face because he wore a mask. So again, I say you don't have a thing on me."

Jesse now steps forward and slams her hands on the table. Max and Mike both jump, startled. "Come on, Mike, you know we have you for the Bjornson murders, that young girl Amber, Doctor Patel, the whole Newman family, and the florist. Just tell us why. Come on, Mike, you know you want to tell us," she says, in a scolding tone of voice.

Mike is not only startled, but angry again. "I told you, bitch, I never killed anyone. I don't know the Bjornsons. I don't know any girls named Amber. I never met Doctor whatever-Indian-name-you-gave and I certainly don't know Rosie, the florist. So get out of my face."

Jesse eyeballs Max. "I didn't say the florist's name was Rosie. Did you, Max?"

Max shakes his head. "Nope, I sure didn't say her name was Rosie."

Mike seems flustered and starts to stutter when answering questions. "I must have read it in the paper. It doesn't matter. I don't know her either."

Jesse is pretty confident now. She knows that they have the right guy. "Yeah, well, we never released her name to the papers. Her son is on vacation and he is next of kin. So until he comes forward, we can't release the name. You want to lie to us again, or do you want to tell us why you killed all of these people?"

Mike's face is turning crimson. He is biting his lip. He begins to stand up and Max pushes him back down by his shoulders. "You have nothing on me. Rosie is the only florist in town so I must have seen her name somewhere. Besides, she did the flowers for my daughter's wedding last weekend and…"

Jesse stops him mid-sentence. "Your daughter Amanda got married last weekend and we have seen the pictures. You are nowhere to be seen in them. Plus, your daughter told us she hasn't seen you in about—what was it?" Jesse looks at Max, who shrugs his shoulders in return. "…ten years. And that is about the same time that there was a murder in Clinton with the same M.O. as these murders. And that just happens to be the town you live in. Hmm… Coincidence? I think not."

Mike is still steaming while listening to Jesse talk. He knows he has to calm down before he lets something slip out of anger. He takes a deep breath. "Yeah, we had a falling out and no, I wasn't at the wedding. But that doesn't matter. I've said it before and I will say it again: you've got nothing on me. *I am leaving.*" He pushes hard against the table with his hands to stand up, pushing back the table toward the wall.

Max bars Mike's way. His head is tilted to the right and is about an inch from Mike's face. "Sit down. We are not through here yet." Max blocks his way out and doesn't flinch as Mike tries to stare him down. "Sit down or I will sit you down," Max growls. Mike sits down and sighs. He turns his head toward Jesse, his eyes roll up till only the whites are showing and his face is the mask of evil that would make most people cringe in fear. Jesse, however, smiles back at him.

Max grabs Jesse by the arm and leads her out of the room. Before she leaves, she turns to Mike. "We are thirsty and going to get some water. Do you want some, Tom?"

Mike doesn't hesitate. "No, that's fine. I won't be here much longer."

Max and Jesse both stop, turn around, and walk right back into the room. Jesse starts laughing. "So your name is Tom? Not Mike? Or is that just the name you gave to your girlfriend, Rosie? You see, we know all about the alias you gave her. She told her friends she was in love with a guy named Tom that fits your description. Now you answered to that name. Hmm… Now that seems rather peculiar, wouldn't you say, Max?"

Max's head ratchets back and forth between the two of them. "Hey, Mike, what do you say I ask the lady to leave so we can have a man-to-man? She has to be driving you nuts. I know she is getting on my nerves."

Mike is taken aback. "Hell yes. She is driving me nuts, twisting my words and all. Shouldn't she just go get us some coffee and donuts or something?" Mike looks right at Jesse as he says this.

Jesse loses her cool and lunges forward at Mike. "I'll get you a needle for your arm, you piece of…"

Max cuts her off and grabs her. "Hey, Jesse, let Mike and me talk for a few minutes. It will be okay." He stares her in the eyes, and they communicate on a subliminal level.

Jesse starts to walk toward the door. She is fuming and turns to him. "I'll be back, scumbag. Don't get too comfortable." She leaves the room and stands next to McCarren and Captain Perry, watching Max do his thing. "I don't get it, Captain, why would Max kick me out of there? I was just about to get him. I know it."

Captain Perry turns to her and pats her on the back. "You did great, kid. But one thing I have learned in the six years I have worked with Max is that he always has a plan, and now you get to see the full effect of that plan."

Max grabs the other chair opposite Mike and wedges it under the doorknob. Perry is alarmed, as Max hasn't done this before. "That should keep her out of here!"

Max turns toward Mike and moves his hands like a duck quacking. "Women—am I right? The worst part is I have to ride with her all day. Oh and by the way, thanks for selling her that little car. Now my knees will forever be in my chest whenever she drives." Max is laughing like he is talking with an old friend.

Mike starts to laugh along, too. "I don't know how you do it, man. I couldn't handle a woman like that in my life." He shakes his head.

Max gathers his thoughts for a few seconds, taking a deep breath. "Hey, Mike, I need you to do me a favor. If you do this for me, I think I will be able to end this ordeal and we both can stop wasting each other's time." Mike nods assent. "Lean in to me and look me straight in the eyes. That is all I ask."

Mike seems taken aback by such an easy request. What could he possibly gain from this? He leans into Max's face. Mike blinks, and their eyes are now deep in one another's. After a few seconds, Mike pulls away from Max and sits back in his chair. "Great! I did you your favor, so can I go now?"

Max takes in a very deep breath. "I have only one more question for you." Max stands up and faces the mirror, moving his hands in a way that simulates him pushing down on something. He is telling the others to be patient with him. He turns to Mike and kicks the table hard toward Mike. It comes close to hitting Mike but stops short, startling him. He jumps out of his seat. "What the hell, man? You said if I did you that favor I could go!"

Max moves quickly over to Mike and pins him against the wall. Max hears people fumbling at the door, trying to get in. "We don't have much time, so I am going to ask you this question one time and one time only. You better answer it, or it won't matter who comes in here. They will not be able to save your life. Got it?"

"Yeah, I got it," Mike screams out.

"Why did you kill my parents?" The noises coming from the door stop. "Why, Michael, did you kill my parents? Tell me!"

On the other side of the glass, Captain Perry pulls Jesse off to the side. "Care to tell me what the hell is going on here? What is Larkin talking about? He was just at his parents' yesterday. They are still alive."

Jesse gives a thumbnail sketch of the situation. "Captain, you told me to trust Max when he kicked me out. Now I am asking you to trust him. He's in control." Captain Perry, Jesse, and McCarren turn their attention back to the window.

"I have no idea what you are talking about, you psycho cop. I didn't kill your parents." He forces his head to the left of Max so he can see the mirror. "Get in here and get this guy off me."

Max keeps his grip on Mike's shoulders. "Hey Mike, do you remember how I told you there's an eyewitness? Well, I am that eyewitness. I am the little boy you made talk to the 911 operator twenty-five years ago. You killed my parents when I was three years old. I wasn't sure we had the right guy until you stared into my eyes today, just like you did twenty-five years ago. I have had nightmares about you and I remember those eyes staring at me through the ski mask—your eyes, to be exact. Gold flecks in them. I'll never forget. So again I ask you, why did you kill my parents? What could they have possibly done that made you want to kill them? Tell me now, or God help you!" Max rears his right arm back and slaps his hand against the wall right next to Mike's ear so he can hear the force that Max has in his arms.

Mike locks eyes with Max and smiles. "I have no idea what you are talking about, you nut job. I suggest you let go of me before I sue you, the entire department, and maybe even the city."

The door bursts open. Captain Perry and Jesse storm into the room.

Max releases him and uses both of his hands to brush off Mike's shoulders where he had a tight grip only a few moments ago. "You are free to go, Mike. Sorry for the inconvenience. I must be mistaken. You're not the man I thought you were."

Mike shakes his shoulders and walks toward the door. "You are damn right you're mistaken." He walks past Jesse and smiles. "Thanks for wasting my time, gorgeous." He winks as he passes her, whistling as he walks out the squad room door.

Jesse turns to her partner. "What the hell? You and I both know we have the right guy and you just let him waltz out of here, whistling. We need to press him harder."

Captain Perry grabs both of his young detectives by the arm and pulls them into his office. "You two are suspended for a week each without pay until a review board goes over what the hell just happened here." He looks directly at Max. "I expected more from you. You do not hide things like your parents being killed and you being the boy who dialed 911 twenty-five years ago from me. What the hell were you thinking, staying on this case? You almost cost us the whole case against this nut. As it is, we still have nothing and now I have to turn this investigation over to McCarren. Damn it, Max, you really let me down. Now get out of here, both of you." Max and Jesse both take their detective shields out of their respective pockets and place them on Captain Perry's desk as they leave the office.

Max and Jesse leave the squad room and head toward the parking lot. Once outside, he stops Jesse by pulling her shoulder. "I got this, Jesse. We'll have this guy soon. I have a plan."

J esse Fairlane lies in bed tossing and turning as she sleeps, dreaming about what just happened to her in her first week as a detective. She suddenly feels a pinch in her neck. She awakes from her slumber long enough to see a fuzzy figure standing over her. Feeling lightheaded, she realizes she has just been drugged by the man she and Max have been hunting for the last week. She tries to shake the effects of the drugs, but the more she tries, the faster they seem to work, and she drifts off into a drug-induced sleep.

Jesse awakens from a slap across her face from a hand wearing a leather glove. Her eyes pop open, but her vision is still blurry. She blinks a few times, clearing her eyes. She feels the pressure of something heavy sitting on her stomach. The blurry vision starts to subside and she sees a man in a suit wearing a ski mask straddling her. She tries to lift her arms, but as she pulls on them, she can feel the tape adhesive pulling on her skin. She squirms around, trying to shake him off, but he just sits there staring at her. He tilts his head a few times and smiles, his white teeth gleaming like some sort of demon in the dark.

"Good morning, Detective," the man says in a raspy voice.

Jesse thinks that he is trying to mask his voice. "Really, Mike, after all you and I have been through, did you honestly think I wouldn't recognize your smile, your eyes? I can tell it is your voice, even though you are trying to make it sound different. You're truly pathetic." She starts to laugh.

Mike pulls his mask off. "You're right, Jesse. It is just silly of me to try and hide who I am now. You are not going to be able to tell anyone about this anyway, after I finish ridding the world of you and your time-wasting ways." He gets up from her stomach and starts to pace beside her bed. He starts to mumble softly at first, but it gets louder each time he turns around and paces the other way. Jesse can finally hear what he is saying after the third go-round. "You wasted my time. Time is money." She sees him getting angrier as his voice gets louder. "Why did you have to waste my time today? I could have spent that time with my daughter, but you had to push me. I wanted to stop after killing my ex and her dumbass husband, but you had to push me." He pulls a knife from his inside jacket pocket.

Jesse is lying in her bed, her eyes lasering on Mike as he paces. "Mike, I get it. I understand that your ex-wife wasted your time for many years, but you and I both know that if you kill me, Max will find you and he will bring you to justice and maybe even kill you. You saw him today—he almost lost it in front of our captain. Do you really think he will be able to hold back after you kill his partner?"

Mike stops dead in his tracks. He leans into her, his hot breath tickling her ear. "Then it is a good thing that I am heading over to his place right after this. He won't be looking for me because he will no longer be wasting his or my time anymore after tonight." He laughs uncontrollably into her ear. Pulling his head away, he sits on the bed next to Jesse. "You see, Jesse, you and Max will be my final triumph before I retire from helping the world shake off the time wasters like a dog shakes off fleas. I truly did want to stop after my ex. I have everything I want now: my daughter back in my life, the life insurance money from my ex and soon, I'll take my daughter, her new husband, and my new grandbaby away from all of this. I figure they'll all enjoy a nice tropical setting where nobody will ever find me. They will just think it is my way of making up for all of the time I lost with my daughter. In reality, I will have gotten away from this city and the police trying to catch me."

Jesse starts shaking her head. "Like I said, I get killing your ex and her family, but why kill Amber? Why kill the Bjornsons, and why did you kill that young doctor? And I need to know why you killed Max's parents all those years ago. I am sure he is going to ask you the same question later tonight, but I need to know before I leave this world."

Mike hovers closely over Jesse as he places his left hand to her right side He tilts his head down toward her face. "I guess I can give you that satisfaction, at least." He takes a deep breath. "I killed the Bjornson family for wasting my time at the dealership. They spent hours with me and didn't buy the car. The same goes for that Indian doctor kid. He truly wasted my time that very day. He took all of my time and then bought a different type of car from a different dealer. That is pretty much the same story for everyone that I exterminated from this world like the insects they were. Even Max's parents wasted my time all of those years ago. The young girl, Amber—she was different than most of my work. She was unique in the fact that she only wasted about fifteen minutes of my time. She took too long in the coffee shop line the morning before the day of her death. I was in a hurry to go see my girl, Rosie, that day and she just couldn't decide what she wanted. I truly didn't want to kill her, but after killing the doctor, I just didn't feel satisfied and she did waste my time, after all—and as you know, time is money."

Jesse listens intently to his story. "Why did you cut off fingers and thumbs from most of the people? Why did you stick the keys into Max's dad's throat?"

Mike looks down at her. "Mr. Bjornson's fingers were cut off so he could no longer sign checks or contracts. I originally left him alive to tell people to stop wasting time, but he didn't listen and kept wasting people's time, including yours. As for the rest of the people, I cut off their fingers and thumbs so I could use their own blood to write on the wall. I also truly loved the sound of the bone being cut. Max's mom and dad are a whole other story. Max's dad bought a car from someone else after he spent hours with me. So I took the keys to his brand new car and shoved them into his throat so he would choke, not just on his own blood, but on the keys to the car he betrayed me with."

Jesse smiles. "Now that is irony for you—pure genius. One more thing I need to know, Mike. What song did you whistle when you left Amber's apartment and when you left the police station earlier today? Everyone who hears it says it sounds familiar, but they can't place it, and I agree with them. I heard you whistle it and I know I have heard it before, but for the life of me, I can't remember the name of the song." Jesse listens closely as Mike starts to whistle his song. "Yeah, that's it. What is the name of that song? I have had it in my head all day, thanks to you."

Mike chuckles. "*Patience*, by Guns 'N Roses, is the song. They whistle at the beginning and end of the song. It's my way of reminding myself that patience may be a virtue, but revenge is sweet. I whistle it whenever I'm about to do my work and right after I have done it."

Mike pushes himself up from his comfortable position of leaning over Jesse. He is getting anxious. He stands up and paces again. "Why did you have to take time away from my daughter today? Why? Why? Why? You couldn't just let us grieve over the loss of Phoebe? All of you women are alike—all you care about is yourselves. Women are going to be the downfall of this world. I can't take it anymore. Jesse, you need be exterminated like the bug that you are."

Mike climbs onto the bed and straddles her. He drops his butt onto her stomach. This is the same position he was in when he woke her from her drug-induced sleep.

"Wait Mike, I have something I need to say. You need to hear this before I go. Please just grant me this last wish," Jesse pleads.

Mike leans back and puts all of his weight on her stomach. "What are you going to tell me? That I will have to live with what I have done for the rest of my life? Well, the joke's on you, Detective, because I lost my sense of compassion a long time ago, and every single person that I took from this world deserved it. Heck, the good people on this planet deserve better than their time-wasting ways, and I helped provide a better world for all of the people like me—the people that hate when other people waste their time with no regard to how it makes them feel. Haven't you ever stood in a grocery store line while the person in front of you questions the price of every item? Or have you ever sat in a drive-thru lane waiting as the person in front of you takes forever to complete their order? Well, I for one am sick of people wasting my time. So by all means, Detective, tell me what you have to tell me, knowing full well that no matter what you say to me, it will not make me shed a tear, feel remorse, or change how I feel about what I have done."

Jesse puts a smile on her face as she starts to chuckle. "You're right. What I have to say probably won't make you feel remorse, but hear me out." Mike perks up, wondering what she could possibly have to say. "Here goes, Mike. Are you ready for this?" She takes a deep breath and screams, "Get him off me. Now!"

As she screams, her closet door flies open and Max erupts from the closet. His gun is aimed directly at Mike's head. "Go ahead, Mike, give me another reason to blow your head off. Do it, you piece of shit." Mike turns his head around so fast that Jesse and Max both hear his neck crack from the stress. "We've got you now and there is no way out of this. Take a look at the teddy bear on Jesse's night stand. There is a camera in there and we have been recording you this whole time." Max opens the drawer to the night stand, gun still pointed directly at Mike. "And just to make sure we got your confession, we also recorded you with this handy-dandy digital recorder." Max laughs as he grabs Mike and forces him to the floor. "I knew you wouldn't let us keep hunting you. Thanks for being so predictable, Mike."

Max handcuffs Mike. "Great job, Jesse. I am glad you trusted me with this plan. You knew you were never in any danger, right? I would never have let him get that knife anywhere near you." Max pulls Mike up off the floor and stands him up.

Jesse nods her head. "I knew you would never let him hurt me. I was surprised you let him drug me, though. That was a shock, but outside of that, I knew I was safe. I do need you to do me one favor now, Max. Cut me loose from this tape," she says with a chuckle.

Max pulls a pocketknife from his front pocket and cuts the tape loose from his partner. "Let's get this piece of shit to jail and get the evidence to the captain. Call it in, will you?"

Jesse grabs her cell phone and calls Captain Perry. "Captain, it's Detective Fairlane. I need you and a squad car over to my place immediately. Mike Hogan just tried to kill me." She listens for a few moments to Captain Perry. "I'm fine. Max is here and we got the whole thing on audio and video. He is not going to get away with this." Jesse pushes the end button on the screen of her phone and places it back on the table. Max and Jesse look at each other and smile.

Mike struggles with his handcuffs. "I knew I should have killed you 25 years ago when you were a kid."

The detectives exchange satisfied grins.